The police department was trying to ease the minds of the public, but their efforts were futile. In reality, Boggs knew, there was nothing for them to do until they caught him—or he killed again. She turned off the radio just as she pulled into Toni's parking lot.

Toni opened the front door with glass in hand and Boggs stepped inside. She suspected she'd replay the 30 seconds that followed at least a hundred times. She'd arrived expecting to spend maybe an hour with Toni at a costume store. But when that door opened, her heart melted. Before her stood the woman of her dreams. As she crossed the threshold, she felt as though she had walked into a movie. Maybe it was the music and flickering candles. Maybe it was the peaceful and comfortable feeling of Toni's townhouse. Maybe it was seeing her, barefoot, wearing an untucked old shirt and holding a glass of wine. Boggs felt like she had finally come home after all these years.

Visit

Bella Books

at

BellaBooks.com


or call our toll-free number

1-800-729-4992

# ANTICIPATION

## TERRI BRENEMAN

Bella
BOOKS
2006

**Bella Books, Inc.**
P.O. Box 10543
Tallahassee, FL 32302

Printed in the United States of America on acid-free paper

First Printing 2006
2nd Printing September 2007

Editor: Christi Cassidy
Cover designer: Stephanie Solomon-Lopez

ISBN-10: 1-931513-055-4
ISBN-13: 978-1-931513-055-3

## Acknowledgments

This book was a labor of love and would not have been possible without the love and support of many people. A huge thank you to Christi Cassidy, my editor, who was able to make sense of my ramblings. A special nod to Robin Shultz, R.N., who gave me medical insight. And most of all I would like to thank my partner, Cat, for believing in me and making everything I experience ten times better just because I'm with her.

# About the Author

Terri Breneman was born and raised in Prairie Village, Kansas, a suburb of Kansas City. She received a Bachelor of Arts degree in psychology and sociology from Pittsburg State University, Kansas. While living in Germany she earned a master's degree in counseling from Boston University. As a psychotherapist specializing in borderline personality disorders, she worked with high-risk adolescents, juvenile sex offenders and their victims. She decided to change careers and attended St. Louis University School of Law. After graduation she opened her own practice. One year of that was quite enough and she was fortunate to find her current job as a research and writing attorney for the Federal Public Defender's Office in St. Louis.

Terri lives with her partner in St. Louis, where they share their home with four cats—Tigger, Dexter, Felix and Sam. The cat featured in Anticipation, Mr. Rupert, was a longtime companion. Rupert Eugene died two years ago at the age of 17. He is still loved and missed terribly.

# CHAPTER 1

Inside the darkened room, a tormented man sat in silence with his eyes tightly closed. His body rocked back and forth at a steady pace, as if it were keeping time with an unheard song. His hands were damp and clammy, and he continually wiped them on his pants. He rocked faster. A bead of sweat formed on his upper lip.

Although the room was quiet, the sounds inside his head were deafening. The voices were beginning again. They had been silent for almost two weeks, but now they were screaming at him. "You idiot. How could you be so stupid? Don't you know how to do anything right?"

The man rocked harder and faster. He had to gain control. Some nights it was much harder than others. He took a deep breath and focused on his hands. Slowly the sound of the voices faded and his own voice filled his head. He smiled. He was back in control. This had happened before, of course. A lot. It seemed to be happening a little more often now, and a little more intensely, but it had always been this way. It was who he was. It made him brilliant. He could now concentrate on the next step of his plan. And the next woman destined to die.


Toni Barston sat at her desk and smiled. This was her third week as a new attorney in the Fairfield Metro Prosecuting Attorney's Office and she loved every minute of it. It wasn't the biggest prosecuting office in Missouri, but the metro area population was nearly one million. Her office was small and sparsely furnished and there was scarcely enough room for her desk, an additional chair and old file cabinet. The stack of files on her gray metal desk was in danger of sliding to the floor. Every prosecutor had a heavy load and Toni was no different.

Toni ignored all other files except the one in front of her, Dexter Crown. This was her first big case and it was a doozy. Three prominent women had been brutally murdered in the past six months. Each woman had been a respected professional with powerful connections. The murder scenes were gruesome but hard evidence was virtually nonexistent. The perp had entered each woman's home with no signs of force. He had apparently exited through the front door of two of his victims but had used a window to leave the last murder. Toni stared at the crime photos. Each woman's throat had been slashed and the bones in her right hand crushed. Panties were stuffed into their mouths. Toni stared at the pictures again. The photos were good. Too good.

Anne Mulhoney, Toni's supervisor, had given her this case just one hour ago. Toni tried to tell herself that she'd been picked for this assignment because of her dedication and talent. Unfortunately, she knew it was really because it was an open-and-shut case with virtually no chance of a trial. Detective Frank Parker had apprehended the suspect and gotten a videotaped confession. The public defender's office had already indicted him and he'd probably plead guilty. Still, Toni didn't want to make any mistakes. She wanted to know this file inside and out.

Although there was no hard evidence, there was some circumstantial evidence that was very helpful. Frank had gathered two witness statements saying they saw Dexter Crown near one woman's home the day of her murder. There was also a note from Frank that psychological records were available.

Two hours passed before Toni looked up from the file. Frank Parker was standing in front of her desk. As usual he was dressed impeccably in khaki slacks, crisp white shirt and blue blazer. Although this was the standard Fairfield detective uniform, Frank looked like he had stepped from the pages of a fashion magazine. He was about six feet tall with short cropped dark brown hair. His pale blue eyes were cold but seemed to gleam against his year-round tan. Frank Parker was a legend in his own time and he knew it. He had to be the most arrogant, chauvinistic bastard Toni had ever met, but he was the best detective in Missouri. She respected his record, but he definitely wasn't her type. Although he never referred to the women in the department as "babe" or "hon" (at least not since his last warning from the chief), Frank Parker had that certain look in his eyes, one of superiority. Toni felt both rage and intimidation every time she saw him.

"So, *Ms.* Barston, everything set for the prelim?" It wasn't actually a question. He just smiled, winked and left her office.

Toni shook her head and rolled her eyes as she watched him walk away. She did not like him. She glanced back at the file and was again absorbed in her work.

A little later, distracted by laughter, she looked out her window and saw one of the unit's investigators, Sam Clark, laughing with a woman. He was a happy-go-lucky sort of guy. He had been one of the first to welcome her to the department and offer his help. Toni felt very much at ease with him and welcomed his daily smiles and jokes. Sam was one of the few veterans who still had a good outlook on life.

Toni had never seen the woman who was talking to Sam. She was dressed in gray sweats and a sweatshirt with AIR FORCE ACADEMY printed on the front. Toni was instantly intrigued.

Sam seemed very chummy with her and Toni moved her chair closer to the window to get a better look. She couldn't hear their conversation, but at this point she didn't care. For some reason this distraction had her almost mesmerized.

Outside the Fairfield Law Enforcement Building, Sam Clark was talking to Victoria Boggsworth, affectionately known to all as Boggs. Boggs was a veteran investigator for the prosecuting attorney and had spent seven years in the Air Force as a military intelligence officer. She had the reputation of being tough as nails when it came to work. She had a knack for getting information from people and never giving up on a lead. Boggs was also the star shortstop for the prosecutor's softball team. At five feet six, her athletic body and green eyes made her stand out in a crowd. Her hair was light brown, short and stylish. At thirty-nine years old she still turned heads.

"Things just haven't been the same since you've been on vacation, Boggs," Sam was saying. "I've had to buy my own lunch every Monday."

"So, what's been happening on the unit, Sam? Did we finally get that new attorney?"

"Sure did." Sam was grinning from ear to ear. He loved to be the first to pass along new department gossip. "Toni Barston. That's Toni with an *i*, not a *y*. You should see her. Whew! But seriously, she seems to be a real good kid."

Boggs tried not to sound too eager. "So what's this new pup like?"

"Well, she's inexperienced but seems dedicated and thorough. I think she'll be damn good once she gets a few trials under her belt."

Boggs had hoped for a better physical description and decided she might have to wander in and take a look for herself. It might be a good idea to check her messages and water her plants before she had to start back to work on Monday. A pleasant thought for a Friday afternoon. Boggs looked toward the Metro Center and smiled. "I'll catch up with you later, Sam."

Toni had been watching Sam and the woman for several minutes when suddenly she turned, looked directly up at her and smiled. Toni quickly pushed her chair away from the window, knocking over the stack of files in the process. Her cheeks were burning and her heart was racing. A deep gasp escaped. She felt as though she had just got caught peeping into a men's locker room. It took Toni several moments to realize that no one could see her through the window and she began to relax.

She shook her head and began picking up the scattered papers from the floor. She tried to get her mind back to business. For all she knew, that woman was Sam's sister. She had to watch herself. If anyone had seen her drooling like that . . .

"Hey, counselor. It's Friday, five thirty, time to pack up and head for home." Sam tromped into her office and plopped down on the only available chair. "I think you're working too hard."

My God, she thought, how long had she been sitting there staring into space?

"Oh, um, I'm just waiting for a fax from Johnson County Psychiatric Hospital. The records clerk said she'd have it here by six." Toni hoped Sam hadn't noticed her faraway look.

"Well, counselor, you look like you need a break. Tell you what, your investigator is back from vacation, so I'll just ask Boggs to drop off the info at your apartment later tonight. You go on home now."

Toni thought of a dozen excuses. She didn't want "old Boggs" to come by her apartment. She knew Boggs only by reputation. Anne Mulhoney had said that Boggs was an old hand at investigating and one of the best. After hearing this, Toni pictured Boggs as an old geezer with gray hair and leathery skin. No doubt he also drank whiskey straight and chain-smoked. She chuckled to herself. She read too many mystery novels. Anyway, the thought of spending even ten minutes with a hard-nosed investigator didn't appeal to her. Not tonight. Not any night, in fact. Before Toni could verbalize her objection, Sam was out the door.

Toni groaned and began filling her briefcase with the Crown file. She pulled on her jacket and brushed some imaginary lint from her skirt. She made mental notes to pick up Chinese for dinner and drop off her blouses at the dry cleaner. Toni took one last glance at her office and headed to the elevator.

Boggs had just rounded the corner and was heading toward her own office when she first saw Toni Barston. From Sam's description, it had to be her, that and the fact she was coming from the attorney's office area. Toni was walking away from her, toward the elevator. Boggs immediately noticed the legs, and she let her gaze drift upward. Even from this vantage point, she liked what she saw. She quickened her step. Although she considered herself a woman of much experience, she wasn't prepared for what happened next.

Toni was waiting for the elevator to the parking garage. She quickly looked away when she noticed Boggs walking toward her. Boggs saw her blush. Toni turned back toward the elevator and rushed through the doors as soon as they opened. Unfortunately, an incredibly large woman burst from the elevator at the same time. Toni's feet nearly left the floor with the impact and she was propelled backward. Her briefcase crashed to the floor and as if on cue it popped open and spewed its contents.

It took everything Boggs had not to laugh. The woman bursting out of the elevator weighed at least 400 pounds. Her brightly colored polyester sponge pantsuit resembled 1970s motel decor. The elevator woman continued on her quest and Boggs was unsure whether she was unusually rude or simply unaware of the crash.

Toni knelt down and began gathering her papers and assorted items. She looked up when Boggs stopped in front of her.

"Here, let me help," Boggs said as she kneeled next to Toni. "Did you get the license plate of that woman?" Boggs was beginning to chuckle when Toni glanced at her. The chuckle died in her throat. She looked into Toni's eyes and felt like the wind had been knocked out of her.

They were the most striking eyes she had ever seen. An intense royal blue, they seemed to look right through her. Boggs was taken aback. The woman kneeling in front of her was absolutely stunning. Her light brown wavy hair, brushed back, fell almost to her shoulders. Her cheekbones were high and the features delicate. Small gold earrings dangled lightly from her ears. Boggs could only stare. Their eyes locked for what seemed like an eternity before Toni looked back toward the floor. Boggs noticed the flush on her face, then let her gaze trail downward. Under the gray suit jacket and behind the white silk blouse, Toni's breasts were full and seemed to strain at the lace bra. Toni's skirt had slid above her knees as she continued to gather her things. Boggs suddenly realized that she was gawking and began mumbling while helping Toni retrieve her items.

*Damn.* Boggs was admonishing herself for this temporary loss of control. She could not afford to be blatant in the Metro Building. The last thing she needed in her life was some straight woman accusing her of harassment. But, God, she could get lost in those blue eyes and thick wavy hair. And that perfume.

"Thank you. I guess I was in too much of a hurry," Toni said without making eye contact. The elevator doors again opened and she disappeared inside, clutching her briefcase.

Boggs stood outside the elevator doors with Toni's yellow highlighter in her hand and a smile on her face. She was amazed that this brief incident had such an effect on her. She rarely lost her composure or her ability to bullshit with people. She tried to shake the feeling and headed toward her office.

She was sitting in her chair with her feet on the desk, glancing at her messages, when Sam strolled into her office. As usual, he was clutching a Diet Coke and grinning.

"I'm glad I caught you in time, Boggs. I volunteered you for something."

Boggs didn't look up. "Forget it, Sam. I am officially off until Monday. Get that rookie Davis to do your dirty work."

Sam chuckled and plopped down in a chair next to her. "Aw, come on. That new attorney was waiting for a fax, but I told her you would drop it by her place tonight. She's a nice kid. Anyway, no one else is around and I've got to head home for dinner. Betty is fixing spaghetti tonight."

Boggs glanced up from her pile of pink message slips and smiled at him. Sam dearly loved his wife and her spaghetti. Anyway, she wanted to get a closer look at this new attorney and she could spare a few minutes tonight. "Okay. I'll hang around for a little longer and get the fax. Give me the address."

Sam chugged on his Diet Coke and jotted down Toni's address. "Thanks. I know she wants the fax for the weekend. Mulhoney gave her the Crown case and the preliminary hearing is on Monday. It's no big deal, but I think the kid is a little nervous. This is her first big case, you know."

Boggs took the address, glanced at it and then stuffed it in her sock. Sam looked at her as if she were a bit nuts and she shrugged. "No pockets."

Sam grinned and got up to leave. "Okay, see you on Monday. Don't forget, the Chiefs are playing the Broncos Sunday and since Denver is going to win, be prepared to buy me lunch." She and Sam regularly bet on football games in which she usually lost. Their standard bet on anything and everything was lunch at some disgusting restaurant. Winner got to pick and invariably Sam found a diner worse than the one before.

Boggs just shook her head and glanced down at the rest of her messages. Nothing too exciting here. Some woman named Joanie had called on Wednesday but left no message, just her number. Hmm. One of the witnesses she had been trying to reach. Ah, here was the one she was looking for. A message from Dave Berry, a friend of hers, about some college kid she was trying to locate. She pegged the kid as a probable witness to a fraternity rape. She'd been trying to locate him for over a month now.

After a quick phone call, Boggs had a "date" with Dave at a local college bar. Dave was sure the kid would be there and he'd be able to point him out. This was the first break she'd gotten on this potential witness and she grinned to herself. She had located the kid on a computer online service. A bunch of frat boys had been in a chat room a few days after the rape. She'd traced all but one, and tonight she would get him. She looked at her watch. It was almost six. She gave her plants a quick drink and then went to the main office to see if the fax had come in yet.

# CHAPTER 2

Toni opened the front door of her townhouse and stepped inside. It was a small two-level place, but it was just the right size for her. It was a corner unit so she only had neighbors on one side. Mr. Rupert greeted her at the door. Mr. Rupert was her best companion. He purred loudly and rubbed against her leg. At twenty pounds, he had a pretty mean push. She placed her briefcase on the dining room table and went to the kitchen. Her shoes, however, stayed by the front door. Wearing high heels was not one of her favorite things.

She poured herself a glass of white wine, fed Mr. Rupert and went upstairs to the master bedroom. Actually it was the only bedroom. A small desk in the corner held her laptop and assorted books. The queen-size waterbed with its oak headboard took up most of the room.

She quickly stripped off her suit and hung it neatly in the closet. She tossed her blouse on the bed and shook her head. The dry-cleaning bills were going to get her yet. She had to find some

10

blouses she could wash at home, that was all there was to it. She made a mental note to call her mom and add that to her Christmas list. Blouses that did not have to have an allowance of their own. Toni pulled out her favorite outfit from the closet, navy sweats and an old, torn, white sweatshirt. Perfect outfit for a fall evening at home with Mr. Rupert.

She had just finished changing when Mr. Rupert came into the bedroom. It had taken him only minutes to scarf down his dinner. He hopped—if a twenty-pound cat could hop—onto her computer desk and looked at her. This was their usual routine and Toni began to tell him about her day. His enthusiasm was always the same. As she talked, he cleaned his face and every once in a while interjected a meow. He did seem slightly interested in her description of the elevator incident, but maybe that was because she was a bit animated. Hard to read Mr. Rupert's feelings sometimes.

"Come on, boy. Time for me to eat now." Toni picked up her glass of wine and went back downstairs to the kitchen.

Mr. Rupert followed her and watched as she picked up her carton of Chinese and went to the couch. There was a large, old, dark green sectional that curved around the far corner. A square coffee table was centered in front of the couch. Across the room stood a floor-to-ceiling bookcase made from cinder blocks and stained boards. Friends often kidded her about her garage sale/college dorm decor, but it was comfortable and suited her needs. She wasn't one for fashion or style when it came to decorating.

Toni had arranged her TV, mini stereo and large assortment of books on the shelves. She considered this the "livdin," a combination living room, dining room and den. There was a small table in the corner that was supposed to be a dining table, but mostly it contained various newspapers, her briefcase and mail. She always ate her meals on the couch. She had just begun eating when she noticed the light flashing on her answering machine. She leaned over and hit the play button.

"Toni, this is Lea. A bunch of the old gang is going to O'Dooley's tonight. We'll be there about nine and you *better* show up. You have been working too much, girl. Okay, gotta go. See you there."

Toni smiled. She and Lea had been the best of friends throughout law school. They had spent many a late night guzzling coffee while studying or just bitching about school, professors and life in general. It would be good to get together for a few hours. She glanced at her watch. Almost seven. That would give her plenty of time to eat, work for a while and then go out.

The answering machine beeped a few times and then Sam's voice came over the speaker. "Hey, counselor. Boggs should be over pretty soon with the fax. Try not to work too hard this weekend, okay? See you on Monday."

Shit. She completely forgot about Boggs coming over. Toni jumped up and spilled her chicken fried rice on the floor. Mr. Rupert was a mere flash of fur as he dove for the food. Anything on the floor was fair game in his mind. She knew she didn't have much time. In a near panic she looked around the room for possible incriminating evidence. She pushed Mr. Rupert aside while scooping the food back into the carton, then threw the carton into the kitchen sink and ran to the bookcase. She scanned the titles and quickly removed any book or magazine that might give her away. After piling them all in the closet—how appropriate, she thought—she smiled and looked around again. There. Good old Boggs would never suspect a thing. At that moment Toni heard a car door slam shut. She also noticed the small painting that hung above her dining table. She dearly loved that picture, but why would a woman have a painting of that nature in her home? It was tasteful, to be sure, but it did show a woman in a rather revealing outfit. She was putting the picture in her closet when the doorbell rang.

She looked out the peephole of her front door. The face staring at her was a bit distorted, but there could be no mistake. Standing in front of her door was that woman. Toni's heart began racing and her mind was flying. What was this woman doing at her front door? Did she follow her home? Was she able to see through her and had come to give her a piece of her mind? Toni couldn't think clearly. The doorbell rang again.

She attempted to calm down. She remembered what her father

always told her. "Never open the door to strangers, Toni. Ask who it is first." Dad was always giving clichéd advice.

Toni gulped hard several times and then heard herself say, "Who is it?" Her voice sounded weak and far away. She waited for a response.

"It's Boggs from the office. I brought your fax."

Toni could not believe her ears. This was Boggs? Hard-nosed old Boggs? The investigator assigned to her? This wasn't a leather-faced man. Shit. Okay, she told herself, just open the door, take the fax and say thank you. If she didn't make eye contact, Boggs wouldn't suspect a thing. Anyway . . . it was probably just an over-reaction today. *Just stay calm, Toni, and act like a normal person.* She opened the door and smiled.

Both women stood silently for a moment before Boggs looked down at the fax in her hand. "I'm Boggs, uh, your investigator. Um, here you go. I hope you didn't have to wait too long." She thrust the papers at Toni.

Toni took the fax but was unable to break the eye contact. She had promised herself not to meet this woman's eyes, but that was a hard habit to break. Before she could even think of a response— "thank you" didn't even enter her mind—the phone rang.

On the third ring, Toni broke free and turned toward the phone. Boggs remained in the open doorway and Toni could feel her watching her.

"Hey, counselor. This is Sam. Has Boggs come by yet? I got a message for her, but her cell phone doesn't seem to be working. Or else she's ignoring me." He was chuckling.

The sound of Sam's voice snapped her back to reality. "She just got here, Sam. Here . . . I'll let you tell her." She turned to Boggs and motioned to the phone. "It's Sam."

As she handed the phone to Boggs, she felt the electricity between them and her face began to get hot. She turned away quickly, then noticed that Mr. Rupert was ambling toward the opened door. She cut him off in the nick of time.

"No, boy, you are not going out tonight." Mr. Rupert looked

up at her, protested mildly and went to check out the visitor. Toni shook her head. Mr. Rupert was strictly an indoor cat, but that wasn't from a lack of trying on his part.

Toni looked at Boggs while she was talking on the phone to Sam. She felt her gaze drift down and she smiled to herself. When her gaze trailed back up, she was met with a smile. Toni's face instantly flushed and she turned toward the kitchen. She picked up her glass of wine and took a long swallow.

Boggs hung up the phone and turned to her. "My God. That cat is huge!"

Toni grinned. "Boggs, I would like you to meet Mr. Rupert. And he's not huge, just big-boned."

"Nice to meet you, Mr. Rupert," Boggs said as she gently rubbed his head. Mr. Rupert took to her immediately. She clearly gave him the respect he deserved. "I'm glad I finally met you." Boggs was looking at Toni but continued to pet Mr. Rupert. "Sam's been talking about you. How do you like the office so far?"

Toni stepped farther back into the kitchen. "Good. It's really great." *Oh, that was intelligent, Toni. Duh. A real conversationalist here.* She could not believe what she had just said. She was having difficulty thinking clearly and it was obviously showing. She was making a fool of herself again, just like at the elevator.

Boggs seemed determined to stretch this conversation as long as possible. "Hell of a crash by the elevator today." She smiled broadly, as if this would encourage Toni to speak.

Toni was getting even more nervous. She took one more drink and told herself that this was all in her imagination. Boggs had no idea what she was thinking. And if she could keep the conversation focused on work, she would never know. She nodded to herself and smiled at Boggs. "No kidding! I can't believe I crashed into her like that. I don't think she even saw me!" Both women laughed. "Hey, thanks so much for dropping this by. I want to go over some details this weekend before the prelim. I hope it wasn't too much out of your way." She smiled again and glanced at her watch in what she hoped was a hint. She was way too nervous to keep this up.

"Not at all," Boggs replied. She took her cue and turned to the door. "Okay, Ms. Barston. If there's anything I can do for you, let me know." Boggs had her hand on the doorknob when Toni responded.

"Call me Toni," she said. "Please. And thanks again." Toni looked straight into those green eyes and smiled.

Instead of replying, Boggs simply nodded and went out the door.

When the front door closed, Toni sighed. God, that woman was absolutely incredible. She closed her eyes until the picture formed in her mind. Hmm. *Okay, kid. That's where it is going to stay—in your mind.* At least she had until Monday to compose herself. She picked up her Chinese once again and headed for the couch. "Well, I guess this is still edible." She curled herself into the corner section and flipped on the TV. Mr. Rupert crawled up next to her and began to purr. "Okay, boy. We have about an hour of relaxing before one of us goes out, and it's not you. What shall we watch?" Mr. Rupert responded as usual. Toni nodded and turned to the comedy channel. It wasn't until several minutes later that she realized she hadn't even offered Boggs a glass of wine or really even invited her inside. She shook her head in disbelief. She'd have to apologize on Monday.

On the other side of Fairfield the man sat on the edge of his bed. His eyes were closed tightly and he was slowly nodding head. It was dark. Both inside his room and inside his soul. After several minutes the nodding stopped and he sat motionless. Inside his mind he was reliving every glorious detail of his last conquest. His hand moved slightly when he envisioned crushing the woman's hand. When the memory reached its end, a small smile crept onto his face and a deep sigh escaped.

He was proud of his accomplishments. Very proud, but he had more to do. The smile on his face grew larger. There was no doubt in his mind that he would continue. Soon. Very soon.

# CHAPTER 3

Boggs entered her apartment and glanced at the clock on the wall. It was 7:45. She wasn't supposed to meet Dave until about 9:15. She smiled to herself. So far this had been a good day. She met a gorgeous woman *and* found a lead on this college kid. She wasn't thrilled with the idea of hanging out at a college bar, but it would be good to have a couple beers with Dave while they waited. She and Dave had been in the Air Force together and had remained close ever since. She was sure he would have liked to have been closer, but he understood her.

Both of them had become investigators when they got out of the Air Force. Dave had chosen the private sector and was doing pretty well. They often swapped ideas and stories over a few beers.

Boggs peered into her refrigerator. Not much to choose from, but there never was. She had never really gotten the hang of cooking. The refrigerator held several bottles of beer, fruit juices, water, yogurt, grapes, three oranges, a cheesecake and leftover pizza. There was one frozen dinner in the freezer. It was impossible to tell how long it had been there. She grabbed some water and a slice of cold pizza and headed down the hall to the living room. Her one-level apartment was small, but the living room was the size of all the other rooms combined. It held a large couch and recliner with a beautiful glass coffee table she'd bought while stationed in Germany. The opposite wall was filled with an elaborate entertainment center, including a 48-inch flat-screen television surrounded by a stereo system. She flipped on her reel-to-reel and music filled the room. She didn't think anyone else in the world still owned a reel-to-reel, but it was a relic she cherished from her days in the Air Force.

She loved all music. Tonight she had on a sensuous blend of R&B and jazz. She closed her eyes and imagined dancing slowly with Toni. The music seemed to engulf her. It was several minutes before she pulled herself from this fantasy.

Damn. She *had* to get this woman off her mind. She'd never get any work done this way. She flipped off the reel-to-reel. She searched for one of her favorite "working" CDs, popped it in and hit play. The room filled with the sound of 1940s big band. Now she was ready to work. Next to the entertainment center was a 55-gallon aquarium filled with a variety of fish, including a red-tailed shark and an albino frog, her favorite, named Horace. "So, did you pick up any clues for me today?" She fed Horace and the rest their dinner. Probably more appetizing than her own, she thought.

On the far side of the room, there was an L-shaped corner desk. The computer was the latest in technology complete with a video cam. The computer allowed her to tap into various resources, some of which were not quite aboveboard. She also spent many hours entertaining herself with the chat rooms. Above the computer desk there was an alarm clock because she had the habit of getting on the computer and losing all track of time. As she sat down at the desk, she set the alarm for 8:45.

The alarm went off before Boggs had even finished reading her e-mail. Frustrated, she glanced down at her notes. She had some new information about a couple of pending cases and had caught up with a few friends from around the U.S. Not bad for a Friday night. She pulled herself away from the screen and went into her bedroom.

Now, what should she wear to a college bar? She opened the doors to her walk-in closet and stepped inside. Jeans would be good. And a sweater. Anyone who knew Boggs would have picked out the same thing. It was her normal attire for fall. She pulled off her sweatpants and unfastened her ankle holster. It took her about five minutes to change clothes. She switched holsters and placed a pancake holster in her waistband and pulled her sweater over it. She looked in the mirror. Perfect.

Toni and Mr. Rupert had finished watching a standup comedy show when she started up the stairs. She looked in her closet for about ten minutes. She always had a hard time deciding what to wear. She finally settled on jeans, a white brushed denim blouse and her favorite brown Italian boots. She looked in the mirror as she put on her earrings. Shaking her head, she stripped off the blouse and replaced it with an old faded workshirt. Much better.

"Okay, Mr. Rupert. You're in charge of the house tonight. No parties and no Home Shopping Network." Mr. Rupert was not amused. He meowed loudly. It was a cool evening and he had clearly hoped she would stay home. There was nothing like a night spent lying in her lap while the two of them watched TV and ate popcorn.

Toni grabbed her car keys and headed out the door. As she drove toward campus, her mind was again on Boggs. Whew! She would have to tell Lea all about this woman. Although Lea would listen politely and smile, she was never very enthusiastic about Toni's dates—or wishful dates. Lea and Toni were very much alike, but this was one thing they did not have in common.

At O'Dooley's Toni headed toward the familiar table by the dartboards. No one in the group ever played darts, but they had adopted the table years ago. It was one of those high round tables surrounded by barstools. Lea was already seated, sharing a pitcher of beer with several of their law school friends. Toni quickly joined them and soon the five of them were exchanging bits of news and gossip. If it hadn't been for law school, Toni doubted whether they would have become friends. Something had drawn them together their first year, but for the life of her, she couldn't remember what that was.

She sat back and listened to her friends talk about their families and careers. The topic turned to babies and Toni let herself drift into her own world. She couldn't seem to get Boggs out of her mind. She wracked her brain for any information she might have heard around the office. All she could remember was "a hard-nosed investigator." She smiled to herself. No one had ever mentioned a boyfriend, and Boggs wore no wedding ring. Could it be possible? Toni tried to shake this notion from her mind. She didn't want to get her hopes up. But still . . .

She was rudely brought back to reality when Jake Hamilton tapped her on the shoulder. She and Jake had known each other for years, but it had been months since they had seen each other. They hugged as only old friends could and Jake kissed her lightly on the cheek. An architect with a promising career ahead of him, he'd inherited a great deal of money and was considered a very eligible bachelor. He had accompanied her to several gatherings during her law school days and it was rumored early on that the two would get married. Both Toni and Jake knew that couldn't be further from the truth, but they enjoyed all the rumors.

Jake said hello to the rest of the gang and agreed to stay for one drink. He loved being the center of attention. The conversation now became lively as each of the women described the "perfect woman" for Jake.

Boggs met Dave in the parking lot of O'Dooley's shortly after 9:15. They outlined their game plan and headed to the front door. Boggs scanned the tables, mostly out of habit, and she felt her heart skip a beat when she saw her. Grinning, she couldn't take her eyes off her. The grin quickly disappeared when she saw a guy embrace Toni. Shit. Why was she feeling so jealous? As she and Dave headed for a table, she kept Toni in her sights. A scantily clad waitress appeared and took their order.

"Jeez, Boggs, you must be in another world. You didn't make one comment about that waitress. Is something wrong?"

She looked at Dave and grinned. "I guess I have a lot on my mind today. Okay, let's get down to business. See the kid anywhere?"

"No. Not yet. But it sure looks like you've spotted someone." He was chuckling as he poured them each a beer from the pitcher. "Who is she?"

Boggs was momentarily embarrassed. She and Dave often compared notes on women, but this caught her off-guard. Obviously she had been staring at Toni. She hoped no one else had noticed.

"New attorney at the office. Just met her today. She seems really nice. Sam just raves about her. I don't know much, to tell you the truth." Boggs grinned. *Don't know much yet, but give it a few days.*

Dave began talking about one of his cases and Boggs felt herself only half listening. Oh, she made the appropriate responses, but her mind and her gaze were on Toni. She wondered what Toni was thinking. Their eyes had met a few times and Toni had smiled, then looked away quickly. Was she nervous? Maybe she thought Boggs was getting "too friendly." Who were those people she was with? Attorneys? Was that her boyfriend? He didn't seem to be paying her that much attention. How could he sit next to her without touching her every once in a while? Jeez . . . the woman was straight *and* a co-worker. Two big no-nos.

Dave suddenly nudged her shoulder. "Boggs. Back to earth, girl. The kid just walked in. Let's go."

They got up and approached the kid. Within a few moments they were escorting him outside to talk. Boggs took one last look at Toni's table and sighed.

Toni had noticed Boggs and that man walk into the bar. She had immediately felt her heart beat a little faster. She tried to watch Boggs without being overly obvious, but Boggs had caught her glance several times. She hoped that Boggs hadn't seen her disappointment. When Boggs left the bar, Toni felt incredibly let down and wasn't sure why. Oh, well. Just because she'd never heard about Boggs having a boyfriend didn't mean she was available. No chance now, she thought. She hoped she'd be able to concentrate on her work. She didn't have time for a lover anyway. With a new sense of conviction she told herself it was all for the best. She turned back to her group of friends and poured herself another beer.

# CHAPTER 4

Toni awoke on Saturday morning with an unusual feeling. She slowly opened her eyes and looked next to her. No one there. She glanced toward the bathroom door. It was dark. Whew. That had been one hell of a realistic dream. She guessed some part of her brain was still hoping she and Boggs would get together. Gosh, it had seemed so real. She closed her eyes again and tried to bring back the image. She smiled and sighed loudly.

Mr. Rupert responded to the sigh and she said, "Okay, boy. I know. It's time for you to eat. Poor starving boy. You are *so* abused."

She shook the image of Boggs from her mind and reached for her faded red sweatpants. She usually slept in only a torn baseball shirt. She didn't own a robe. In fact, she'd never understood the purpose of a robe except when she lived in a college dorm. Thank God those days were over. Downstairs in the kitchen, Mr. Rupert was waiting for her, although not very patiently. He got very cranky when Toni was late with breakfast. Here it was 8:00 a.m. and he hadn't had one bite yet. He was so vocal this morning that she fed him before making coffee. Then she went upstairs to shower while it brewed.

She let the spray cascade over her body. She closed her eyes and tried to recall the dream in its entirety. An image began to form of Boggs walking toward her . . . slowly. Toni had felt both nervous and excited in the dream. That feeling combined with the jet of water was beginning to arouse her. She was just getting the image into focus when Mr. Rupert barged into the bathroom.

"Mr. Rupert! Thanks for ruining the moment."

He jumped up on the toilet seat, meowed and began to clean his face.

She laughed out loud. "I suppose you're right. I better get my act together. Or did you come in here to tell me the coffee is ready?" She finished her shower, leaving the image of her dream behind. She threw on some shorts and a sweatshirt and headed downstairs.

Toni spread out the Crown file on her dining room table, arranging it in neat piles. With a fresh cup of coffee in hand, she was ready. She picked up the fax Boggs had delivered last night. Where was her highlighter? She looked through her briefcase again. Nope. Must have left it at work. Puzzled, she went upstairs to her desk and picked up a new one.

The first few pages of the fax were composed of simple demographics. Dexter Crown had been a patient at Johnson County Mental Hospital several times. He was 35 years old. She remembered an image of Crown on his emotionless videotaped confession. Toni wanted to know what made him tick. She scanned the report for the diagnosis and prognosis.

DIAGNOSIS
AXIS I: 302.84 Sexual Sadism
300.29 Simple Phobia (acrophobia)
305.90 Substance Abuse

AXIS II: 301.70 Borderline Personality Disorder
AXIS III: N/A
AXIS IV: Psychosocial Stressors = 4, Severe
AXIS V: Global Assessment = 40, impaired in reality testing

Toni began reading the assessment from Dr. Jamison.

Dexter Crown displays classic symptoms of Borderline Personality Disorder. He is unable to sustain consistent work behavior and often travels from place to place without a clear goal. His relationships are usually brief and intense and he suffers from a sense of abandonment. Mr. Crown has no regard for the truth as indicated by repeated lying and use of aliases. He can be very aggressive and has a history of assaulting women. He also has a long history of property destruction and stealing. Mr. Crown lacks all remorse for his past behavior and feels justified in having hit women. He stated to this interviewer that "women have too much power for their own good." He also suffers from depression.

Mr. Crown reported a physically and verbally abusive childhood. He expressed a hatred for his mother, stating, "She used my father. She was a whore." He stated that his father was often absent, but he got along well with his older brother. Mr. Crown had sporadic attendance in high school and dropped out at age 15. He has held a variety of jobs, none lasting more than six months.

The remainder of the report consisted of notes by the social worker assigned to Crown. Toni scanned these notes briefly, then reread the diagnosis. She tried to recall her past work as a psychotherapist. She had a Master's degree in psychology and had worked mostly with teenagers, but the terms of the diagnosis made sense. Crown's behavior seemed to fit the bill here. He had a history of assaulting women and obviously there was no love lost for women with power. All three of the victims were women in executive positions. There shouldn't be much trouble getting a conviction, she thought, especially because he had confessed to all the murders and was apparently going to plead. She turned to the next pile on the table. The first victim was Helen Carter. She had been the CEO of ECONTRON, a huge telecommunications company in the city. She also sat on the board of several other corporations, had a voice in city politics and was active on the crime prevention committee. It was rumored that Helen would stop at nothing to get what she wanted. The people close to her said that she was a driven woman but rewarded those who worked hard.

Helen was divorced and had lived alone for several years in a condo on the west side of town. There was an elaborate security system in the building, but unfortunately for Helen, the system had been malfunctioning for several days. The condo association had hired private security guards to walk the grounds, but none of them saw anything unusual the evening she was murdered.

Helen was found the next morning by her cleaning woman. Toni looked at the crime scene photos and a shiver ran down her spine. She flipped to the ones showing the condo. Helen had apparently been working that evening at her desk. There were several contracts and notes arranged neatly in piles next to a half-full cup of coffee. *Gee, just like I work at home . . .*

There had been no signs of a struggle in the home office. The kitchen and dining room looked as though they were rarely used, as if decorated merely for show.

The bedroom, however, was another matter. For a moment Toni was fascinated with the quality of the pictures. The colors were vivid and the lighting almost perfect. The queen-size bed, positioned at an angle in the corner, was covered with a rose-colored duvet and accented with half a dozen pillows arranged against the delicately carved wooden headboard. A small table stood next to a cozy overstuffed chair in the opposite corner. A magazine sat on the table, just waiting to be picked up. Helen was on the floor. Toni shuddered. These were the perfect photos to show a jury. Helen had left the world with a look of terror on her face. Her eyes were wide open and her mouth was frozen in a scream. Her panties were stuffed in her mouth.

Toni closed her eyes and shook her head in an attempt to rid her mind of the image. She got up and headed for the kitchen. As she poured herself another cup of coffee, she let out a deep sigh. Mr. Rupert responded with a loud meow. He was sitting on the kitchen counter next to a bottle of Kahlua.

"What a good idea, Mr. Rupert." She added a generous shot to her mug of steaming coffee, stirred and added milk. She continued to stir while standing there in the kitchen, surprised at her reaction to the photos of Helen Carter. She had seen them several times, but this time she seemed to feel the fear and horror. She also had a nagging dread in the back of her mind. What was it? Something just wasn't right.

She went slowly back to her table and sat down. The hot coffee and Kahlua soothed her nerves a bit. She looked back at the file and again experienced that uneasy feeling. Mr. Rupert joined her by jumping up on the table. Although he was incredibly graceful for a "big-boned" kitty, he nevertheless scattered most of the papers.

"Gee, thanks, Mr. R. I needed to reorganize this file. You are so helpful." She laughed out loud. If anyone ever heard her talk to her cat like this, they would think she was off her rocker. God, she needed to get a life.

She reorganized the file and sat back in her chair. All she really needed to do was present the facts at the preliminary hearing on Monday. The prelim would set out the basic facts and establish probable cause for the charge of murder. She would put Detective Parker on the stand and he would describe the confession and witness statements. Usually the defense counsel would ask a few questions, but it would most likely be over in less than thirty minutes. The judge would then hold Crown in jail until his next court appearance. If everything went according to plan, that appearance would be a "change of plea" and Crown would plead guilty. Toni was certain that this case would not go to trial. Dexter Crown would no doubt take the offer of three life sentences in exchange for a guilty plea instead of facing the death penalty. Toni didn't need to find out what made this man tick. All she had to do was present the facts.

With this new realization in mind, Toni began to make notes on the evidence, or lack thereof; motive, his hatred of women; and the transcripts from the confession. Her opening statement, per se, was simple. The state would prove that Dexter Crown murdered three woman.

A pot of coffee and several hours later, Toni finished her notes. She looked at her yellow legal pad and smiled. A job well done, she told herself. She felt as though she would present her case at the prelim with no problems. She knew all the facts cold. She always liked to be well prepared. She got up, stretched and yawned. It was such a good feeling to accomplish so much on a Saturday morning.

Toni looked at her briefcase on the floor and the papers on the table, thinking how far she'd come in the last three years. She had begun law school with a feeling of confidence and a sense of direction. She had worked as a psychotherapist for high-risk teens for several years. Although she had enjoyed her work in the beginning, it wasn't what she felt she wanted to do for the rest of her life. With the support of her partner, Sadie, she quit her job and went back to school full time. Little did she know, that step would forever change her life.

She and Sadie had been partners for seven years. Together they shared a house, a dog, a cat and their lives. She knew to their friends they seemed to be the ideal couple. They rarely argued and seemed to be happy. In reality, *comfortable* would have been a more appropriate description.

Sadie was a well-paid electrical engineer and spent her days, and many nights, designing new systems for a consulting firm. She was brilliant and Toni admired her knowledge and abilities. Sadie was not, however, a source of emotional support. As the first year of law school took its toll, she felt the relationship begin to slip away. Sadie didn't understand the pressures of law school. In fact, she never even saw the building. She also wasn't interested in meeting any of Toni's new friends. The gulf between them grew larger every day.

Toni tried to tell herself that she could comfort herself. She tried to talk to Sadie, to explain how she was feeling, but it did no good. Sadie merely shrugged her off. Months passed. Long talks into the night over coffee in their kitchen produced no results. Toni finally gave up. A few months later, Toni was living in an apartment with Mr. Rupert. A friendship and relationship lost forever. She wished only the best for Sadie, but it had been time to move on.

For the last year and a half of law school, she survived on her own. She dated occasionally but mostly concentrated on school. The time seemed to go by quickly. Then came graduation and immediately she began studying for the bar. Now she had her dream job.

She realized that she'd been lonely the past two years, but no lonelier than she had been before that. How sad, she thought. She smiled to herself. It was time to stop feeling sorry for herself. She had a great job and a great cat. It was time to have a little fun. She was determined to get a life.

# CHAPTER 5

Toni arrived at the office early Monday morning. As usual, she was the first one there. She had an hour before the prelim, so she began going over her notes.

At 8:45 Detective Frank Parker appeared at her desk with a videotape in his hand and a condescending look on his face. "Boning up on the Crown case?" he asked. Gee. What a subtle innuendo.

Instead of responding directly, she gathered her notes. She glanced at Frank as she walked past him toward the door. "See you in there, Frank," she said lightly.

Frank frowned and went in the opposite direction. She knew he didn't like women attorneys. He thought women should be secretaries and leave the "real work" to men. She chuckled to herself. Too bad, pal.

Toni sat alone at the prosecutor's table in Judge Haley's courtroom. Martha Haley had been a judge for almost ten years. She was known to be very tough, according to the prosecutor's office, but fair. Prior to becoming a judge, Martha had been a well-known civil rights attorney. Some of the police force thought she carried that background into the courtroom, thereby giving defendants more breaks than the cops thought they should have.

Judge Haley was also influential outside the courtroom. She and her husband owned one of the two major newspapers in the city. The daily editorials never carried a name in the byline, but Toni and no doubt most of the city figured they carried her thoughts and ideas.

Toni had just finished spreading her notes out on the table when Carol Bledsoe flew into the courtroom. Carol had been in the public defender's office for fifteen years. Her caseload was enormous, as was Carol herself. Rumor had it that Carol had never been seen without food—either in her mouth or just inches away. Toni was amazed that a woman of that size was able to move so quickly. She always seemed to be on the verge of being late, and her dramatic entrances were legendary.

Carol dropped her huge briefcase on the opposite table and smiled. Toni noticed she was munching on something.

"So, Carol, pretty interesting case, don't you think?" Toni asked.

Carol took out a large file. She began glancing through it and said, "I don't know. I'll let you know in a second."

Toni was dumbfounded. Not only had Carol just inhaled an entire Twinkie during her short response, but she wasn't even prepared. How could anyone come into a courtroom with the hopes of defending someone without even knowing the case. Toni knew this was just a prelim, but jeez.

She was still in shock when Carol closed her file. She leaned back in her chair, which protested loudly, although Carol didn't seem to notice. She popped a Ding Dong into her mouth and looked over at Toni. "Looks like my guy admitted to the whole thing," she said between chews. "With charges like these, Judge

Haley will never allow bail. I guess we'll be out of here pretty quick."

Toni nodded. Carol was known to be good at her job. A little burned out maybe, but still a good public defender. Carol didn't seem to be too concerned. She continued to munch. It looked like another Twinkie, but Toni couldn't be sure. Carol's hand moved like lightning from her briefcase to her mouth. Amazing.

Frank entered the courtroom at the same time as the sheriff and Dexter Crown, who looked much as Toni had expected. He was wearing dark blue work pants, a white T-shirt and slip-on tennis shoes. This is what all prisoners were issued. He was about six feet tall and had long wavy hair. His arms were muscular and displayed at least six tattoos. Toni noticed that Crown looked almost indifferent to the whole proceeding. He was escorted to Carol's table and sat down, his hands still handcuffed in front of him. He never even glanced at his attorney, just looked out the window.

Frank came over to the prosecutor's table and tossed the video down next to her. He was just beginning to sit when the bailiff called, "All rise."

Judge Martha Haley entered the courtroom with confidence and sat gracefully at the bench. She nodded first to Carol, then looked at Toni. Judge Haley nodded and smiled. She instructed all to be seated and then asked her clerk for the Crown file.

Toni was both excited and nervous. This was her first prelim on her own. She had sat in on dozens, but this was all hers. She tried to calm herself and looked up at the bench. Judge Haley was still looking at the file. Toni was glad her first appearance as a prosecuting attorney was before Judge Haley. Toni admired her greatly. Martha Haley had been a guest lecturer at the law school on several occasions. Toni was always the last to leave the lectures, oftentimes engaging the judge in conversation after class. Although they disagreed on a number of issues, Toni was impressed with her sense of justice.

Judge Haley closed the file and looked directly at Toni. Silence.

Toni froze. Oh, my God. What was she supposed to do? What was the name of the defendant? Dexter something. Dexter Shoes? Shoes! What the hell was she thinking about? She could hear her heart thumping. She was going to be sick. *Brilliant debut as an attorney, Toni.* Maybe she should have stayed with psychology.

Toni glanced down at the table and saw her notes lying neatly before her. It all came back in a flash. Apparently only seconds had passed, but it had seemed like hours.

"Ms. Barston, you may begin." Judge Haley smiled as if she remembered all too well what it was like the first time she came before a judge by herself.

Toni stood up, thanked Judge Haley and began her statement. Within fifteen minutes she had stated all the facts in a concise and clear manner. She then called Detective Frank Parker to the stand and questioned him regarding the arrest and the evidence against Crown, including the subsequent confession of Dexter Crown. She was about to get into details when Carol objected.

"Your Honor, my client was coerced into this so-called 'confession' and I move to have it suppressed."

Toni was surprised by the objection. She hadn't thought Carol was even paying attention. The last time she'd glanced at Carol, she was looking out the window. Toni frowned. This was a preliminary hearing. If Carol wanted to move for suppression of the tape, that would be done later, first as a written motion and then at a hearing. What was she doing?

Toni regained her composure quickly and informed the court that she wasn't offering the confession into evidence at this time. And just to put it on record, she told the court that Dexter Crown had been given his Miranda rights twice, signed a waiver and again waived his rights on videotape.

Judge Haley called both attorneys to the bench. "Now, Ms. Bledsoe, is there something you want to say?" she asked softly. "Normally this would not be an appropriate time, but I'm a little curious."

Carol went into a five-minute speech about her defendant's

rights in particular and civil rights in general. Toni's mind was racing. For a moment she couldn't remember the names of any cases dealing with Miranda or custody.

Judge Haley just smiled. "I am very impressed with that line of thought, Ms. Bledsoe. In fact, if I'm not mistaken, I made a similar argument many years ago. It was very persuasive, as I recall." She looked as though she was remembering a very satisfying moment in her life. She looked at Toni and her face once again became that of a judge. "Ms. Barston, any response?"

Toni paused for a moment and then gave a brief recap, including the reading of Miranda rights. She also pointed out that Carol hadn't filed any written motions. Toni did, however, summarize all relevant case law on the subject. She wasn't sure how she did it, but the argument was effective.

Judge Haley turned to Carol. "Ms. Bledsoe, although in principle I believe in your theory, in this case it has no bearing. Your client has signed a waiver and I believe he reiterated that waiver on videotape. The confession will probably be admitted at the proper time. Since this is merely a preliminary hearing, Ms. Bledsoe, you may want to consider further research and submit a memo before trial, if there is one. Unless, of course, you merely wanted to rattle the new prosecuting attorney. As you may have guessed, I'm holding this defendant over for trial. Now please step back and let us resume."

Both Toni and Carol returned to their tables. On cross-examination, Carol asked Frank only a few questions. There were no other witnesses. Judge Haley nodded to signal the end of testimony and then stated again that Dexter Crown would be held over for trial. Carol then rose from her chair and requested bond at $50,000, a ridiculously low figure. Judge Haley looked to Toni and raised her eyebrows.

"Your Honor, the State recommends no bond. Mr. Crown is charged with the mutilation and murder of three women. He has no known address and is a risk for flight. The State respectfully requests that he be held in the Metro jail pending trial."

Judge Haley nodded and jotted down some notes. Moments later she denied bail, dismissed court and disappeared into her chambers. The whole ordeal had taken less than 30 minutes. Frank got up, spoke briefly to the sheriff, and left. He never even looked at Toni. Dexter Crown was then escorted from the courtroom.

Carol was chewing something as she addressed Toni. "We'll probably be talking to each other on Friday afternoon, or maybe next Monday. Once you guys get your recommendations on paper, give me a call." With that said, she gathered her huge briefcase and flew out of the courtroom.

Toni compiled her notes and began filling her own briefcase. All in all it went pretty well, she thought. She felt a sense of purpose in doing a good job, especially if it meant keeping a guy like Crown off the streets. Her smile turned into a big grin.

Boggs slipped out of the back of the courtroom. She hadn't been able to resist the urge to sit in on this prelim. Although she was pretty certain of the outcome, and would have normally never even considered sitting in on this, she just *had* to see Toni in action.

She smiled to herself as she made her way back to her office. Toni had been a bit nervous at first, but she did well. Big Carol had done her best at throwing Toni off the track, but she didn't take the bait. Sam was right. Toni was going to make a good attorney.

Boggs had just sat down at her desk when Sam appeared. With a can of Diet Coke clutched in his hand, he plopped down in the adjacent chair. "I guess lunch is on me today. Who would have thought the Chiefs would pull it off with only twelve seconds left?"

She laughed. "It's about time. It's been so long since I've gotten to pick the restaurant that I've forgotten how. Let's see, how about Greek? Yes, that sounds splendid."

"Ah, come on, Boggs." He groaned. "You know I can't stand that stuff. At least I always pick somewhere that has edible food."

"Just kidding, Sam. How about that little Italian deli on Fifth?" They agreed.

"Now that that's settled," Sam said, "let's get down to business." As head investigator, it was his job to make sure the other investigators had a fairly even caseload, as well as supervision. "When are you going to get together with Toni?" he asked.

Boggs was momentarily taken aback. What the hell was he talking about? Did he know something she didn't? Sam had spent time with Toni while Boggs was on vacation. She hoped he hadn't told the new lawyer about her personal life.

"Hello? Boggs? Earth to Boggs." Sam was looking at her with questioning eyes. "Did you hear me? When are you going to go over your cases with Toni?"

"Oh," she said. Of course. What had she been thinking? She was assigned as Toni's investigator.

"Come on, Boggs, show a little enthusiasm." Sam laughed. "Toni is a good kid. Give her as much help as you can. She doesn't know the ropes yet. I know you hate to hang around the office, but how about sticking close for a week? Give her some insight. It'll make your job easier in the long run. Let Davis do some of your running around."

"Sure. No problem. I can handle that for a week." She tried to sound nonchalant. This would be great. A week to get to know Toni.

"Thanks. See you at lunch." Sam started to leave, but turned back toward her. "Don't forget to mark your calendar for a week from Saturday. It's our annual Halloween party. This year Betty and I are going to outdo ourselves." He was beaming. He and Betty dearly loved Halloween and went all out every year. Boggs always had a great time at their parties.

"Great!" she said. "Maybe this year I'll win the prize for best costume." Both of them laughed. For the past four years, Boggs had come to the Halloween party dressed as a 1940s detective, complete with hat and trenchcoat. Sam had given her hell for her lack of imagination, so last year she had added a special touch, sticking a huge piece of chewed gum on her shoe. Gumshoe.

❧

Toni was standing at the soda machine in the hall when she heard Sam laughing. He was still chuckling when he reached her side.

"Good morning, counselor," he said as a new can of Diet Coke tumbled out of the machine. "How did things go this morning?"

Toni smiled. "It went great, Sam. Thanks. Hey, what has you laughing on a Monday morning?"

"Just chatting with Boggs," he said as he gulped his drink.

Toni immediately caught herself looking over Sam's shoulder toward the investigator's office. Was Boggs in there? She had heard that Boggs spent most of her time working outside the office. Toni refocused on Sam as he began talking again.

"Listen, Betty and I have a Halloween party every year. We just love Halloween, you know. But this year it falls on a Monday and that's no good for a party. So, we're having it two days early, a week from Saturday, and we would love for you to come. Just a bunch of fun people, no stuffed shirts, no politics. The food is great. It's a lot of fun. Whaddya say?"

Although Toni usually made it a point not to socialize with people she worked with, Sam was different. He had really made her first weeks at the office comfortable.

"Sure, Sam. It sounds great. Is there anything I can bring?" she asked.

"Not a thing. Just bring yourself. Oh, if there's someone you want to bring, that's okay too. We start the festivities at about seven thirty. I'll give you a map later this week. See you later." Sam began walking toward his office and called over his shoulder, "By the way, it's a costume party."

Toni headed to her office. She had less than two weeks to think of a costume. This would be fun. She remembered her decision to get a life. Although this wasn't what she'd had in mind at the time, at least it was a start.

She sat at her desk and looked at the huge stack of files. She had quickly learned that the majority of a prosecutor's time was spent with files, not in a courtroom. There were requests for discovery to be answered, petitions to be filed, witness statements to be deciphered and an occasional brief to write. She also fielded numerous phone calls from victims, the public defenders, private attorneys and now and then angry family members of someone who'd been charged with a crime. Sometimes the day went by so quickly that she would realize it was almost time to go home and she hadn't even stopped for lunch. Today was no different.

At 4:30 the phone rang. It was Boggs. "I was wondering if we could set up a time to go over your cases?"

At the sound of Boggs's voice, Toni had a vivid recollection of her dream several nights ago. Her face became flushed and her heart began to race.

"Toni? You there?"

What? Oh, God. What did she just say? Toni shook that image of Boggs from her mind and stammered, "I'm sorry, Boggs. What did you say? I was just finishing writing a brief and I guess, um, I was pretty absorbed in my argument." She tried to sound professional but feared that she failed miserably.

"I just wanted to set up a time to go over your cases," Boggs repeated.

Toni looked at her datebook. Aside from a few staff meetings and a couple of interviews with victims, there was nothing scheduled for the rest of the week. She didn't want to sound too eager, even though she wanted to scream, "Now!" She even fantasized about asking Boggs to meet outside the office, maybe even at her apartment. Not very professional, she reprimanded herself. She cleared her throat and spoke calmly into the phone. "Well, my schedule is pretty light this week. Any suggestions?" Excellent. Now the ball was in her court.

"Well," Boggs answered after a pause, "we'll probably need a couple hours at least, so today is out. How about tomorrow afternoon? Let's say three?"

"That would be fine," Toni said in a voice she barely recognized. "I'll see you then." Boggs agreed and they hung up.

Toni leaned back in her chair and stared at the receiver in her hand. Damn. She had sounded like a snotty, arrogant woman. What a great impression she just made! She replaced the receiver, shook her head and tried to console herself. Heck. She had been caught off guard, that's all. Things would go much smoother tomorrow. She had an entire night to put her hormones in check. Anyway, they would be talking about cases and her work always held her full attention. Tomorrow would be no problem. Satisfied that would be the case, Toni began to close up shop for the day.

Boggs hung up the phone and sighed. Toni was very professional. There was no hint of interest. Oh, well. Maybe the meeting tomorrow would be shorter than she hoped. Still, Toni seemed like the kind of person she would like to have for a friend. She cleared her desk and headed for home.

# CHAPTER 6

Toni woke up a full hour before her alarm buzzed and hadn't been able to go back to sleep. She tried on four outfits and drank five cups of coffee before her alarm actually went off. Mr. Rupert seemed puzzled when he stretched and opened his eyes. Toni was fully dressed. He meowed once, for good measure, and ambled down to his bowl. Toni followed him. He was just about to make his morning "Feed me now" meow when he saw that his dish was full.

She laughed. "Well, good morning, Mr. Rupert. I see you slept in this morning. Breakfast has already been served." Mr. Rupert cocked his head, then dove into the bowl.

Toni arrived at her office, early as usual. She felt more nervous today than she had yesterday. The image of Boggs would not leave her mind. Oh, sure, she was able to put it aside for an hour or two, but it would not go away completely. All she had to do was close her eyes and her dream would reappear.

They were in her apartment. Toni was wearing jeans, boots and a white button-down blouse. Boggs was wearing jeans, a yellow blouse and an ivory cardigan sweater. Toni could feel the electricity in the air. Boggs was talking, but Toni couldn't hear the words. Both were standing, and Boggs began to come slowly toward her. Nervous and excited, Toni felt herself take one step backward.

The ringing of the phone made her jump. Oh, my God. She shook her head. Boy, was that real or what?

The phone rang again and Toni managed to answer in a calm voice.

"Hi, Toni. Jake here. How's life in the great criminal justice system?" He laughed.

"Oh, jeez, Jake. It's you." She let out a long sigh.

"Well, that's a warm welcome! Expecting Janet Reno to finally return your call?" Jake was laughing, then he stopped and said seriously, "Hey, Toni, are you okay?"

"Sorry, Jake. Caught me off guard. I'm a mess, really. It's a long story, but nothing serious. I've just been dateless for too long. When you called . . . well, let's just say you brought me back to earth."

"Ahh. Fantasizing while sitting at your desk, huh? Anyone in particular?"

"Jake!" she cried. "Can we change the subject? Now, what's up?"

"Just the best news ever." He was obviously very excited and just about bursting. "My sweetie is being transferred *here*. Can you believe it? After almost two years of long-distance romance, we will finally be together. Isn't that marvelous?"

"Oh, Jake," Toni said. "I am *so* happy for you both. You two make such a sweet couple. When's the big move?"

"In two months. It's going to seem like forever. Anyway, how about celebrating with me tonight? My treat. The usual?"

"Sounds wonderful. I should be out of here by five or so."

"Perfect. I'll pick up the food and wine, and I'll be at your place around six thirty. That'll give us plenty of time to eat, drink, celebrate and talk about the new lust in your life. See you tonight."

Toni laughed and hung up the phone. She and Jake had a long-standing ritual. It began years ago when Toni got her first "real" job as a psychotherapist. She had called Jake and they decided to go out to dinner. Later that day, Jake sprained his ankle and had to stay home with his foot propped up on a pillow. Toni arrived that evening with take-out Chinese and a bottle of wine. Although this was a far cry from what they had planned, they had a wonderful time. They talked for hours. At the end of the night they decided that whenever one of them had something to celebrate, he or she would bring Chinese and wine to the other's house.

The rest of the day passed quickly. She was talking on the phone to one of the attorneys in the public defender's office when Boggs appeared at her door. Toni's heart involuntarily skipped a beat. She waved her in, motioned to the only chair in her office and continued her conversation, thankful that she would have a couple minutes to compose herself. While still listening on the phone, Toni reminded herself to keep her emotions in check. Not an easy task with this incredible woman a mere three feet away.


Toni jotted down a few notes before ending the call. She noticed Boggs looking around her office and then she wiped her hands on her pants. Toni wondered what Boggs was thinking and if she could tell how attracted she was to her. Jeez. She felt like a teenager, jittery and a little scared. Toni ended her call.

"Hi, Boggs. Sorry I was on the phone. Thanks for setting up this meeting. I have a printout of all my cases. I guess we should just start at the top." Hmm. Not bad, Toni thought. Very professional. Maybe she could make it through this after all.

Boggs agreed and for the next fifteen minutes they discussed the cases and took notes. Boggs wrote down the names of various witnesses to locate. The next file was Dexter Crown's.

"I guess there isn't much to do on this one. Carol Bledsoe thinks he'll take the life sentences." Toni had the file in the center of her desk.

"I guess you didn't have to use that fax after all." Boggs glanced up from her notes and looked at Toni. Their eyes met and time seemed to freeze.

Toni couldn't speak. She felt a powerful connection that she didn't quite understand. Several seconds passed before Toni was able to look away. She cleared her throat and continued as though nothing had happened. For the next hour, Boggs and Toni pored over the files. Toni refused to allow herself to think about what had happened. They finished at 4:30.

Boggs leaned back in her chair and stretched. "Well, I guess that about does it." She made no move to leave.

"Guess so," Toni replied. She didn't want Boggs to leave. Not just yet.

Both women's attention turned to the hall outside Toni's office. The voice of the mail clerk, Brittany, could be heard clearly. No one could mistake that voice. It squeaked. Brittany was a very nice young woman, but she had not been blessed with the brain of a rocket scientist. She had been working in the building for more than two years but continued to get lost. No one seemed to know her job description, except that she delivered mail. Oh, yes, she did have one other task. She was in charge of decorations for the various holidays. Evidently Brittany was talking to one of the secretaries who worked for the prosecutors.

"Where do you want me to put these at?" she squeaked to the other woman.

"Asshole," Toni murmured.

Boggs looked at Toni with disbelief. "What did you just say?"

Toni giggled, embarrassed to discover she had said that out loud. "Oh, Boggs." She laughed. "It's not what you think." She continued to laugh while Boggs just stared. Toni regained composure and said, "It's an old joke. Remember in school we were always taught never to end a sentence with a preposition?"

Boggs nodded. She clearly had no idea what Toni was talking about.

Toni could hardly contain herself. "Okay. Well, Brittany just said, 'Where do you want me to put these *at*?' So, because you should never end a sentence with a preposition, I added 'asshole.' There, better grammar for all." With that said, both Toni and Boggs burst into laughter.

They were still laughing when Brittany knocked on Toni's door. Toni waved her into her office. "Here are your decorations," she squeaked proudly. She waved good-bye and left. Toni could hear her five-inch heels click down the hall.

She looked at her "decorations." They consisted of a cardboard ghost measuring four inches high and a small plastic pumpkin. She looked at Boggs with disbelief.

"Wow." Toni feigned awe. "These are wonderful. I never dreamed my position here warranted such incredible fringe benefits."

"Unbelievable, isn't it?" Boggs was struggling to keep a straight face. "You should see what she brings you for Thanksgiving." Finally, she couldn't hold it in any longer. Both laughed so hard, tears streamed from their eyes.

Toni attempted to be serious again. "Brittany is really sweet, but every time I hear that voice, I have this awful image. I know this is really tacky, but I imagine her living in a trailer, listening to old country music and wearing a tube top. Isn't that terrible of me?"

Boggs remained silent for a moment. Toni thought she might have offended her and was just about to apologize when Boggs began laughing so hard, Toni couldn't understand what she was saying. After several minutes, Boggs said, "She does! I swear she does!"

"She does what?"

Boggs was beginning to laugh again. "Brittany really does live in a trailer, loves country music and, get this, she wore a tube top to the department picnic last year!"

"No." Toni gasped. Both she and Boggs covered their mouths with their hands and laughed some more. "God, we're bad. We are going straight to hell!" Toni stopped and looked at Boggs. That was all it took. More laughter filled the office.

When she and Boggs recovered, they noticed Sam standing in the doorway and gripping his Diet Coke. He had a huge grin on his face. "Must be good," he said. "Do you want to let me in on it or did you have to 'be there'?"

"Sorry, Sam," Boggs said. "I guess you just had to be here. What brings you down here?"

"Well," he replied, "I just came to drop off a map to the counselor here. She has graciously accepted an invitation to *the* Halloween party." As he handed the map to Toni, he pointed to the "decorations" on her desk. "I see you've received your allotted Halloween decor. Pretty tacky, huh? It almost gives Halloween a bad name."

Boggs chuckled and turned toward Toni. "Sam and Betty are Halloween fanatics," she explained. "They have the most incredible decorations and continue to outdo themselves every year. They *do* Halloween like most folks do Christmas. So, you're going to be there?"

"Wouldn't miss it for the world," Toni replied. The three began exchanging ideas on party games, decorations and food, Sam's favorite topic. Several minutes passed before he looked at his watch. "Gosh, it's after five. I've got to head home. It's my turn to cook. I'm making lasagne. With Betty's leftover spaghetti sauce, it turns out great. Would either of you like to join us for dinner?"

"Sorry, Sam." Toni sighed. "It sounds really delicious, but I already have plans."

"Me too, Sam," Boggs said. "Maybe you could bring some leftovers in for lunch tomorrow?"

Sam shrugged and took a long swallow of Diet Coke. "Maybe." He grinned. "If you're lucky. See you two tomorrow." With that he was out the door.

"Well, I guess I better head home too," Boggs said. "Thanks for a really enjoyable afternoon. Who knew going over cases could be so much fun."

"You are very welcome," Toni replied. "It felt good to laugh. I don't think I've laughed that hard in a long, long time. Thanks, Boggs. I forgot how good it can make a person feel."

Boggs stood, and Toni looked directly into her eyes. Neither said another word. They didn't have to say anything. Boggs nodded and left.

Toni left her office shortly after Sam and Boggs. She opened the door to her apartment and was met, as usual, by Mr. Rupert.

"Hiya, big boy! How was your day?"

Mr. Rupert replied enthusiastically, as if he sensed the happiness in her voice. She chuckled. It had been a long time.

She began telling him about the events of the day while filling his dish. She then went upstairs and changed into her sweats. As she hung her suit in the closet, she smiled. She'd make this her lucky suit from now on.

She went back downstairs and plopped down on the couch. Mr. Rupert joined her and together they went through the day's mail. There was a lot of mail today. Toni separated it into three piles. The first one was for bills. Yuck. The second was personal stuff or professional junk. There was also a letter from Sandy, an old colleague from her psychotherapy days. The third pile belonged to Mr. Rupert. It contained mostly catalogs and junk mail, but he didn't mind. Once placed in front of him, he dove in headfirst, scattering envelopes everywhere. He just loved getting mail.

Toni glanced at her watch. "Jake will be here any minute." She had just finished picking up the mail when the doorbell rang. "Hi, handsome," she said as she opened the door.

Jake glided inside, one arm gripping a huge bag of Chinese food and the other carrying a magnum of wine.

"My gosh, Jake. How much food did you bring? Are you planning on sharing this with the whole complex?"

He laughed. "No. Just us. I couldn't decide what I was hungry for, so I got a little of everything."

While Toni got out plates and napkins, Jake began filling her in on details of the upcoming move. He was so animated and happy, she couldn't help but grin. In all the years she had known him, he had never seemed so genuinely content. They drank white wine and nibbled food. After nearly two hours, Jake was finally winding down.

"You know, it feels so good to tell someone how I feel." He sighed. "I have to keep pretty closed-mouthed at work. I have to keep up my reputation as an eligible bachelor, you know." He winked. "Well, now that I have monopolized the entire night, why don't you tell me about this woman you're interested in?"

Toni leaned back on the couch and put her feet on the coffee table. Mr. Rupert curled up next to her and purred contentedly. "There's nothing to tell," she answered truthfully. "My investigator—her name is Boggs, is, well, very nice. But that's all there is. She is not interested in me. I saw her the other night with her boyfriend. I was disappointed at first, but not now. We talked today, about work of course, and, I don't know, it's hard to describe. I guess I felt some sort of bond. I think we can become friends. Maybe even good friends."

"So, what are you going to do?" he asked. "I mean about your dateless situation. You can't spend every night working. And on the weekends, you can't possibly look forward to watching *Cops* with Mr. Rupert."

"Come on, Jake," she protested. "It's not that dramatic. I date."

"Hell, Toni," he said, "you can't fool me. When was the last time you went on a real date?"

She immediately opened her mouth to respond but said nothing. My God, she thought. Had it been *that* long? The more she thought about it, the wider Jake's grin became.

"Okay, you win. It was sometime this past summer. So what's your point?" She was beginning to laugh. She had to admit that her personal life was somewhat comical. At least, she would rather think that than the alternative.

"Well." He was getting that matchmaker look in his eye. "There is a very interesting woman who just started working for us. She's attractive, brown hair, and she has a great sense of humor. She would be perfect for you. Why don't you let me try and set something up?"

Toni moaned. "Jake, you know I hate setups. They always end in disaster. Anyway, what makes you think she'd be interested?"

He rubbed his hands together as though he was plotting a devious crime. "Just leave the details to me, and leave Friday night open."

With that remark, he announced that he had to head for home. She congratulated him for the hundredth time about his good fortune and they said good night.

After Jake left, Toni busied herself cleaning up. There was a ton of food left. No need to cook for a while. She poured herself another glass of wine, sat down on the couch and put her feet on the table.

She gently scratched Mr. Rupert's head and thought about the dream she'd had about Boggs. It had seemed so real, so vivid. Oh, how she longed to have someone in her life who truly understood her. Someone who knew why she smiled, why she cried. Someone with whom she could share her life, her hopes, her dreams. Was there such a person for her? Was she looking for someone who didn't exist? She thought about the exchange she'd had with Boggs earlier that day. Maybe a real friend was what she was looking for. A lover never seemed to fit that bill. There were friends and there were lovers. Never both. With that realization, Toni went to bed.

# CHAPTER 7

Toni sat at her desk and stretched. Boy, what a week this had been. She had completed more paperwork in a week, it seemed, than she had in a whole semester of law school, although the pile in her in box was only slightly smaller than when she began. She had just reached for another request for discovery from the pile when the phone rang.

"Hiya, crime fighter," Jake said. "You didn't forget about the big date tonight, did you?"

"Well, to tell you the truth," Toni replied, "I sure did. It's probably a good thing, too, or I would have found a way to back out. I hate blind dates."

"Listen," he suggested, "just think of it as a few fun people going out for the evening. Since I thought you'd back down if it were just the two of you, Bob and I will go along. Your date is Linda. We'll leave from here and pick up Bob, then we'll swing by and pick you up around seven, okay?"

Toni smiled. Maybe this wouldn't be such a bad evening. She really liked Bob. He had been a childhood friend of Jake's and they had gone out often. He had a great sense of humor and they always had a good time.

"Okay, Jake," she said. "Where are we going? So I have an idea on what to wear."

"We'll grab dinner at Winston's, then we're going to the new club in town. Gotta run." Without even saying good-bye, Jake disconnected.

Toni finished the next few requests on her desk, glanced at her watch and decided to finish up for the day. It was past 5:30 and she still had to get home, feed Mr. Rupert, shower and get dressed.

When she reached her apartment, she was in a pretty good mood. It was a gorgeous fall evening, and she was about to go out on the town. Although she was not what she considered "really excited" about the evening, she was sure it would be enjoyable.

By 6:40 she was dressed and ready to go. Amazingly, it had taken her only a few minutes to pick her outfit for the evening. She chose her favorite jeans, a rust-colored sweater and her brown suede bomber jacket. She turned on some upbeat music and settled on the couch to wait for Jake, Bob and Linda to arrive. Mr. Rupert joined her.

"Well, boy, this is the big night. I am finally going out on a 'date'! I know you aren't thrilled, but be nice when she gets here, okay? Maybe this will lead to a second date, and I want to make a good impression." She paused. "You know something? I don't even feel nervous. I suppose I should be worried about how things will go, but I'm not." She was more nervous about seeing Boggs around the office.

Mr. Rupert was about to respond when the doorbell rang. Toni shrugged at Mr. Rupert and got up to answer. When she opened the door, her heart began pounding and her jaw dropped.

"Hi, Toni," Boggs stammered. "Sorry to just pop in on you like this, but I have something I thought you might want. Carol Bledsoe filed these motions just before close of business today and

I thought, well, you might want to take a look over the weekend. I was in the clerk's office when she filed and, um, well, I know you like to keep up on things."

Boggs was clearly doing her best to act casual and failing miserably. There had been no justifiable reason for her to deliver these motions and memos, Toni thought, but she appreciated the gesture. Did this mean something? Both women smiled at each other.

"Gosh, that was awfully nice of you," Toni said. "I mean, for you to go out of your way and all. I'm really glad you did. This will give me more time to look them over and decide what I want to do. This is really great. Thanks."

Another brilliant dialogue! God, why was she so tongue-tied around Boggs? She thought she'd gotten past this. What should she do now? On the outside she tried to appear cool, calm and collected. Was she stammering? Did she look like a complete fool standing there? Her cheeks were burning. *Damn it Toni, say something!*

"Um, uh, would you like to come in?" *Smooth, Toni, very smooth.* Wait, had she replaced the books and the pictures or were they still in the closet? No, they were still in there. Okay.

Before Boggs could respond to that poor excuse for an invitation, Mr. Rupert was heading for the front door. Both Toni and Boggs instinctively reached for the fleeing feline and promptly bumped heads.

"Oh, my gosh, are you okay?" Toni asked.

Boggs was rubbing her head and grinning. Both women immediately burst into laughter. It took almost a minute before Toni realized that Mr. Rupert was nowhere to be seen.

"Mr. Rupert. He's gone!" Toni pushed past Boggs and ran into the courtyard. No sign of him. Boggs headed for the parking lot.

"He's not over here," she yelled. Toni was returning from the courtyard when she met Boggs at the front door. "He couldn't have gone too far, Toni. Let's circle the building."

Toni was about to close her still-open front door when she spotted him. There he was, sitting on the couch, washing his face.

She looked at Boggs, motioned toward Mr. Rupert and grinned. "The little shit. He never left."

Boggs followed Toni into the apartment and shut the door.

Toni sat on the coffee table and began lecturing the big furball. "You scared me to death, young man. You know you aren't supposed to go outside without your leash. You are grounded! That means no TV."

She scratched behind his ears, glanced over at Boggs and smiled. Boggs met her eyes and began grinning again.

"Gosh, Boggs. I'm really sorry about this. Here you go out of your way to bring me those motions and end up on a wild cat chase. I'm sorry." Toni rubbed her forehead. "How's your head, by the way?" she asked.

Boggs gingerly touched the side of her head. She then extended both arms to her sides, closed her eyes and touched one finger to her nose. She opened her eyes and looked at Toni. With incredible seriousness she said, "There seems to be no permanent damage. I believe I can continue to lead a normal and productive life." The two of them laughed. Even Mr. Rupert seemed amused, or at least he put on a good show.

They were still laughing when the doorbell rang. Toni had completely forgotten about her evening on the town. Suddenly she began to panic. What if Jake said something wrong. What if her "date" was dressed completely in leather? What if Bob decided to be a real flamer and swoosh into the room? Oh, God! How was she going to explain this to Boggs? Shit. The doorbell rang a second time. Boggs shot her a questioning look as if to say, "Aren't you going to answer that?" Toni went to the door, took a deep breath and hoped for the best.

"Hi, honey. I'm home," sang Jake as he glided into the room with his group. Toni breathed a sigh of relief. All three of her guests arrived in "normal" attire. What had she been thinking? Jake was conservative and closeted at work. Bob *always* wore jeans and some type of sports shirt. Gee. Panic. What a fun emotion.

"Hello, dear," Toni quipped. "Beaver and Wally are upstairs. How was your day?" Everybody chuckled.

Jake, charming as ever, began the introductions. "I'd like you to meet Linda Matthews. She's new to our firm and new to our fair city. Linda, this is Toni, my darling housewife."

Linda and Toni laughed and shook hands. Toni did a quick appraisal. Good handshake, weak on eye contact. Attractive. A little taller than her, long brown hair, brown eyes, nice smile. Seemed to have a sense of humor.

Jake interrupted Toni's thought. He was gesturing toward Boggs. "Linda, this is an unknown person to me," he said matter-of-factly. "She appears to be in her thirties and is quite attractive. I would also venture to say she is a very nice person—due to the fact that Mr. Rupert is rubbing against her leg. By the way, Mr. Rupert is that thin and trim handsome beast. He owns the building."

"My God, he's huge," Linda blurted out.

Toni regained her role as hostess. "Everyone, this unknown person is Boggs," she said with a smile. "She works with me down at Metro. Boggs, you've been introduced to Linda, and this is Bob Clayton, our very own resident accountant. Don't talk about rounding off numbers or estimating costs in front of him. He breaks out in hives. This other person, well, I've never seen him before in my life."

As greetings were exchanged, Jake approached Boggs with a huge grin, his hand outstretched. "My name is Jake Hamilton. Very pleased to meet you."

"The same," Boggs replied. "I've never met a fifties sitcom father before." Jake smiled even more broadly and after a moment or two of general chitchat, she moved toward the door. "It was very nice to meet you all," she said. Her eyes met Toni's. "Sorry to drop in on you like that, but—"

"Oh, I appreciate your bringing me those motions. You saved me from a major headache on Monday. Thank you." Toni smiled.

There was a slight pause. It lasted only a few seconds, but it was electric. Toni wanted Boggs to stay but knew it wouldn't work.

Neither of them had said a word. Boggs said good-bye and left. Bob and Jake were chatting. Toni was closing the door. They all seemed unaware of what just happened.

Bob was the first to ask. "So . . . what's the scoop on her?"

"Boggs?" Toni said. "She's one of the investigators at work. Very nice and apparently damn good at her job. She is also straight as a board. So, are we ready for dinner or would you all like a glass of wine before we go?"

"Food!" was the chorus Toni received in response. The four of them then headed out.


When Toni arrived home later that night, or actually early Saturday morning, she replayed her night on the town. She had actually enjoyed herself. During dinner she and Linda agreed that they could become good friends, nothing more. Toni was unaware Linda had made that assumption earlier. With the pressure of a "date" gone, they had fun.

After dinner the four of them headed for the new club in town. It had been open over a month, so the initial huge crowds had waned a bit. The place was called Gertrude's Garage. No one knew why. The outside was nondescript, as most gay bars were, but the inside was colorful, both in its decor and clientele, from queens to old feminists. Gertrude's seemed to attract all facets of the gay community. The music was loud and the dance floor was huge. Toni normally didn't care for loud bars, but she had a great time. Everyone was in a wonderful mood.

It had been a long time since she'd gone to a bar and she and Linda danced quite a bit. They also played several games of pool— Toni was horrible, but Linda could have gone pro—and even two games of darts. By the end of the evening, the whole group was exhausted.

Jake had dropped off Toni first. Linda walked her to the door and they agreed to go out again soon, as friends, of course. A quick hug at the front door and Toni was again at home with Mr. Rupert.

She curled up on the couch with him and turned on the TV. She flipped through a few channels and stopped on an old Alfred Hitchcock movie, *Vertigo*. It had been a long week and a long day. An idea began to form in Toni's mind, but within minutes both she and Mr. Rupert were sound asleep.

# CHAPTER 8

It was still early on Monday morning and there was a nip in the air. The man walked briskly down the sidewalk, trying hard to contain his happiness. Everything was going exactly as he had planned. He took a deep breath of the cool crisp air and picked up his pace. As he rounded the corner he spotted a small coffee shop and decided to treat himself. Minutes later he was sitting on a bench in a park in the middle of downtown and sipping a cup of coffee. Several people hurried past on their way to work. No one even glanced his way. Perfect. His master plan was working.

Toni had been working at her desk for over an hour when all hell broke loose. She was summoned to her boss's office. By the time she picked up a legal pad and walked down the hall, Anne Mulhoney's outer office was filled with police officers, attorneys and God only knew who else. Toni made her way to the secretary's desk. Dorothy Whitmore was guarding her boss's door like a mother lion. She had been "Secretary to the Prosecuting Attorney," whoever that might be, for as long as anyone could remember. She was close to retirement but sharp as a tack. She remembered all faces and names. Nothing got past Dorothy, not people without appointments or subtle cues from a judge.

"What's going on, Dorothy?" Toni asked. She knew it had to be something big, but she had no idea why she had been called. She was the newest attorney in the office and there were several more senior attorneys being held at bay by Dorothy.

"It's a biggie," Dorothy replied as she ushered Toni to Anne's door. "Mix-up over at the jail. Looks like your boy Crown is gone."

Before Toni could respond she was inside Anne's office.

"Okay, everyone," Anne said as she saw Toni come in. "Let's settle down and get to business." The prosecuting attorney did not have a loud voice, but it was full of authority and confidence. She had always been able to capture the full attention of a jury and now the group gathered before her stopped talking and fumbled for chairs.

Toni felt a little out of the loop with this cast of characters. Sheriff Ramos, who was in charge of the jail, was visibly uncomfortable, but not nearly as fidgety as the two deputies standing behind his chair. Both appeared very young and scared to death. The taller one was rocking back and forth in his squeaky new black shoes. Toni thought the other one was close to losing his breakfast. Sitting to the left of the sheriff was Paul Capelli, chief trial attorney and first assistant prosecutor, busy writing notes to himself on his ever-present legal pad. He had been with the office almost twenty years and seemed to take most things in stride. He was a superb trial attorney and loved law but apparently hated the politics. Toni knew Paul would have no official position at this meeting and that he was there for moral support. Detective Frank Parker was sitting near the window. As always, he looked smug, confident and handsome. The only vacant chair in the room was next to Frank. Toni elected to remain standing.

"Thank you all for coming on such short notice," Anne began. "As you know, we've had an unfortunate mix-up this morning. Dexter Crown was mistakenly released from jail about an hour ago. In a nutshell, here's what we think happened. He apparently requested medical attention early this morning. He was then taken to the main holding cell to await transportation to the med facility. This holding cell is the same one used to house all of our overnighters, folks waiting to be released on bond, the usual drunks, et cetera. Anyway, when the deputy called the list of names of those folks being released, Mr. Crown came forward. He was let go with the others. By the time the mistake was noticed, Mr. Crown was long gone." She paused. "Sheriff Ramos, would you like to add anything?"

Sheriff Ramos shifted slightly in his chair and cleared his throat. "Thank you, Ms. Mulhoney. Um, yes, the perpetrator was released. He, um . . . Mr. Crown answered when the name John Collins was called. No one else came forward, so the deputies processed him out. Mr. Collins was being held for public intoxication, no bond or anything. Deputy Williams then noticed a man sleeping in the cell after the others were released. He assumed that was Mr. Crown and tried to wake him. When the man wouldn't come to, he called for assistance. The desk sergeant is the one who recognized that the man was Mr. Collins, not Crown." The sheriff glanced at Anne and then lowered his eyes. Toni almost felt sorry for him. She could tell that he felt personally responsible.

Anne shook her head slightly and took a deep breath. "Sheriff, is there any indication of foul play regarding Mr. Collins?"

"No, ma'am, not that we know of," he replied. "He just was still passed out from the night before. He's been in a few times. He was really drunk, I mean, intoxicated this time. He was taken to the med center for observation."

"Okay," Anne said. "But to be on the safe side, have them run a tox screen." She turned her attention to the rest of the group. "I'm holding a press conference in about an hour with Chief Jackson. It will be brief. From our standpoint, we're continuing to put together our case for prosecution. I'm sure Chief Jackson will talk about apprehending Mr. Crown." She looked around the room. "If any reporters ask any of you questions, your response will be 'no comment,' okay?"

Everyone nodded.

"That's all for now."

As everyone got up and headed toward the door, Anne gestured for Toni to stay. Toni remained standing by the door, exchanging brief hellos with the departing group. Frank winked at her as he went by. Paul Capelli was still writing on his pad but he stopped long enough to look at her and smile. As the last person left, Anne asked her to shut the door.

"Toni," Anne began, "sit down for a minute. As you probably know, I gave you this case because, well, basically it was going to be a plea. It's not that I think you're incapable, it's just that you haven't tried a case like this before."

Toni smiled and nodded. She had a feeling she was about to be pulled from Dexter Crown's case.

"Anyway," Anne continued, "we plan to proceed as before. I'm hopeful that Mr. Crown will be rearrested sometime today. Because it seems to be the jail's mistake, I don't see the need for any additional charges being filed at this time. I'm going to leave you on this case for now, but be prepared to having the press hound you. You're the prosecuting attorney of record. I just thought you should have a heads-up. Talk to Paul. He's had lots of experience in high-profile cases and knows how to handle the press."

"Thank you, Ms. Mulhoney," Toni replied. She noticed that Anne was looking through papers on her desk and took that as a sort of dismissal.

When Toni reached Anne's outer office, Paul was waiting for her and motioned for her to follow. They went into his office. She had met Paul while she was still in law school. He was a friend of her criminal law professor and had spoken to her class on several occasions. She'd made a point of talking with him after class and had grown fond of him. His enthusiasm for his work impressed her, as had a speech he'd given at a seminar during her last year of school, discussing the prosecutor's office. After that seminar she had talked to Paul about pursuing a career at his office.

Toni sat down and glanced around his office, which was neat and organized. Hanging on the wall were several framed photographs that each featured Paul and some important person. His degrees hung behind his desk alongside several awards. On his desk was a picture of a woman who Toni guessed to be his wife.

Paul began talking but never looked up from the legal pad on which he was writing. "I assume Anne told you what to do," he said.

"She told me not to talk to the press," Toni responded. She assumed that was what he meant.

"Are you having any problems?" he asked.

Again she wasn't sure what he was referring to but answered in the negative.

"Anne may be a little busy, so go ahead and give your sheets to me this week." He was still scribbling on his pad. Finally, he looked up. He blinked several times then smiled. "Anything else?"

Toni sat motionless for a moment. He still looked stressed but a little of the Paul she remembered from law school shone through. She shook her head and stood up. Paul started writing on his pad again and Toni left. She knew he was one of the best trial attorneys in town. Maybe that's because he didn't waste any time on small talk. Even so, there was something strange about him today. He didn't seem like himself.

As she made her way back to her office, she noticed the halls were almost deserted. Now that the initial excitement had passed, everyone had gone back to the daily routine. There was nothing she could do about the current situation either, so she decided that she too would return to her desk.

In the short time Toni had been working at Metro, she had become comfortable in her daily routine. Although she realized she had much to learn, she was definitely getting the hang of the basics. She glanced down at her daily calendar—1:30 Billings plea before Judge Keith, 3:00 Jackson plea before Judge Stafford. She had two arraignments tomorrow and the rest of the week was clear, so far. She was working on one of the arraignment files when Sam knocked.

"Good morning, Toni," he said. "How's life in the public eye?" He chuckled.

Puzzled, she frowned at him as he plopped down in the vacant chair.

"You know . . . Crown is missing?"

"Oh,` yeah." She sighed. "But he's the one in the spotlight, not me."

"You will be." He smiled. "The camera crews are already set up outside. If you plan to go anywhere for lunch, I'd suggest going out the side door. Reporters can be such a pain in the ass."

She laughed. "Thanks for the tip. So, what do you think about this mess? Do you think it'll take long before they pick up Crown?"

He leaned back in the chair and took a drink from his can of Diet Coke. "Well, if Frank is on the job, it shouldn't take long. He's the best damn detective I've ever seen."

Toni raised her eyebrows only slightly at that last comment, but Sam saw it.

"I know he's an arrogant son of a bitch, and he treats most women like sex objects, but if you can look past that, he's good. He plays by the rules and his reports are clear and concise. He's the best cop we can put on the stand. Even though there's folks who can't stand him socially, no one questions his professionalism."

Toni nodded and smiled. "I've heard about his record, Sam, and I know he's one of the good guys, but sometimes . . . ugh! I know I've only been here a few weeks, but he can sure grate on my nerves."

"I know," Sam said. "He comes on pretty strong at first, but he'll mellow out after a while. Once he knows you better he won't try so hard. But anyway"—he shrugged—"on to a more important subject. Betty and I need to take a headcount for this Saturday. Her brother is running this wild haunted house and invited all of us for a special tour. It's going to be great. So, should I put you down for one or two?"

"One," Toni said. "Just me, unless I can convince my cat to dress up."

Sam headed to the door and was jotting something down in his notebook when he turned toward her. "Oh, how are things working out between you and Boggs? Is she giving you everything you need?"

Hell of a loaded question, Toni thought. *I wish.* Instead she just said, "Great, Sam. She's on top of everything. Thanks."

Toni watched Sam amble down the hall and smiled. He was a very nice guy and maybe he was right about Frank. In the future she decided she'd try to look past Frank's obnoxious exterior. After all, there was no question about his professional abilities and she could care less what he did in his personal life. It takes all kinds, she thought. There. A personal realization on a Monday. She laughed out loud. And she needed to come up with a costume in less than a week.

By the time she was ready to leave work that day, the media had tripled their ranks outside the building. They had been given a barrage of "no comments" all afternoon. The morning press conference had been short and sweet, and there had been no further developments. Dexter Crown had not been seen. Toni wondered if the media would be in the parking garage too.

Just then Boggs arrived at her office door. "Are you parked out front or in the garage?"

Toni was momentarily taken aback. What timing. "I'm in the garage," she said. "Are they there?"

"Not on the east exit."

Toni motioned for her to come in and sit down, which Boggs did immediately. "Well," Toni said, "I assume we're both talking about the media?"

Boggs laughed and nodded. "I don't think they'll bother you, but I wanted to let you know. They're mainly waiting for Anne to leave, but it'll be a long wait. She slipped out about forty-five minutes ago. It should be all over pretty quickly. If I know Frank, he probably knows all of Crown's haunts and will pick him up tonight."

Toni thanked her for the information while she packed up her things. "Hey, did Sam tell you about the haunted house?"

"No. What's the scoop?"

Toni lit up. It was great to feel like part of the gang and pass along news. She was almost as animated as Sam as she told Boggs what she knew. The two women then exchanged stories of favorite haunted houses. Nearly a half-hour had passed before Boggs glanced at her watch.

"Gee, Toni, it's a quarter to six. I'm sorry I kept you. I guess I better pack up and head out." She rose from her chair but didn't leave.

"Thanks again for the media update. I guess I'll go through the east exit." Toni thought about the prospect of going home to her quiet apartment and wished she could think of a viable reason to invite Boggs. Could she tell her she needed help on one of her cases? No, there was nothing urgent. Boggs would see through that. Maybe she could ask for help with her computer. A lame idea. It was a laptop, for Pete's sake, and all she did was word processing. Shit.

Boggs broke the silence. "Boy, I'm starved. I could really go for a burger and a huge plate of fries. You know, the kind you get in a bowling alley or corner tavern? Disgusting, but delicious! Doesn't that sound good?"

Toni grinned. Gee, what a novel idea. Ask her for dinner. Harmless enough. Everyone eats. *Why didn't I think of that? Way to think on your feet, Toni.*

"That does sound good, Boggs. How about it? The two of us can treat ourselves to a real grease fest. Do you know any good spots?"

Toni watched as Boggs attempted to disguise her surprise at the invitation, as if she never dreamed Toni would want to go. Boggs stammered, "Well, I know a great hole in the wall over on Clark Street. It's good, cheap and greasy. Are you up for it?"

"You bet," Toni replied. "I'd like to change into some comfies first, if you don't mind. Where on Clark is this place? Should I meet you there?"

"Well, it would be just as simple for me to pick you up. It's on my way. How about we both head home, change clothes, and I'll pick you up at seven. Would that be okay?"

Toni nodded. "As long as I don't have to dress formal, that will give me plenty of time. I just need to feed Mr. Rupert."

"Greasy burgers it is," Boggs said. "The dress code is comfy. See you at seven." With that Boggs left Toni's office with a bounce in her step.

As Toni drove home that evening, she mentally pictured and discarded seven outfits. Jeez, this was just dinner at a hole in the wall. But still, even though she and Boggs would never be more than friends, she wanted to look good. As she pulled into her parking space, she realized she was humming a nondescript tune. She glanced in the rearview mirror and laughed when she saw her own reflection. How long had she had that ridiculous grin on her face? *What a goomer!*

As soon as Toni entered her apartment, Mr. Rupert knew something was up. The energy and excitement was contagious. He hopped up on the back of the couch and began meowing loudly. Something good was going on and he wanted to be involved.

"Hi, handsome," she sang. "How's my boy?" The words were the same, but he seemed to know something was different. Mr. Rupert frowned as if he considered himself pretty good at reading humans, especially her, but just couldn't put his paw on it. Chuckling, Toni ruffled his head and went to the kitchen to fix his dinner. She spooned cat food into his dish and then announced, "Soup's on," as he stared at her for at least two seconds before the call of food overtook him.

Upstairs, Toni stripped off her suit and those damn pantyhose in a flash and jumped in the shower. She was already toweling off when Mr. Rupert entered the bathroom. Instead of her normal dialogue with him, she was humming. From her walk-in closet she grabbed her oldest jeans and a sweatshirt and glanced at Mr. Rupert as he watched her with fascination.

Toni pulled on her clothes and grabbed some socks and tennis shoes. She ran a brush through her hair, glanced at the mirror and smiled. As a last-minute thought, she sprayed on a touch of her favorite cologne and headed back downstairs.

She glanced around her livden. Everything looked okay. She took her driver's license and cash out of her briefcase and stuffed them in her pocket. She was ready. She looked at her watch. Six thirty. Not bad. She poured herself a glass of iced tea and settled down on the couch with the day's mail. She saw the letter from Sandy stuck in a flyer on the table and realized she had never read it. Jeez. Her mind must not be operating as usual. She couldn't believe she hadn't opened that immediately. Mr. Rupert took his usual spot next to her.

Toni tore open the letter from her old co-worker. It was full of the basics—Sandy's new husband, their honeymoon in Hawaii and their new apartment in Chicago. Toni was so happy for her. Sandy had been through a bad marriage years ago and Toni was afraid she would never get involved with anyone again. Apparently Sandy had a new job as a therapist dealing mostly with phobias. Toni stopped. Now where had she just read something about phobias? She shrugged and finished the letter. The rest of today's mail was pretty routine. Her thoughts turned to the evening ahead.

"Well, boy, I'm going out to a greasy spoon for dinner," she explained. "Boggs will be picking me up at seven. I know, but it's not a date. She's really nice, don't you think? Anyway, I've got to eat, don't I?" After giving Mr. Rupert the grocery store flyers, she went through the remainder of the pile. Bill. Bill. Alumni newsletter asking to please donate money. Ha! She could barely pay her student loans and they wanted money? Bill. Sweepstakes—"You're a winner." Community newspaper. Toni gathered the bill pile and put it on her table. The remaining mail, except for the paper and

Sandy's letter, was ceremoniously placed in the trash. She returned to the couch and had just begun reading the paper to Mr. Rupert when the doorbell rang. It was 6:50.

"Sorry, I guess I'm early," Boggs said. "I didn't expect to make all the lights and there was hardly any traffic."

"No, that's great." She waved her in. "I'm ready. All I need to do is grab my coat and I'm ready to roll." She went to the closet and retrieved an old jacket. It was faded and well worn with the year '42 sewn on the sleeve and the letter "W" on the front.

"What a great jacket. Where did you get it?"

"It belongs to my dad. He was manager, i.e., water boy, on the football team in high school. I borrowed it from him ages ago and I haven't had a chance to return it yet."

Boggs laughed. "Oh, do your folks live out of town?"

"Well, I suppose they do . . . technically. They live about fifteen miles outside the city limits. In all honesty, I hope I never have to give this jacket back to him. This may sound corny, but it makes me feel good, almost hopeful. Anyway, enough about my odd little quirks. Are you ready for food?"

Boggs readily agreed and after a quick pat on Mr. Rupert's head, Toni led the way out. Boggs seemed in a cheerful mood and chatted easily as they walked toward her SUV. It wasn't until they were driving to Aunt Hattie's, the hole in the wall, that Toni felt the electricity between them. There was no question. They were sitting less than two feet apart. The music on the radio was slow and sensual. Toni wondered if Boggs felt it too. She was acting more than a little nervous and flipped the radio to an all-talk station. There was no conversation until Boggs hit a somewhat large pothole. That began what could only be described as a painfully dull discussion of the fascinating subject of street repair. By the time they pulled up in front of Aunt Hattie's, Toni was breathing a sigh of relief and questioning the wisdom of this whole idea.

She got out and looked up and down the sidewalk. Although there were several cars, all she saw was an old warehouse and a few closed shops. Puzzled, she glanced over at Boggs.

"I told you it was a dump," Boggs said. "Are you sure you're up for it?"

Toni nodded slowly. "Sure. I trust your judgment, and I can actually smell food, but where in the hell is it?"

Boggs laughed and pointed to a tiny sign hanging above the door to the warehouse. It was made of wood and barely discernible from the building itself. She headed for the door and Toni followed. Unsure of what she would find inside, Toni took a deep breath, then crossed the threshold. She was surprised to discover a remarkably quaint diner inside. There were about 20 tables, each with its own candle and mismatched silverware. A sign by the cash register informing customers to seat themselves. Boggs headed over to a corner table. A waitress appeared almost immediately. She was dressed in jeans and a flannel shirt that had obviously been shrunk in the dryer. It clung to her like saran wrap and was unbuttoned dangerously low.

"Hello, ladies." She smiled seductively. "Menus are on the table. Can I get you something to drink?" she asked as she leaned down. Both Toni and Boggs averted their eyes.

Toni grabbed a menu and stared intensely for a moment. She then casually looked at the waitress. "I think I'll have the house white wine."

Boggs suppressed a giggle and without looking up said, "Me, too." The waitress nodded, smiled and disappeared. There was a momentary silence at the table. Boggs was the first to speak. "Very interesting outfit, don't you think?"

"Oh, yes. Fabulous plaid pattern. It really set off her . . . eyes," Toni replied with all the seriousness she could muster.

That was all it took. Both of them started laughing and continued to giggle like teenagers until the waitress returned with their glasses.

After they had regained their composure, Toni said. "I guess I wasn't expecting that. At least not here, but I suppose I didn't know what to expect. But I will say that she certainly made an impression." She smiled slightly. "And she did fill out that shirt well."

Boggs nodded. "Aunt Hattie's *is* different. Aunt Hattie herself does a lot of the cooking and she's known for having an interesting clientele. But the food is cheap and really hits the spot. I highly recommend the burger basket. It's two patties with cheese, lettuce, tomato and onion and comes with more fries than you can possibly eat."

After the waitress returned and took their order, Toni and Boggs began chatting. It started with superficial talk of wine and food but quickly turned to telling about their lives. Toni carefully avoided the subject of relationships but otherwise gave a detailed account, as did Boggs. They were relating college dorm stories when their food arrived. Toni thought for sure a few more buttons would pop as the waitress balanced their plates, two glasses of water and a bottle of ketchup.

"Can I get you anything else? Maybe some hot sauce? Or how about some more wine?" The two assented to more wine and the waitress left.

Toni looked down at her "burger basket." "My God, this is huge. There must be a least two pounds of fries here." She quickly ate a few and let out a sigh. "Heaven. Simply heaven."

They continued their conversation between bites of crispy fries and juicy burgers. At some point the waitress left the wine bottle on the table. By the time Toni declared she could eat no more, the wine bottle had been drained. They pushed their plates with the remaining pound of fries to the edge of the table and Boggs moaned.

"I am so stuffed," Toni said. "I don't think I can walk. That was the best burger I've ever had. How did you ever find this place?"

Boggs smiled. "An old friend of mine brought me here years ago, and I've been addicted ever since. I come here at least every two weeks to get my grease allotment. The majority of the time I come alone and entertain myself with people-watching, although I bring a book to disguise my intentions."

"Gee," Toni said. "I guess I threw a wrench in your routine." She smiled.

"No, no," Boggs stammered. "I wanted you to come." Her face flushed. "I mean, it's nice to have company when you eat."

Toni immediately felt the electricity. She suddenly realized that throughout dinner, although she had avoided the subject of dating, she had not refrained from leaning close and touching Boggs's arm as she spoke. Had Boggs noticed? Was she flirting? Oh, God, she was so attracted to this woman. Could Boggs see it in her eyes? Had she been making a fool of herself? Gee, maybe she shouldn't have drunk so much wine.

She purposefully leaned away from Boggs. She shook her head slightly in an attempt to clear the alcohol haze. Unfortunately, the only result was pure paranoia. She became painfully aware of her attraction to Boggs and attempted to counteract what she viewed as blatant flirting. Her change of behavior was so abrupt, in fact, that it clearly alarmed Boggs.

Just then, the waitress appeared. "Can I get you ladies anything else? Another bottle of wine or some apple pie?" Each word spoken seemed to strain the buttons on her shirt. She grinned.

"I think that's all, thanks," Boggs said quickly.

"Yes," Toni added. "Could we have the check please?"

The waitress whipped the ticket from her back pocket and placed it midway between Boggs and Toni. When they both reached for it at the same instant, their hands met. Both jerked away, suffered a moment of embarrassment and then began to giggle. The tension eased.

"Well, obviously we're both very anxious to part with our hard-earned money," Boggs said. "Since this is my hole in the wall, why don't you let me treat?"

"Absolutely not," replied Toni. "In fact, I feel I owe you just for the experience alone."

They laughed and agreed to split the check. Each of them placed fifteen dollars on the table to cover the food, wine and a healthy tip. Smiling, they stood up to leave. The sexual tension had lessened and Toni felt the warm bond between them. They chatted easily on the ride home. When Boggs dropped her at her town-house, Toni waved broadly. She had made a new friend.


On Friday evening, the man was walking the city streets. There was an intense argument raging inside his head. At the moment both sides were holding their own. He struggled to keep his composure. Tonight he needed to blend into the crowd. He couldn't afford to be recognized. He should have stayed inside, but something more powerful compelled him to walk. The voices became louder.

"It's over. They know it's you. Do the right thing." That was his left side talking. The voice of reason. Sometimes he hoped that side would win. It always started off with the left side being more powerful.

"That bitch doesn't know her place." The right side was getting louder. "Sitting up there, like she's better than anyone else. She thinks she can tell me what to do. She's a whore. I'm the one who is running the show."

He continued to walk but his pace had quickened. He knew that he must gain control. If he kept walking, he'd be able to concentrate. Just a little farther. The arguing shouldn't last much longer. He began to focus on his breathing and the cadence of his step. As the voices waned, he smiled. The next stage of his master plan was so close now. His destiny was clear.

As he continued walking down the populated streets, no one gave him a second look. He blended in well. To the passing gaze, he knew he could have been anyone. Anyone.

# CHAPTER 9

Another week passed quickly for Toni, although it had been stressful. Everyone in the office seemed tense. Dexter Crown had not been found. The media had been unrelenting in their coverage, accusing the entire Fairfield justice system of everything from corruption to just plain stupidity. By Friday it was obvious that nerves were frayed. Anne Mulhoney had canceled the staff meeting and the new cases had simply been assigned by Paul via a short memo. There had been no chitchat in the halls. The other attorneys seemed to be as overloaded with work as Toni was. With the media onslaught, everyone was making sure every *i* was dotted and every *t* was crossed. Toni had followed suit.

Toni realized that in the last few days she hadn't had a normal conversation with anyone. Sure, she had exchanged information with the other attorneys, gotten reports from the police and asked Boggs for various things, but that was all. Everyone seemed to be overloaded, rushing to court or back to their offices. There was kind of a panic in the air—not on the outside, but more like an undercurrent. It was all very unsettling. She had spoken to Frank that morning and he looked like hell. She knew he was under the gun to find Crown, but it looked like he hadn't slept since Monday. Even Paul Capelli looked dazed. She had seen him several times walking briskly down the halls with a strange expression on his face. He never acknowledged her, but then again he didn't seem to notice anyone. It was probably because he was handling a lot of Anne's work this week. Anne had been attending several closed-door meetings but still appeared to be composed and in control. Toni admired her greatly.

Now here it was Friday and she felt as though she hadn't gotten anything done. Sure, she had been in court, written letters, motions and requests, but there was still an underlying feeling that she had forgotten something. She tried to go through all pending projects in her mind. Nothing jumped out at her. Even though Dexter Crown hadn't been located, that wasn't what was troubling her. At least she didn't think so.

Hmm. Maybe she was just thinking about her costume for the party. She should call Mom and Dad and see if they'd finished working on her jacket. The party was tomorrow. Probably that's what was bugging her.

After a quick phone call Toni felt better. Her mom had just completed the finishing touches. Dad had to run some errands downtown and would be happy to drop by the office *if* Toni promised to take pictures of the finished outfit. Toni promised. She smiled. Her folks had been eager to take on this project when she called a couple days ago. She had apologized for the late notice but asked for some ideas. Actually, she only asked to borrow a large jacket, but after telling them her ideas, they insisted on doing more. They were both retired now and dearly loved "projects." Although they had undoubtedly bickered about the details, Toni knew they enjoyed working together. And after 40 years of marriage, that was quite an accomplishment.

Toni gathered some paperwork and stopped off at the receptionist's desk. Chloe smiled and held up one finger when Toni arrived, indicating she was on the phone. Chloe wore a wireless headset and it was often difficult to tell whether or not she was talking to you or a caller. Toni watched in amazement. Chloe was able to answer 12 lines, transfer, take notes and give info without ever making a mistake. She remembered voices as well as names, all while working on some unrelated project on her computer.

After about two minutes she turned back toward Toni. "Good afternoon, Ms. Barston. What can I do for you?"

Even though Toni had insisted she call her by her first name, Chloe was adamant about referring to all personnel as Mr. or Ms.

"Well," Toni said. "I wanted to let you know I was running down to the clerk's office for a few minutes. My dad is supposed to drop by this afternoon, so could you let him know I'll be back in a jiffy?"

Chloe smiled and nodded but was again answering the phone. Amazing, Toni thought. She had trouble keeping track with just one phone. She hoped they paid Chloe well. With that, Toni headed to the second floor.

She returned almost 30 minutes later, mildly frustrated. The clerk, Slow Lucy, had been unusually drained of energy today. Her steps had always been slow, but today it was almost painful. She wasn't disabled in any way—just deliberate. The walk from her desk to the counter, 15 feet at most, took almost a full minute. That was after she acknowledged your presence, sighed, rearranged the papers on her desk, sighed, then pushed her chair back. On days when Toni was in a hurry, it was infuriating, and on days when she was not, it was almost comical. Today Toni's mood fell somewhere in the middle. As she approached the receptionist's desk on her return, Chloe again raised one finger. Toni waited.

After a few seconds, Chloe handed her a large paper grocery sack. "Ms. Barston, your father dropped this off for you. I told him you'd be back very soon, but he didn't want to bother you at work. He sure was beaming, though. He seems very proud of you."

Before Toni could respond, Chloe was back to the phones. Toni headed for her office and once there dove into the bag. She pulled out a large blue workman's jacket and held it up. Although it was at least four sizes too big, it was perfect. Neatly embroidered on the front left side was the name "SLIM." She turned the jacket around and giggled. The back was emblazoned with "REFRIGERATOR REPAIR." She dug farther into the bag and found one of her dad's shirts and a huge tool belt, complete with tools. There was also a pair of used blue jeans, size 42. She was elated. She now only needed one more item to complete the look. This would be her best costume ever. While she was continuing to admire her parents' handiwork, she was startled by Boggs's voice coming from behind her. She quickly stuffed the items back into the sack.

"What's this? Did you go shopping during your lunch hour?" Boggs was attempting to look over Toni's shoulder.

"Just admiring my prize-winning costume," Toni replied. "Hey, no peeking."

She turned to face Boggs as she folded the top of the grocery sack. Although she wanted her costume to be a surprise, she also desperately wanted to share her excitement. She struggled with this dilemma for an entire 30 seconds before her excitement overtook her. She'd always had trouble with surprises.

"Okay. I can't stand it any longer. Shut the door."

Boggs responded without question.

Once it was shut, Toni said, "Promise you won't tell. I'm going to be a refrigerator repairman."

Boggs's expression could best be described as, well, blank, as if she was trying to imagine how dressing as a repairman could be a great costume, let alone prize-winning. Clearly feigning enthusiasm, she said, "Boy . . . that sounds really great."

Toni didn't let Boggs's total lack of comprehension and understanding dampen her enthusiasm. "Okay. Picture the guy from *Saturday Night Live*." Boggs's expression remained a blank. Toni continued, "Remember? A huge guy with his pants so low in the back you could see his crack?" Toni was laughing now.

It took only a minute or so before Boggs got it. A broad grin broke out on her face, but she still looked a bit puzzled. "How? I mean, well, you're not planning on . . . you know . . ." She was stammering and seemed slightly embarrassed, her cheeks reddened.

Toni opened the paper sack and retrieved her jeans. She held them up. "I'm going to strap on a couple pillows and wear these." She grabbed the jacket from the sack. "This is my jacket." She beamed. "I've got the whole outfit. My folks put it together for me. Of course, I still need to pick up my rubber butt, but it will be absolutely perfect."

"Your what?" Boggs's eyebrows shot up.

"My rubber butt. It's on hold at Jack's Costume Shop," Toni replied.

"Your butt is on hold?"

After a slight pause, they both realized how outrageous that sounded and began laughing.

Toni said, "I'm going over to pick it up after work. Do you want to come along? Maybe there's something there to add to your costume." Even as she spoke, she realized how unrealistic her suggestion had been. She was sure that Boggs would have plans tonight. Hell, it was Friday night. How pathetic, Toni thought. Her big excitement was to pick up a rubber butt. And she was so jazzed about it that she'd invited Boggs. *Boy, I really do need to get a life.*

Boggs seemed surprised by the offer. "That sounds like fun. I've never been to Jack's. What time?"

"Well, how about seven?" Toni thought for a moment. "It's only about a mile from my place, so if you just want to drop over, we'll go from there." Boggs agreed and they returned to their work.

The rest of the afternoon passed quickly, but by the time 5:00 rolled around, Toni was packing her briefcase. She didn't relish the thought of working over the weekend. She looked at the files she had placed inside, then looked at her calendar and decided she'd have time to finish the work on Monday. No need to do it over the weekend. She took the files out. She began to close her empty briefcase, but at the last minute she put Dexter Crown's file inside. She wasn't sure why she did. Maybe it was because it didn't feel right carrying an empty briefcase.

The man was tired, very tired. It had been a long week. The voices had gotten so loud at one point that he was afraid others could hear. The left side had put up a fair fight, but he had known from the beginning that it would lose. Now the left side was just an occasional murmur. It wouldn't be long now. Maybe tonight. Maybe tomorrow.

As Toni drove home from work she remembered she was out of milk, so she stopped at the grocery store. Her plan was to just run in, grab a quart and go. Big mistake. Never go to the grocery store when you're hungry. She entered the store, picked up a shopping basket and headed to the dairy section, via the snack aisle.

Wow. Wavy Lays were on sale. Buy one get one free. What a deal. She grabbed two bags. Wheat Thins. Oh, yum. She hadn't had those in ages. They'd be great to have in her desk at work. Into the basket they went. From the dairy section she got her milk. It was right next to the cheese. Ooh, Gouda cheese. That would be perfect on the crackers. Satisfied, she headed to the checkout, bypassing the chips. Instead she perused down the aisle filled with beer and wine. A huge sale sign caught her eye. Gosh! White wine for only $5.49. Great price. And it was a pretty good label. She really should keep an extra bottle or two on hand. She grabbed three. No, make that four. The basket was full now, so she got in line. While waiting, and after reading the headlines of all those weekly gossip papers, she noticed a display to her left. Hmm . . . Little Debbie's oatmeal pies. She used to eat those in college. Boy, were they good. She added a box to her basket. The cashier rang up her items. As Toni lugged the bags to her car she was shaking her head. That was the most expensive carton of milk she had ever bought.

Toni arrived home, fed Mr. Rupert and started putting the groceries away. Of course, she had to open one bag of chips. She looked in the fridge. She already had one bottle of wine in there. She glanced at her watch and realized she only had 45 minutes before Boggs was due to arrive. Enough time for a light snack. She poured herself a glass of wine and cut off a hunk of cheese. Cheese, chips and wine.

"Healthy fare tonight, Mr. Rupert," she said. "Protein, dairy, grains and, um, fruit." She giggled and put the rest of her things away. The four bottles of wine went in the fridge.

Toni went upstairs to get ready. She quickly showered and pulled on her favorite jeans and an old faded denim workshirt. She would put her shoes on later. Comfy and relaxing clothes. Back downstairs, she took her chips, cheese and wine to the living room. Instead of turning on the TV, she flipped on the stereo and lit a couple of candles. With her feet on the coffee table and Mr. Rupert by her side, she let out a sigh.

"Ah, this is nice. Tasty treats, good wine, mellow music and my handsome boy. A perfect way to relax. It's been one hell of a week."

Boggs turned on the news as she drove to Toni's. She hoped to get the forecast but instead heard the latest report about Crown, which noted that many of the city's residents were becoming more anxious. After hearing that "a serial murderer is on the loose," one resident had called in and complained about "our inept police department." Apparently some of the women were arming themselves with everything from mace to guard dogs to automatic weapons. Husbands and boyfriends were masking their anxiety with talk of killing Crown themselves. The police department was trying to ease the minds of the public, but their efforts were futile. In reality, Boggs knew, there was nothing for them to do until they caught him—or he killed again. She turned off the radio just as she pulled into Toni's parking lot.

Toni opened the front door with glass in hand and Boggs stepped inside. She suspected she'd replay the 30 seconds that followed at least a hundred times. She'd arrived expecting to spend maybe an hour with Toni at a costume store. But when that door opened, her heart melted. Before her stood the woman of her dreams. As she crossed the threshold, she felt as though she had walked into a movie. Maybe it was the music and flickering candles. Maybe it was the peaceful and comfortable feeling of Toni's townhouse. Maybe it was seeing her, barefoot, wearing an untucked old shirt and holding a glass of wine. Boggs felt like she had finally come home after all these years. Those intense feelings lasted less than a minute, but it was as if they left a permanent mark on her. As if she had glimpsed into the future. She was brought back to reality by the sound of Toni's voice. What had she just said?

"Boggs, are you okay?" Toni asked, clearly concerned.

"What? Oh, sure." Boggs shook her head. "I guess my mind was somewhere else. I'm sorry. What did you say?"

"I just wondered if you wanted a glass of wine before we go," Toni said. "I mean, if you're pressed for time we can go ahead and leave."

"A glass of wine sounds great," Boggs agreed.

Toni motioned for her to sit and went into the kitchen. She began describing her evening, including a trip to the grocery store that got out of control.

"So it felt so good to sit here and just get lost in the music and wine." She handed Boggs the wineglass.

Boggs leaned back on the couch, took a long, slow drink and sighed. "This is nice." Two minutes passed. "Really nice."

The two of them sat in comfortable silence, drank their wine and listened to the music. Boggs enjoyed the soothing voice of Norah Jones.

She liked the look and feel of Toni's apartment. The walls were a light sage green with accents of tan and red. The old couch was comfortable and welcoming. The candles gave the room a warm glow.

When their glasses were nearly empty, Toni said, "Well, how about you and me heading to Jack's to pick up my butt?" They laughed. "I'll get my shoes and coat."

Boggs put on her jacket as Toni got ready.

"I'll drive if that's okay. I know the way," Toni said. Boggs didn't mind. Toni unlocked the passenger door first and opened it for her, then walked around and hopped in her side. The gesture was not lost on Boggs. One eyebrow instinctively shot up. Toni's car was small. Toni could have easily unlocked the door from the inside. Later, when Toni shifted into third gear Boggs realized Toni's hand was about six inches from her knee. Her heart beat faster.

When they got to Jack's, Boggs was confused. It looked like any other card shop, decorated for Halloween. There were only about six people inside, which didn't correspond to the large number of cars parked outside. Toni led her to the back of the store and down a flight of stairs. Boggs gasped when she reached the basement, huge and literally crammed full of Halloween "stuff" and people. One entire wall was dedicated to hats. There were gruesome statues and full-size monsters peppered throughout. As they wove their way around various displays, she saw every type of costume imaginable, from Snow White to Bondage Betty. There were also thousands of accessories including wigs, makeup and jewelry. They squeezed by an animated group of teenagers and through another doorway. Boggs scanned the walls and chuckled.

"This is the body parts room," Toni explained as she headed over to the clerk. That was a major understatement. Hanging on the walls was every body part imaginable. All shapes and sizes, some were true to life and others were huge. On the floor were boxes of severed arms and legs with ragged red edges.

Boggs picked up a foot. "This one looks familiar." She tossed it back and went to take a closer look at the wall. She was studying one of the "parts," the torso of a muscular man with lifelike chest hair, when Toni appeared at her side holding a large rubber butt, which she handed to her. It had Velcro straps on the side. Boggs held it up for inspection and laughed. This big butt even had dimples.

"Won't this be great?" Toni chuckled.

Boggs was finally able to visualize the entire refrigerator repairman outfit and she couldn't help but laugh. Toni had been right . . . this would be a prize-winner.

They began wandering through the aisles and spent at least thirty minutes in the mask section, trying on one after another. Some were goofy like Wilma Flintstone, some gross and some hideous. Next they headed to the hats. After Boggs had tried on a bright yellow Dick Tracy hat, Toni asked, "Are you going to be a gumshoe tomorrow?" She tried on a flowered hat with blond pigtails.

Boggs was admiring her glow-in-the-dark hat in the mirror. "Of course! I would like to add a twist, but I haven't been able to come up with anything. Hard to top the gum. Any ideas?"

Toni tried on a baseball cap with a jumbo propeller on top. "I don't know." She flicked the propeller. "Maybe you need a prop?" She pointed to her hat.

Boggs glanced over at Toni and a light went off in her head. "That's it! Perfect. I need a miniature umbrella. Do you think they have one here?"

Without a word, Toni grabbed Boggs's arm and steered her to another part of the store. They found huge umbrellas, parasols and a pair of sunglasses with wipers. Toni dug around on the shelf and located two miniature umbrellas. One was hot pink and the other was black, Boggs's choice. She was still wearing the bright yellow hat and she held the umbrella above her head.

"Now I'm an 'undercover' gumshoe. If I can figure out how to attach this thing to the hat, I'll be all set," she said.

Toni looked thrilled. "Oh, Boggs, it's perfect." She moved closer to examine the props. She was standing very close now and Boggs could smell her perfume. "I think with some tape, staples and maybe a glue gun, you could attach it with no problem. I've got everything at home if you need it." Toni shifted her focus from the hat to Boggs. Their eyes met and they both smiled. Damn. After a moment, Boggs reluctantly broke the gaze. "That would be great. Would you help me?" Toni agreed and they headed to the cashier. After Boggs paid for her hat and umbrella, she stood to the side waiting for Toni to pay for her rubber butt. Was that a Gertrude's Garage card in her wallet? No way. Gertrude's was the new gay bar in town. Was it possible? She was determined to find out.

On the short drive back to Toni's townhouse Boggs noticed a number of pizza delivery cars. That was probably because she hadn't eaten and was hungry.

As if reading her mind, Toni said, "I don't know about you, Boggs, but I think I'm going to have to order a pizza."

"That would really hit the spot. Since you volunteered to help me with my 'hat project,' I'll treat."

Within minutes of arriving at Toni's townhouse, a major decision had been reached. A large, thin-crust, ham and mushroom. Toni called in the order, then asked, "Would you like some wine?"

Boggs nodded vigorously. She definitely needed a drink. As Toni poured them each a large glass of wine, Boggs glanced around the room, looking for clues.

"Make yourself comfy. Feel free to put on some music," Toni said.

Boggs headed to the CD rack. For sure she'd find some hint here. Maybe a CD labeled "lesbian music." Just a thought.

"Take off your coat and stay a while," Toni suggested.

Boggs just nodded while perusing the music selection. She wanted something mellow, something conducive to conversation. She was also thinking about Toni's suggestion that she take off her jacket. She was still wearing a pancake waist holster. When she'd gone home to change her clothes, thinking she'd only be out about an hour or so, she hadn't bothered switching to her ankle holster. She was always a little leery about taking off her jacket around people she didn't know well. Some people, even attorneys, became somewhat nervous seeing a gun. She was always cognizant of this fact, even though she regarded it as just a necessary piece of equipment. You never knew.

She selected a CD labeled *Mellow Mix* and popped it in the stereo. She held up the case for Toni's inspection. "Is this okay?" she asked.

Toni looked up. "That's great. I haven't listened to that in quite a while. A friend of mine burned it for me. It's got a lot of oldies but goodies."

Satisfied, Boggs sat on the couch and sipped her wine. As the first song began, she smiled broadly. "My God," she said. "This sure does bring back memories."

"No kidding," Toni said. "Freshman year at college . . . all-night party at the dorm. How about you?"

Boggs chuckled. The song had been playing during an incredibly romantic evening with Sally many years ago. She was momentarily caught up in a wave of emotion. What a wonderful night that had been.

Toni leaned over and touched her arm. "Back to earth, girl. Must be one hell of a memory. Come on, I shared. Now it's your turn."

Jolted back to the present, she shifted her attention to Toni. Shit! What the hell was she going to say to her? She groped for a plausible scenario. Best to stick as close to the truth as possible, she decided.

"Well, it was playing during a romantic dinner." She smiled but said no more.

Toni cocked an eyebrow and looked as if she expected her to give more detail. "A romantic dinner, huh? Where did you go?"

Boggs hesitated. They'd been in Sally's studio apartment, sitting on the floor, surrounded by candles. She smiled. "Actually, it was in a tiny studio apartment." She didn't mean to be coy, but Toni was her colleague and she wasn't sure if she was gay or not.

Toni didn't respond, which was fine with Boggs. She took a long swallow of wine and the conversation had turned to fashion when the next song played.

"Ugh," Toni grunted. "This one reminds me of parachute pants and big hair. Yuck. And we thought we were such hot shit."

Boggs laughed. "No kidding. Everyone used so much hair spray that you'd be afraid to light a cigarette within five feet of them." She was still laughing. She had been in the Air Force during that time and never wore her hair that style, but she had always been fascinated by the look on other women.

After another glass of wine, the doorbell rang.

"Food!" Toni leapt up, but instead of walking around the coffee table to get to the front door, she stepped over Boggs's legs.

Boggs froze. She even held her breath. This had taken her by complete surprise and she wasn't prepared to have Toni suddenly within inches of her. She felt her body react. She wanted to grab her, kiss her, touch her. Anything. The whole interaction lasted maybe three seconds. She snapped out of it and quickly got to her feet, reaching into her pocket for the money. She hoped she hadn't been too obvious.

After Toni paid the pizza guy, she set the box on the coffee table and said with a flourish, "Madame, your main course. Please wait just a moment while I get the fine china."

Boggs grinned. She loved Toni's sense of humor. Toni returned from the kitchen with paper plates, napkins, a corkscrew and a new bottle of wine, which she presented to Boggs.

Boggs pretended to inspect it carefully. "Yes, this is just fine," she said. "A very good month."

Toni laughed and began to serve the meal. Boggs opened the wine and filled their glasses. As they ate and drank, Toni steered the conversation toward work, for which Boggs was grateful. She was feeling a little nervous, incredibly attracted to Toni and yet still not sure if she was gay. And even if she was, it didn't mean she was interested. Keeping the topics to work was good.

"So, Boggs," Toni said after a while, since I'm now an old-timer at the office, what can you tell me about the folks there? Is there any good gossip? People I should shy away from?"

It was a leading question but Boggs didn't mind. She thought for a moment before answering. "Well, overall I think we have a pretty good team. Some are obviously more experienced and some have huge egos, but no bad eggs." She took a few more bites of pizza. "Anne Mulhoney is very good, both as an attorney and as a boss. She has a lot of clout and people truly seem to respect what she says. I wouldn't be surprised if she became a judge in a few years." She paused to drink more wine. "Let's see. Paul Capelli is an excellent trial attorney. He can memorize every detail. He's amazing to watch. Otherwise, I don't know too much about him. I do know that his wife has tons of money. She's always in the paper, at some charity ball or something."

"I met him when I was in law school," Toni said. "He is a fantastic speaker and I talked to him a couple times. He seems a little more distant now than he did then. I guess it's because of this Crown mess."

Boggs agreed. "It's been rough on both him and Anne especially. Let's see. Who else. There's David something the third. He's pretty new. He gives me the creeps, but I think he's a decent lawyer."

"What about Frank?" Toni seemed curious.

"I know you've already formed an opinion of him. He's never given me much trouble, mostly ignores me. He's definitely a member of the old boys' network. He never gives me leads, but he gives them to Sam, so that's okay. Rumor has it that Frank has a checkered past and that's why he always knows what's going down on the streets. When I first started working at Metro I did a little digging but came up dry. I got bored with him. I think maybe he started the rumor himself."

They laughed. "That sounds like him," Toni said. "Mr. Studball. The dude who knows the score. I know he's good, but he still annoys me."

Boggs nodded. "Most of the other detectives are okay. There

are a few who barely work but always seem busy. But they're all right. I play softball with a few."

Toni's eyes lit up. "Oh, you play softball? I love softball."

"Do you play?" Boggs asked, surprised.

"No." Toni shook her head. "I'm a professional fan. I got hooked years ago. This past summer I would just show up at a ball field and watch whomever was playing. It was a good way to enjoy myself without spending money."

Boggs grinned. This was interesting. "Did you follow any particular team or league?" she asked.

Toni sipped her wine, then looked directly at Boggs and smiled. The wine surely had played a part in her boldness. "I went to a Wednesday night league mostly. A friend of mine used to play and after she moved I just kept going."

Upon hearing that, Boggs had a feeling. A strong feeling. She couldn't quite pinpoint it, but she knew, or at least she thought she knew. At the very least, Toni was open-minded. Boggs knew exactly who played on the Wednesday night league. She looked at Toni, winked and said, "I understand the women's league is a lot of fun. I'm thinking of playing on it next summer." She waited for a response and she got more than she had hoped.

Toni grinned from ear to ear, held Boggs's gaze and said, "I'll be there, cheering for you."

Nothing else was said. It didn't have to be said, but it was as though neither wanted to break the spell by saying too much. She had a strong enough inkling and was thrilled. They finished their pizza and continued to sip wine. Toni was positively glowing.

Boggs reluctantly broke the silence. "Well, I suppose we should work on my hat. If I drink much more wine I'll be utterly useless. As it is now I'll probably laugh incessantly."

Toni nodded, adding that she too had reached her limit. "I'll either embarrass myself or fall asleep if I keep this up." She went upstairs to retrieve the necessary supplies while Boggs got her hat and umbrella. Toni returned with a box crammed full of various crafts paraphernalia.

"My gosh. I would have never pegged you as a craftsperson," Boggs said. "You've got enough stuff in there to make just about anything." She began poking through the items in the box.

Toni shook her head. "Actually, I hate doing anything remotely crafty. My folks insist I keep this stuff here. When they come to visit they always have such grand ideas and they like knowing they have supplies readily available. I did, however, use the staple gun last week to tack down a corner of the carpet."

Toni placed all the items on the coffee table and they began their project. Both acted as though they knew what they were doing, but that ruse lasted only a few minutes.

"I am absolutely clueless." Toni laughed. "What the hell are we doing?"

Boggs was sitting on the floor trying to figure out how to work the glue gun. She was failing miserably. She raised her arms to the heavens and moaned. "Martha Stewart, I need you."

Toni, who had been sitting on the couch, was laughing so hard she rolled to the floor, nearly spilling the contents of the box. "We're two very intelligent, charming and somewhat tipsy women," she said emphatically. "We should be able to handle scissors and glue." As she held her side and wiped tears from her eyes, she looked over at Boggs.

Boggs was still on her back, laughing hysterically. It was contagious. After a few minutes, she was exhausted. She sat up and began studying the hat and umbrella intensely. "We must look at this logically," she said after a minute or two. "It must be straight and secure."

"Don't look at me," Toni said.

It took almost a half-hour, but between the two of them they were able to securely attach the umbrella by removing the black band from the hat and using duct tape, which was hidden when the band was replaced . . . almost.

After seeing a small ring of tape showing above the band, Boggs sighed. "This is good enough for me."

"Martha Stewart would be so proud. Why, in one evening you

were able to create a completely new ensemble for a festive Halloween gathering. And while you were busy doing that, I made some decorative plates from the used pizza box, carved a beautiful ornament from the wine cork and made the wine bottle into a retro vase!" Toni was cracking herself up.

Boggs just shook her head. "You know, I can't remember when I've had this much fun."

"I know what you mean," Toni replied. "In these past few weeks, I've laughed more and, well, had more fun than I've had in the past few years. Boy, that's a pretty sad statement." She paused for a moment and got serious. "It's strange, but I feel so comfortable with you."

Boggs smiled softly. "Funny, I feel that way too." Both were silent for a few minutes, then Boggs laughed. "I never thought I'd enjoy spending time with a Martha Stewart protégé." Then she told Toni about last year's Halloween party and described some of the costumes. "This year should be even more fun. No one has ever worn a huge rubber butt before."

"I'm really looking forward to a fun night," Toni said. "Do you want to ride together?"

Boggs jumped at the chance. She never did like going to parties alone. "Sounds great. Sam said to come around seven, so how about if I come over about six thirty?"

Toni thought for a moment. "Make it six fifteen and you've got a deal. I may need your help. I'm not quite sure how I'm going to strap on the pillows."

Boggs sensed that she should go. It had been a great evening. She didn't want to move too fast. When she began picking up the dinner dishes, Toni quickly stopped her.

"Don't worry about that," she said. "I'll have the maid take care of it."

Boggs smiled and moved toward the door. "Do you mind if I leave my hat here . . . since I'll be back tomorrow?"

"That's fine." Toni followed her. At the door, Boggs felt the moment turn slightly awkward. Toni said quickly, "I'll walk you out," which broke the tension.

Boggs quickly unlocked and opened her car door. Lingering for a moment, she turned to Toni and smiled. She then looked at the ground and kicked some imaginary rock. She felt like an awkward teenager and was cursing herself. Jeez. Why was she so nervous? It's not like they were on a date. *Think, damn it. Say something.* She felt stupid doing the "kick a rock" routine.

Before she could think of anything intelligent to say, Toni said, "Thanks for a great evening, Boggs." Toni was looking straight at her and smiling.

*Damn!* Boggs thought. How did she do that? Nothing seemed to rattle her. It was as if she was looking right through her.

"And thanks for the pizza," Toni continued. "It really hit the spot. Next time dinner is on me. Although it may be hard to top tonight. I kinda like fancy apartment dinners on the good china." She winked.

Boggs grinned but said nothing. She felt her cheeks flush. Whew! If this was a small example of Toni flirting with her, she was in trouble.

"So," Toni went on, "I appreciate your coming early tomorrow to help me get dressed." She was clearly enjoying herself. She moved a few inches closer and said flirtatiously, "You know, I could put out"—a long pause ensued—"a few snacks . . . we could nibble on before we go tomorrow."

"That sounds grun. I mean frate. I mean great. I was thinking great and fun, you know . . ." Boggs was stammering. *Jeez. I'm a mess. I can't even talk!*

"Are you okay to drive?"

Boggs looked at her. "Oh, sure. It's not the wine. I'm just tired," she lied. And Toni was driving her crazy. Totally blowing her mind. She couldn't even think straight. She needed to head home and regroup. She hopped in her car, rolled down the window and shut the door. There. She felt a little more in control. She took a deep breath and started the engine. Toni was standing next to her door. Boggs stared up at her. "Thanks again for your help tonight. I'm really looking forward to tomorrow night. Maybe we can get something going in the haunted house." She raised an eyebrow. Two could play at this game.

"Hmm," Toni replied. "Interesting. I wish I knew the floor plan so we could have some fun with Sam. It would be great to get in front of the others so we could scare them." She paused and then looked up with that smile of hers. "But since we don't know the layout, I guess we'll just have to feel our way through. What a shame."

Boggs shook her head and grinned. Damn, she was good. Here she thought she was out of practice. She put the car in reverse as Toni waved and went back to her townhouse.


Toni was still grinning while she cleaned up the plates and pizza box. This had been one of the most exciting evenings she'd had in recent memory. She was bombarded by emotions. It had been a hectic and hard week at work, so she was exhausted. She had spent the evening with a new friend with whom she felt very comfortable. She'd purchased a big butt and was preparing for a wonderful party. All those things combined would have made it a great Friday night. But wow! Add to that the fact that she found Boggs incredibly attractive and they had exchanged winks, smiles and double entendres, and the result was fabulous. Toni felt like a new woman. Oh, the possibilities. As she washed the wineglasses, she suddenly began to question Boggs's reactions.

Oh, my God, she thought. What if she was reading her wrong? Maybe all the sexual tension was coming from her, Toni. Maybe Boggs was nervous because it was obvious she was flirting. Was it obvious she was flirting? Duh. Maybe Boggs wasn't good at reading people. Toni supposed that was a possibility. Boggs was an investigator, for Pete's sake. Ugh! *Did I just make a complete fool out of myself?* Damn. Here's what she'd do. Tomorrow, when Boggs came over, Toni would be friendly and cheery, but no flirting. That way, maybe Boggs would think the flirting was in her imagination. That was it. No harm, no foul. Toni smiled.

As she crawled between the sheets that evening, she allowed herself to relive the events of the night. She closed her eyes and felt a smile slowly creep across her face. Reality blended with fantasy as she imagined how the night could have gone. She drifted off to sleep and that same erotic dream from weeks ago began to form. She was standing in her living room. Boggs was facing her, only three feet away. The electricity in the air was palpable. Toni was excited but nervous. Boggs took one step closer, and Toni backed up. Another step. Boggs was smiling and keeping direct eye contact. They were talking, but Toni had no clue what they were saying. She took another step back and found herself against the wall. Her knees felt weak. If Boggs took one more step . . .

Boggs drove home that night with a wide grin on her face. She had a mission. One way or another she was going to confirm her suspicions about Toni. She was pretty sure, but that wasn't good enough. As soon as she walked in her apartment she turned on her computer. She settled into her chair and her investigative skills kicked in. She ignored her e-mail and began with a list of her own. The facts were few. Toni was single and lived alone. No question there. Past relationships? No names ever mentioned. Affiliations? Maybe. Memberships? Friends?

She hopped online and began her search. She found that Toni was a member, in good standing, of the Missouri state bar and American Bar Association. She was also a former member of a professional mental health workers' association.

Well this was going nowhere. Boggs accessed another online service. Nothing. She sat back for a moment, then grinned. She found the site she needed, keyed in a special password, one she wasn't supposed to know. Despite the miracle of firewalls—and courtesy of a good friend who worked for the government—she was able to tap into Toni's financial records and assets. She did feel a tad bit guilty knowing this was not exactly legal, but she was like a bulldog who wouldn't let go once she had her teeth in something. She just had to know. She paged through current balances and other financial data. Then she hit paydirt. A closed bank account from two years ago. A joint bank account with Sadie Donaldson. Very interesting. Boggs continued to page through the information. Previous homeowner, jointly, with Sadie Donaldson. A sister? She didn't think so. Friends may own a home together, but they rarely shared a bank account.

Boggs sat back in her chair. Bank account and house. Closed account about the same time she moved into the townhouse. Coincidence? Membership card to Gertrude's Garage. Sketchy about past relationships. Winked at her several times. Flirting, at least she thought she was flirting. Boyfriend? What about Jake Hamilton? Was that a double date last week? Since Boggs had also seen Jake with Toni at the bar, her theory had a small hole. On a whim, and despite the hour, she called up a friend of hers.

"Dan? This is Boggs. How are you doing?"

"Boggs! How the hell have you been? We were just talking about you. Jim thinks he's found the absolute purr-fect girl for you. We're planning our annual pre-Christmas soiree. Should I pencil you in? December twentieth?"

Dan and Jim had been friends of hers for many years. They were known for their lavish parties and genuine good hearts. They also seemed to know all the dirt in town.

"I wouldn't miss it for the world, Dan, but I'm working on a date of my own. Listen, I was wondering if you knew a guy named Jake Hamilton. Architect?"

Dan sighed. "Well, honey, if you're thinking of jumping the fence for that gorgeous hunk of man, you're out of luck. Not only is he as queer as me, he's taken."

Boggs grinned. "What about Bob Clayton?"

"Available," Dan quipped. "Really sweet guy. What's up,

Boggs? Is this for work? Don't tell me you're on a witch hunt or something."

"Oh, absolutely not," she said. "It's just that there's this woman who . . . well, I'm now sure she's gay. She hangs out with Jake. I was just trying to eliminate the possibility that they were an item. Her name is Toni Barston."

"Doesn't ring a bell, but I don't keep up on you girls. But, ooh, tell me all about her."

Boggs filled in Dan on what she knew and felt about Toni. After she finished, Dan whistled.

"Oh, girl. You've got it bad! I hope things turn out great at that party tomorrow. Maybe you two could drop over for Sunday brunch soon. We'd love to meet her."

Boggs thanked him and promised she would be at the annual party. After she hung up the phone, she threw her fist into the air in a victory salute. Tomorrow was going to be a great day.

# CHAPTER 10

The man was walking. Not too fast, not too slow. He blended in perfectly. He knew exactly where he was going. There was no arguing in his head now. It was a singular voice, full of praise and encouragement. He was no longer tired. In fact, he had difficulty keeping himself composed. Part of him wanted to run to the house. He was almost there. He suppressed a giggle.

Tonight was a special night. He was going to preview one house before arriving at his destination. He had never done that before. But tonight was different. The voice said this was his reward. Both houses were within his "perimeter." He would go to the first . . . just for a quick look. The thought of previewing it made his hands tingle. As the house came into view, he had to remind himself to walk normally. His breathing quickened. He scanned the area. He was an expert now. He was able to spot any discrepancies. He knew exactly how everything should be, even down to the shadows. Perfect.

No one saw him. Good, his timing was impeccable. He knew just which window was his. With little effort, he hopped the chain-link fence and slipped to the side of the house. He knew there was no dog. He knew she would be sitting in that big chair in the family room, reading a book. He knew everything. His hands were tingling and he was salivating. He inhaled slowly and deeply. Every sense in his body was heightened. He positioned himself at the window between the small shrubs. There she was. Just as he knew she would be. He smiled and licked his lips. She was next. He was in control and she would be the next. One day people would realize how he had rid the world of filth. He would be recognized as a hero and they would be in awe of his brilliance.

He stared at the woman. She was oblivious to him and the truth. But soon she would know. Just like the others, she would learn the truth. He licked his lips again. It was time to go. The preview was over. It was time for the feature presentation. He smiled. He liked the sound of that.

He walked back the way he came. Just as he began to hop the fence, a car full of teenaged girls turned down the street. For a split second he was illuminated by the headlights. The car had caught him completely off guard and his pant leg snagged the fence. He dropped to the ground and turned his face away. As the car drove by, he heard the girls laughing at him.

A moment later he was walking down the sidewalk. His leg was throbbing and he could feel blood trickling down his calf and into his sock. He kept walking. He couldn't draw any attention to himself by stopping to examine his leg. The voice in his head was screaming, "You idiot! Can't you do anything right? If I've told you once, I've told you a thousand times, concentrate. You'll never be as good as the others." To the screaming he added his own condemnations. He had lost control. He had lost focus. It would never happen again. He concentrated on his walking. Concentrated on his breathing. Within minutes he was back in control. His inner vision came back into focus. He was in control again. He smiled. He turned the corner and saw the house. It was perfect. The second floor was dark. There were only a few lights burning on the main floor. The front porch was dark. He couldn't help but smile. He had been at this house the night before. He had removed the light bulb and carefully wedged a piece of plastic into the base of the socket. Even if someone had noticed the light was out and put in a new bulb, it wouldn't work. He was brilliant. He had thought of everything. He scanned the area. There was no one in sight. He slipped around to the side of the house. He looked in the window. He could see there was a light on in the study. He knew she'd be there. He felt his hands begin to tingle again. He felt the saliva on the corner of his mouth. He felt alive. The feature presentation was about to begin. He walked to the front porch and rang the bell.

Anne Mulhoney sat in her favorite chair reading an Agatha Christie novel. She'd read it many years before, but she adored her style. The stories were never gruesome and red herrings abounded. At the end of the chapter she looked up from the worn pages and smiled. It was strange being in the house alone. With both kids grown and on their own, she and Bill had slowly transitioned to an "empty nest." At first, the situation had felt awkward, but in time they grew closer than they had in years. They spent many a weekend remodeling and redecorating to fit their new lifestyles. Sarah's room had become her treasured study and Jack's room was now the "gym." She and Bill spent time there almost every morning. Both of them were active weightlifters and Anne especially took pride in her progress. They were now experiencing a whole new wonderful life together.

Anne closed her book and sighed. Oh, how she wished Bill was home tonight, but he had flown out on Wednesday to a dental conference in San Diego and wouldn't be home until the next morning. They had planned on going together and extending their stay over the weekend. She looked at the brochures still lying on the coffee table and remembered the fun she and Bill had had planning their getaway. She shook her head. If all this mess surrounding Dexter Crown hadn't happened, she'd be on the beach with Bill this weekend.

She took a few minutes to feel sorry for herself, then started to plan. Instead of moping around, she would prepare a welcome-home greeting. Bill would love this, she thought. She went to the kitchen to check for supplies and to plan a menu. She decided on Bill's favorites: steak, salad, baked potatoes and a nice red wine. The atmosphere was the important thing—music, candles and a small fire burning. Nothing extravagant, nothing overwhelming. She knew he'd be tired when he arrived home tomorrow. She just wanted to wrap him in love. She was sitting on a stool at the kitchen island feeling both excited and content. The sound of the doorbell made her jump.


Betty Clark plopped down in her favorite chair in the study. She had just gotten home from a 12-hour shift at the hospital. It had been an unusually hectic Friday in the E.R. This was the first chance she had to sit down and relax. She kicked off her shoes, wiggled her toes and sighed. She opened her can of Diet 7-Up and took a long drink. She instinctively picked up her novel that was lying on the table, but after a couple of pages, she put the book back down.

Betty was used to working long hours and coming home to an empty house, but tonight seemed different. She'd had an uneasy feeling all day, one she just couldn't shake. If Sam were home, he would be her sounding board. She leaned back in her chair and took several deep breaths in an attempt to clear her head. She was probably just tired. She wished Sam were home. He had taken the afternoon off to drive up to his mother's house. Today was her birthday. Normally Betty would have gone with him, but they were short-staffed at the hospital. Because tomorrow was their big

Halloween party, they agreed Sam would come home tomorrow morning in time to spend the day preparing for the night's fun. Betty looked at her watch. Nine in the morning was too far away. Aside from this horrible feeling, she was missing him. After 20 years of marriage, she still rushed home to see him.

She decided to make a list of the things they needed to do tomorrow. Surely that would keep her mind occupied. She got up to get a pad of paper and pencil and checked all the doors and windows. She even put the chain on the front door. It was pretty useless, but it made her feel better. With pad in hand, Betty headed back to her recliner, stopping to grab a bag of chips. Party food, she thought. Grinning, she settled in, chips and soda nearby, and began her list. The feeling of doom had not left, but she was able to focus on the big party. When the doorbell rang twenty minutes later, a shot of pure fear engulfed her. She was momentarily paralyzed and thought about remaining very still and quiet. A horrible scene passed before her eyes. That image, however, was overcome by a compelling urge to answer the door.

The door opened only a few inches due to the chain, but she could feel the door being pushed from the other side. She instinctively pushed back in an attempt to close the door again. The voice she heard didn't register for a moment.

"Honey, it's me. Are you okay?" It was Sam.

Betty fumbled with the chain, tears rolling down her cheeks. Sam wrapped his arms around her as she collapsed into his chest. He held her tightly.

"What's wrong? Did someone hurt you?" His voice seemed calm. Betty regained enough composure to tell him she was okay, just scared. They went into the kitchen and sat down, holding hands across the table.

Betty spoke first, "I guess I just got spooked, honey. I've had this creepy feeling all day and then I came home and just couldn't shake it."

She was still trembling and Sam moved his chair closer to hers their hands still entwined.

"It's okay now," he said. "I'm home. You're safe."

The idea that Sam was actually home finally registered with her. "Why are you home so early? Why didn't you call?" she asked. "I'm so grateful, but I thought you'd be home in the morning."

He reached up and gently caressed her cheek. His eyes were damp with emotion. "I was just missing you," he replied. "Anyway, Mom was tired and wanted to go to bed early. I just couldn't stand the thought of us each spending the night alone. I figured I'd just jump in the car and surprise you. I'm sorry. I should have called."

Betty began telling him about her day and how this awful feeling had overwhelmed her. Sam made them some hot pizza rolls. He listened intently to her description. After about an hour in the kitchen, she announced she was ready to "move on," and they began talking about the party. She retrieved her list and the two of them spent the next hour making final plans. When they finally went upstairs to bed, Betty was feeling safe and secure. She hung on to Sam's arm all the way to the bedroom. She noticed he was limping slightly.

"What happened to your leg, honey?" she asked.

Sam squeezed her arm and smiled. "Oh, I opened the car door and my leg was in the way. It's nothing."

As she lay in bed next to the man she loved, she prayed a bit longer than usual. Tonight she was especially grateful that they were both home together. Still, part of that horrible feeling lingered.

Anne Mulhoney was disturbed by someone ringing the doorbell this late. In this day and age, no one just "came over" unannounced. It was simply unheard of. She got up from her stool and went to the front door. Apprehensive about answering the door at night—it was after ten—she looked through her peephole. Although the face of the man was somewhat distorted, there was no doubt it was him. She shook her head. What the hell did he want at this hour? She opened the door.

"Good evening, Anne. I hope I'm not disturbing you," he said.

Anne tried not to look too perturbed. "What can I do for you, Ralph?"

"Well," he answered quickly, "I'm not one who puts his nose in other people's business. I always say that what other people do is between them and their maker, but some things you simply can't ignore. Take for instance just last week. I was out in my garden, minding my own business, when that Simpson dog came over. I don't hate dogs, mind you, but people shouldn't let them run wild like they do. Well, I had about had my fill—that dog had dug up one too many flowers for my taste—so I grabbed him by the collar and marched right over to those Simpson people. They looked at me like I had ten heads. No respect. Those people have no respect."

Anne stood there listening to him prattle on and on. He was the neighborhood busybody. Always complaining about something or somebody, he would talk for hours if you let him. She said, "Ralph, what brings you here tonight? Is there something wrong?" Thankfully this brought him back to his reason for coming over.

"Oh, yes. That Simpson girl. She and her friends were making all sorts of noise when they pulled in their driveway, laughing and carrying on. Naturally I went over to speak with them—"

"Ralph. What does that have to do with me?"

"Oh, yes. The girls told me they saw a man jump over your fence. They said he was coming out of your yard. I thought you should be told immediately . . . with all those crazy people and all. You should have the police come over. I'd be happy to tell them what I know."

Anne thanked him for the information and promised him she would look into the matter. She shut the door and locked the dead-bolt. She laughed to herself. Ralph was always trying to be involved. He had a good heart, but he drove everyone crazy. She returned to the kitchen and poured herself a glass of wine. She decided to read her Agatha Christie book for a while before going to bed.

The man had prepared for tonight much in the same way as he prepared for the other nights. His hands were covered with clear latex gloves. He wore a nondescript navy jogging suit, a type that was sold at every discount store in the city. His jogging shoes were ordinary. The baseball cap atop his head was also navy and contained the logo of the NYPD. Nothing about his appearance would draw attention. It was perfect.

When the front door opened he grinned and apologized for the late-night intrusion. The woman seemed a little perplexed at the reason he gave but stepped aside to invite him into her home, just as he knew she would. Play to her expertise and she would be happy to share her wisdom. Bitch. How dare she think she knew more than he did. She should be more concerned about her family —her husband—and stay out of the way. Tonight she would learn.

The woman closed the front door and led him to her study. His hands were tingling as his fingers closed around the cold, hard steel of his knife. It was time. He licked his lips. With a practiced move, he reached around her with his left hand and grabbed her chin. At the same time, his right hand wielding the knife, he sliced her throat. She made only a small sound before falling to the floor.

She had sensed danger too late. In a split second everything no doubt made sense, but there was nothing she could do.

He stepped back as she fell. He started giggling and dancing around the study. Perfect. Her eyes were open just like the last one. He stepped back and quickly checked himself. Except for the one glove and knife, there seemed to be no blood on him. He was good. He left her on the floor and went to her bedroom. He opened the first drawer of the dresser. Women always kept their underclothes there. She was no exception. He chose a very pretty pair. They had to be pretty. Satisfied, he returned to the woman. There was a slight gurgling noise, but he paid it no attention. He took the panties and stuffed them into her mouth.

He stood back and grinned. He frowned as he began to list all the crimes she had committed. The list was long, but her life of crime had ended. She would be happy now because she was helping him better the world. Her death would help teach other women how to behave. When he finished his explanation to her, he reached for her lifeless hand. He shook her hand and congratulated her on her acceptance of the truth. Power and anger surged through him. He could hear the bones break. This conflict of emotions always confused him. Part of him felt that wonderful sense of accomplishment and achievement of a job well done. There was a tremendous sense of relief . . . that he could rest for a while. Another part of him was filled with rage and hatred for this piece of filth lying on the floor. He scanned the room. Everything was perfect. He became once again filled with confidence and the rage drained from him. He walked calmly to the front door and left Judge Haley's house without looking back.

# CHAPTER 11

Toni awoke early on Saturday morning and went through her usual routine of making coffee and feeding Mr. Rupert. A few minutes later, with coffee in hand, she sat down and started her to-do list for the day. There were the regular Saturday chores—laundry, paying bills and vacuuming. Maybe she should do more of a fall cleaning today. That would keep her mind off tonight. She was both excited and anxious about seeing Boggs again. She looked at Mr. Rupert, who was carefully cleaning the last bit of breakfast from his face.

"Okay, boy. Here's the plan. We're going to clean this place from top to bottom. I'll start upstairs and you start down here. We should be finished in no time." She grinned. Mr. Rupert completely ignored her. She topped off her mug of coffee and headed upstairs. Within minutes she had stripped the sheets from her bed and gathered all the dirty clothes. When she got back downstairs, Mr. Rupert was in the middle of the floor in the living room, on his back with his feet in the air. He stretched and meowed as she walked by. Ah, the life of a cat. She lugged her clothes through the kitchen and put the first load in the washer.

Returning upstairs she placed fresh sheets on the bed. Satisfied, she turned to the bathroom and began the dreaded task of cleaning the toilet. She worked methodically and was finished in no time at all. She went back to her bedroom and looked at her desk. What a mess. Books were stacked on the desk and the floor. She shook her head. This called for a fortified cup of coffee.

Toni went downstairs and filled her mug with coffee . . . and a splash of Kahlua. She started the next load of laundry. Mr. Rupert had not budged from his spot on the carpet. She gathered the assorted papers and mail from the dining room table and returned to her desk upstairs. She sat down and sighed. This task alone could take an hour. There were assorted law books, novels, magazines, catalogs and even a few old psychology textbooks from her undergrad days. The mundane job of sorting and stacking all this stuff onto her tiny bookshelf took an hour and she barely made a dent. Her "throw away" pile contained a candy wrapper, one old brochure and a dried-out highlighter. For some reason, she felt compelled to keep catalogs "just in case" she needed to order something. She rarely did, even though Christmas wasn't that far off.

On her third cup of coffee now, dangerously close to her limit on an empty stomach, she began stacking her books. She arranged them by topic after flipping through each one. It wasn't that she didn't know the contents, it just brought back memories of a particular class or time. Criminal law. That was a tough class, but she had loved it. Administrative law. Ugh! Why did she still have that book? She should have sold that sucker the day of the final. In fact, she should have never bought the darn thing. She'd remained clueless throughout that class the entire semester. Ooh! Abnormal psychology. That was a great class. Mmm. Great professor, too. Toni recalled how she'd had a crush on Dr. Veronica Anderson. She paged through the book and found an old exam dealing with phobias. She remembered going into Dr. Anderson's office to ask for clarification, just so she could be close to her. Toni removed the exam and glanced at the questions. Acrophobia. Wasn't that one of the diagnoses for Crown? The ringing of the phone interrupted her train of thought.

"Well, good afternoon, honey." It was her dad. "I hope I didn't get you out of bed."

"Oh, Dad . . ." Toni glanced at the clock. "It's only eleven o'clock. But I guess if I'd been up since five like you and Mom, it would seem like late afternoon by now." She and her dad had a long-standing joke. No matter what time she would get up on a Saturday morning, he would already be sitting at the kitchen table. When she was a kid, she had tried desperately to get up first but never did. His greeting to her was always the same, "Good afternoon!" She grinned.

"Just calling to remind you to take pictures of your costume before you go tonight."

"I will, Dad. Are you all staying home tonight?" she asked. Since her parents had retired, they were always on the go.

"As far as I know, yes," he said. "We just finished painting the living room and dining room. After lunch we're going to the grocery store. It's time to start the Christmas baking. There's also a sale we wanted to check on."

Toni rolled her eyes. Her parents could cram more in one day than she could in a week. It was exhausting.

"Hang on, honey," her dad continued. "Here's Mom."

"Hi, sweetie," her mom said. "How are you? Are you getting enough sleep?"

Toni answered affirmatively.

"Make sure you take good care of yourself. Now, how are you for blouses? There's a good sale going on. How about we pick up a couple for you?"

Toni hated to shop for clothes and her parents had great taste. They also had a nose for sales. "That would be wonderful, Mom. Especially ones that don't need to be dry-cleaned."

"Done," her mom replied. Toni could hear her scratch that off her list of things to ask. "Next, we're going to the warehouse store to buy ingredients for my Christmas baking. I'm making the usual, of course, plus a few new kinds of fudge, although I won't start that until Thanksgiving. Do you have any special requests this year?"

Toni smiled. Her mother was famous for her baking. In fact, that's all anyone who knew her wanted as a gift for Christmas. She began on November first and made one type of goodie each day. Then she and Dad would carefully package and freeze or refrigerate the dozens of cookies and candies at the end of each day. As Christmas arrived, they would get out the fifty or so containers and create an assembly line. With Christmas tins in hand, they would fill each one with at least two of every sweet.

"Gosh, Mom, just the usual I guess," Toni said. "I would like to order a large tin for work, if that's okay."

"Of course, sweetie. It's already on my list. Okay, well, we've got to scoot. I've got to fix lunch before we run our errands. Love you."

With that, her mom signed off. Toni shook her head. What a pair. With all that talk about food, she was hungry. She went downstairs, switched the laundry and looked in the fridge. Cold leftover pizza. She was in luck. She poured herself a glass of iced tea, took the pizza box to the couch and turned on the TV. Mr. Rupert still occupied the same spot on the living room floor. He was snoring. The sound of the TV woke him and he protested loudly. With all the energy he could muster, he got up, stretched and hopped up on the couch next to her. He immediately fell back asleep. Toni munched on her pizza and flipped through the channels. By the time she had gone through the cycle twice, nearly 45 minutes had passed.

A glance at her watch told her it was nearly noon. She had plenty of time. She could finish cleaning and shower before 3:00. Then she would treat herself to an afternoon of college football. With that decision made, she tossed the pizza box into the trash, grabbed her clean laundry and headed back upstairs.

Sam and Betty arose early Saturday morning. There was still a lot left to prepare for the party. By noon they had finished the decorations. They had done the family room together but had worked on the other areas individually. They were as excited as two kids on Christmas morning, Betty thought.

"Let's do a walk-through," Sam suggested, "so we can get an idea of how everything looks."

She agreed and they went to the front yard and looked around. Cobwebs covered the porch, complete with huge spiders. There was a pumpkin on each side of the door, waiting to be carved. Tombstones leaned against the front steps and gargoyles were perched on the corners of the roof. Sam had set out sand-filled paper bags along the sidewalk, each with a votive candle to be lit later. Betty expressed her appreciation of his work with a long "ooh."

He grinned. "I think I got the knocker to work. Try it, hon."

She went up on the porch. A huge gargoyle door knocker looked like it was made of granite with two beady eyes that glowed red. She reached up and tried it. The sound was tremendous. It sounded like it knocked on a huge, empty mansion . . . or dungeon.

"Perfect," she cried. "I love it." She hugged him and then ushered him inside.

The foyer, adorned with cobwebs, was small but sufficient. Betty had decided to remove the majority of the ordinary furnishings and replaced them with ghoulish substitutions. Instead of umbrellas in the stand, there were "severed" arms and legs. Family photos had become ghost portraits. Near the family room, a portrait on the wall said, "Hey, where are you going? I see you." Sam gave her a long smile.

She was ecstatic. "It works great, Sam. As soon as someone walks by, he talks."

They peered inside the downstairs guest bathroom, right off the family room, where Betty had left an assortment of "normal" decorations on the vanity and the walls. She was almost to the point of jumping up and down.

"It looks great, hon." But he was clearly puzzled.

Finally she couldn't stand it any longer. "Open the shower curtain!"

He slowly pulled back the curtain. Then his jaw dropped. "Holy cow! This is incredible." He stood admiring her handiwork. "I absolutely love this. How in the world did you do it?"

She had used an entire spool of fishing line, but she had to admit the effect was unexpected. It would be even more fun at night.

Standing in the shower was a life-size skeleton made of plastic. She had placed a shower cap on his head and secured a long scrub brush to his hand. The designer of the skull had taken some anatomical liberties so that he had somewhat of a face.

"It looks like it's looking straight at me," Sam said.

She eagerly showed him how Mr. Clean was attached to the ceiling, curtain rod and faucet.

After a moment or two, they squeezed themselves out of the bathroom and walked arm in arm to the family room. Silently they surveyed the room.

A late addition to the house, the family room ran the entire width of their home. To the left of the entryway was a sliding glass door that led to a small deck. The back wall held a modest fireplace and the right wall boasted two windows. There was also another doorway that led back to the kitchen.

Even in the daylight, the room had a festive Halloween feel to it. Betty preferred "funny" to "horror" when it came to decorating, as did Sam. Suspended from the ceiling was an upside down cardboard casket. It contained a skeleton, held in by cobwebs, with one arm dangling free. The skeleton was grinning.

Sitting in an old rocker by the fireplace was a witch, a rather rotund figure made from stuffed pillow cases, dressed appropriately with a cape and pointed hat. A large stuffed black cat sat on her lap. A small motor was attached to the rocker and when turned on, she slowly rocked while humming a tune. Next to her was a large black cauldron in the fireplace. Tonight there would be dry ice placed inside so that it would appear to be "brewing."

Scattered about the room were a variety of decorations including pumpkins, severed body parts, candles and wall hangings. On the corner table was a black raven that said, "The end is near," when someone walked by. One of Sam's favorite decorations, however, appeared to be an ordinary mirror that replaced the painting above the fireplace. Betty chuckled. Most folks didn't really notice the mirror until they looked in it. Then, to the surprise of everyone, the reflection included not only that person, but also a grinning ghost. The effect was both startling and amusing. Sam adjusted the mirror and admired himself. Next to him was a reflection of an obviously happy ghost, literally beaming. Betty smiled.

"I think the three of us look great!" Sam laughed.

Betty shook her head. "Okay, you two. Let's get a move on. We've got a lot of hors d'oeuvres to prepare this afternoon." She had already baked a cake and a few dozen cookies.


After cubing a variety of cheeses and cleaning fresh vegetables, the two began working on the hot food. Soon the kitchen was filled with the aroma of onions and garlic, the sound of laughter and, for Betty, the overwhelming feeling of love. Time passed quickly as they worked side by side. By late afternoon there was a huge pot of chili on the stove and three Crock-Pots lined up on the counter. Barbequed Smokie Joes, hot wings and Swedish meatballs—perfect for a crisp Halloween night, she thought.

"Everything turned out great, Sam. How about bringing in the pumpkins? I'll fix us a quick sandwich and then we can carve the pumpkins after we eat."

Sam nodded and trotted outside. By the time he carried in the pumpkins, Betty had prepared turkey sandwiches and placed a fresh can of Diet Coke by his plate.

Sam glanced at his watch. "Let's see. It should only take about an hour to do the pumpkins. Then I'll run out and pick up the dry ice. That will still give us lots of time."

Betty nodded and finished the last of her sandwich. "I told most people to come around seven. Then we'll have plenty of time to mingle and snack before we head out to the haunted house. I am *so* excited. Bill said we should all go to the employee entrance and he'll take us in that way." Bill was Betty's younger brother who loved Halloween as much as they did. "This is going to be so much fun."

"The best ever." Sam picked up the big knife. "Okay, let's get these pumpkins carved. I need to have time to transform myself into Gomez Adams."

Betty laughed. This year they were dressing as Gomez and Morticia. Although it wasn't the most original idea they'd ever had—last year they were rotten fruit—it was a bit more practical. They'd had difficulty maneuvering around the guests last year and sitting was nearly impossible. This year they would be able to wear their costumes the entire evening. She smiled. This was going to be the most memorable party yet.


That afternoon the man walked briskly past several shops, then stopped in front of a newspaper machine to read the headlines. There was no mention of his latest victory, but maybe tomorrow. Disappointed, yet smug, he continued on his way. It was a beautiful crisp fall afternoon and he was feeling very proud and content. On a whim he stopped at a coffee shop and bought himself a cup to go. Digging in his pocket for change, he smiled at the young cashier. She smiled back then lowered her eyes. Ah, a girl who knew her place.

He took his cup and sat outside. He blended in quite well. Pleased with his surroundings for the moment, he took time to relish his last accomplishment. It had been the work of an artist. As he replayed the events in his mind, there was a momentary feeling of anger and shame when he recalled jumping the fence. He unconsciously touched his leg. The cut had been deeper than he first thought. He had worried that it might require stitches, but the bleeding had finally stopped. He shook his head and then chuckled ever so softly. He thought about how incredibly inept the police were and how brilliant he was. Here he had made a big mistake and the police were clueless. So clueless, in fact, that he could probably give them a hundred clues and they would never catch on. In the end, this would make them all realize how advanced he really was. They would know, of course, by what he'd done, but this would help illustrate the depth of his mind. He decided to explore this idea further while he enjoyed his coffee. He didn't linger too long. He had to get back home or he would be missed.

# CHAPTER 12

Toni glanced at her watch. Time to shower and start to get ready. She turned off the football game and ruffled Mr. Rupert's head. She still hadn't vacuumed or dusted, so with a wary glance back at Mr. Rupert, she quickly cleaned the room. Although it wasn't the most thorough job, it looked nice enough. She replaced the vacuum cleaner in the closet and went upstairs. After showering she surveyed her costume as it lay spread out on her bed. She decided she would wear shorts underneath, just in case. She had decided earlier that a few couch pillows would suffice for her stuffing but was having difficulty figuring out how she would keep them in place. Mr. Rupert, as if sensing his expert advice might be needed, jumped up on the bed. He promptly took charge and with his huge head tossed the pillows off the bed. He looked around at Toni's costume and curled up next to her long body pillow and began bathing. Toni retrieved the pillows from the floor.

"How rude, Mr. R.," she said. "I'm trying to be creative here."

Mr. Rupert glanced up from his task and meowed loudly.

Toni laughed. "You are so pushy sometimes, young man. Look at you. It's not like I'm in your way or anything. You just barge on through, then plop down on my big pillow." An idea flashed. "Hey, my big pillow. I could wrap that around my waist and use a rope or bungy cord to hold it in place."

She yanked the big pillow off the bed, causing Mr. Rupert to roll. She wrapped it around her waist and ran over to the mirror. Satisfied, she dropped the pillow and went to her huge closet and searched through several boxes. In the third box she found a pile of bungy cords. She hooked them together and rewrapped herself in the pillow. With a slight tug she was able to fasten the ends. Grinning, she pulled on the blue jeans. A little snug. Perfect. That would keep them in the best position so that her rubber butt would show. She strutted around her bedroom.

"What do you think? This is turning out great." She sat down at her desk so she could put on her shoes. This was not an easy task. She decided she should bring a change of clothes with her to the party. There was no way she would be able to get around in this outfit all night, especially at the haunted house. She grabbed a pair of overalls and tossed them in a bag. Then she stripped back down to her shorts and a T-shirt before heading down to the kitchen. She wanted to fix a plate of snacks before Boggs arrived.

Toni trotted downstairs and tossed her bag near the door. Realizing she would need a regular coat, she took her letter jacket out of the closet and put it in the bag also. Then she flipped on the stereo and went to work. In no time she had created a plate of sliced cheese, sliced apples and crackers. A far cry from Martha Stewart, but it would be fine. She laughed and poured herself a glass of wine. She spotted a pumpkin candle on the shelf in the living room and remembered her parents had sent her some Halloween candles. She placed them all on the coffee table and lit them. It looked nice. She leaned back on the couch and put her feet on the table.

Now all she had to do was wait for Boggs, she thought. Several minutes passed before she noticed her foot twitching. Mr. Rupert was now sitting across from her, staring intently.

"What? So I'm a little nervous. I'll get over it."

He continued to stare.

"I'm just going to play it cool," she said, more to herself than to him. "I'm sure I blew everything out of proportion last night, but I think I'm okay. Everything I said could be taken very innocently, don't you think?"

Even though it was a rhetorical question, Mr. Rupert must have felt compelled to respond.

"Exactly." Toni nodded. "So when she gets here, I'll just be my plain old fun self. It's going to be a great party. Even if it breaks up early, I can still go to Gertrude's Garage. Jake said he'd be there all night."

Mr. Rupert shook his head as if to say, "Like that would ever happen."

And it was true. She'd never go to a bar by herself.

"I don't know why you get so worked up about these things, boy." She grinned and leaned over to pet her lovable cat. It sure was nice to have someone who listened to her. She was still scratching his head when the doorbell rang. It was 6:10.


Edward pulled into his driveway and glanced at the clock on the dash. It read 6:10. He was so glad to be home from his business trip. The flight from New York had seemed longer than usual and his body ached from being confined in a plane. He hoped Martha was home by now. He'd called her before leaving the Big Apple, but she hadn't answered. He gathered his bags and headed to the front door, pleased to see there were lights on inside. As he fumbled with his keys, he expected Martha to open the door for him. It was then he noticed that the porch light wasn't working. He thought that was odd because it was on a sensor. He let himself inside.

"Sweetheart, I'm home," he called. He set down his bags and

stood there for a moment, smiling. He knew she would be walking out from the study just about now. A few seconds passed. "Sweetheart, I'm home," he repeated.

No response. He took a few steps through the foyer. Maybe she was upstairs, or ran an errand.

"Martha?"

Nothing. The quiet seemed to hurt his ears.

He closed his eyes. Something was terribly wrong. He slowly opened his eyes, said a small prayer and went to the study. He knew. At the doorway he froze. Nothing made sense. There she was. He could see her, but he couldn't seem to reach her. It was as though he was trapped behind a thick sheet of ice. He could see her, but he couldn't move. His best friend. His lover. His partner. His life. He could see her. Tears began pouring from his eyes, melting the wall and freeing him from that spot. He walked slowly to her and knelt down. There was no question she was gone. Nothing he could do. He gently touched her arm and wept. Without leaving her or letting go of her, he pulled his phone from his jacket and called the police.

Seven minutes later officer Patty Green pulled up in front of the house. The dispatcher had said a man called crying, mumbled something about his wife, gave the address and hung up. The call had come from a cell phone. The address was 317 Claymore. It was the home of Edward and Martha Haley. Patty had met Judge Haley and hoped it wasn't serious. She glanced around. Nothing seemed out of place. One car in the driveway. She touched the hood of the car, still warm. She went to the porch, listened at the door for a moment and then knocked. No response. Just as she started to call for backup, another officer pulled up.

"Hey, Steve, how's it going?"

"Slow night so far," he replied. "I heard the address and thought I'd come by. This is Judge Haley's house."

Patty nodded. "No one answered the door and the car is still warm." She knocked again and yelled, "Police." No response. Steve tried the door. It was unlocked. Patty nodded and he slowly opened the door.

Patty scanned the area. A suitcase and coat were lying on the floor. There was a light on in the first room to the left. Patty called out again but got no response. She held up her hand to keep Steve from speaking. She listened for a moment, then gestured for Steve to follow.

Patty quickly assessed the situation. There was no doubt the body on the floor was that of Judge Haley. She was lying on her back in a pool of blood that had turned to black. Her face was now purple and her eyes—wide open—were a milky white color. Panties had been shoved in her mouth. Patty could see her body was frozen with rigor and that Martha's right hand looked distorted. Patty swallowed hard twice, attempting to keep her focus.

She also recognized Edward Haley as he knelt beside his wife, weeping silently. She asked Steve to call the dispatcher and to use the Dexter Crown code. This would lessen the chance of a media onslaught. She knelt beside Edward, careful not to disturb anything.

"Mr. Haley?" she asked. "My name is Officer Patty Green. You need to come with me, sir."

Edward continued to weep, oblivious to the intrusion. She gently took his hand and repeated herself. His deep emotion touched her heart. The contact brought Edward back. In the background sirens could be heard.

Patty spoke again, a little more firmly. "Mr. Haley. You need to come with me, sir. You need to let go of her and come with me."

Edward looked at Patty and blinked several times. Tears still streamed down his face. The paramedics arrived, although there was nothing they could do for the judge. Patty raised her hand to keep them back from the crime scene.

"Mr. Haley," she said gently, "The paramedics need to check you over."

Edward looked at Patty through half-closed eyes. He looked confused, as if he couldn't bear leaving Martha. Patty sensed his turmoil and gently pulled his hand.

"I'll take care of her for now, Mr. Haley," she said. "You go over there with the paramedics."

Edward nodded and Patty led him back to the foyer. She suggested to the paramedics that they take Mr. Haley out to their unit to "check him out." One of the guys nodded and seemed to understand it was best for Mr. Haley to be removed from the scene. Steve was standing in the doorway. "Well," he said. "I did a quick look. Nobody around and no forced entry."

Patty shook her head. "That bastard is back at it again. Okay. Let's rope off everything. I don't want anyone else contaminating the scene. Is Sarge on her way?"

"Should be here any minute," he replied. "Along with anyone else who can get here. I heard on the radio that Detective Parker is on his way. Because this is obviously the work of his boy, I'm sure he'll take over."

Patty rolled her eyes. Like most of the female officers in the department, she couldn't stand Frank. His "God's gift to women" attitude grated on her. Thankfully, she rarely came into contact with him. Just then Frank drove up.

"Well," said Patty, "speak of the devil."

Neither Steve nor Patty said anything as Frank approached the front porch. His blazer was wrinkled and it looked like he hadn't shaved that morning. He was limping ever so slightly.

"Evening, Detective," said Patty.

Frank ignored her and looked at Steve. "What do we have?" he asked.

Steve glanced at Patty. She was the first on scene and it was her case until she turned it over. Patty shrugged her shoulders ever so slightly and smiled, indicating that Steve should answer.

"Judge Haley. Her throat was slit . . . panties in her mouth." Steve gestured over his shoulder. "She's in the study, first room on the left. Husband called it in. He's a mess. Over at the unit. Did a quick perimeter check, no forced entry. Green here secured the scene."

Frank nodded as he pushed by both officers.

Patty followed him to the study and shuddered seeing the body again. She saw Frank look at the judge and sigh. He shook his head as if to clear his mind. By the time the crime scene unit arrived, Frank appeared to be back to his old charming self.

The crime scene team that arrived was the best in the department. Three guys who were not only the best in the business, but truly loved their jobs. Patty knew they had worked the other Dexter Crown cases but had turned up nothing.

Less than five minutes had passed when officer Bannon, one of the crime scene investigators, called out. "Hey. Take a look at this."

Patty and Frank looked at the spot where he was pointing.

"Blood," he said. "But I don't think it's hers. Looks like it dropped straight down but not from the height of her neck. You can tell by the shape. Maybe we caught a break this time. Maybe she wounded the son of a bitch."

Patty was encouraged by the find but Frank looked stunned. He just nodded and stepped back. The other techs came quickly. One photographed the area while the other waited to collect samples.

Patty went back outside, followed by Frank. He called Steve over. "Canvass the neighborhood," he instructed. "If you get any bites, let me know immediately. Don't let them ramble on. I'll be doing all the interviewing of witnesses."

Steve nodded and he and Patty relayed the information to Sergeant Cooper, who said, "You two go ahead. When you're done, give the info to Frank, then go back on patrol."

Steve and Patty turned to go.

"By the way, Green," added Sergeant Cooper, "good work on securing the scene. And Wilson, good job using the Crown code over the radio. Looks like we've avoided the media for now."

"Thanks," Patty replied.

Steve shrugged. "Patty here gets the credit, Sarge. She's the one who told me to call it in that way."

Sergeant Cooper nodded to Patty and walked away.

# CHAPTER 13

Toni looked through the peephole. Ah, a distorted Boggs. She laughed and realized she wasn't nearly as nervous as she thought she would be. Making the conscious decision that she would just have fun and be herself had certainly made a difference. She opened the door and waved Boggs inside. Except for the fact that Boggs was obviously a woman, and wore no hat, her costume was perfect. She looked just like every 1940s private investigator portrayed in the movies. Toni raised her hands to her cheeks and said in her best baby doll voice, "Thank heavens you're here, Detective. The coppers say I killed Big Jim, but I didn't. I adored that big lug."

Boggs shook her head and grinned. "Cute." She eyed Toni's outfit. "Well, that's an original costume. What are you supposed to be? A college student? A protester against the wearing of Halloween costumes?"

"Very funny yourself." Toni laughed. "I discovered that my

outfit, although prize-winning, was difficult to get around in. I thought I'd be comfy until we were ready to go. Have a seat and I'll serve the pre-party hors d'oeuvres. Would you like a glass of wine?"

"Sure," Boggs replied as she headed for the couch.

Toni went to the kitchen and returned with a glass of wine and her plate of goodies. "I want you to know," she said as she placed the plate in front of Boggs, "I've been slaving in the kitchen all day."

Boggs looked at the plate and laughed. "Toni, you shouldn't have gone to *so* much trouble. Thank you."

Toni sat down and sampled the cheese. "Marvelous, if I do say so myself."

They chatted for a bit until Toni looked at her watch.

"I better get a move on. It should only take me a few minutes." She rose from the couch. "I think I can secure the pillow by myself, but I'll yell down if I get in a jam, okay?"

Boggs nodded as Toni left the room.

"Make yourself at home, Boggs," she called over her shoulder.

Toni dashed up the stairs, pleased with herself. She had detected no tension in the air and she was sure the evening would be a lot of fun. She wrapped her big pillow around her waist and struggled to secure it with the bungy cords. Twice they slipped from her hands and flew across the room. On the third try she was successful. Next, she carefully attached her rubber butt and backed up to the mirror. It was a little high, but it needed to show above her jeans. She pulled them on, thankful she had left her shoes on. Bending down was a bit tricky. After a little squirming and read-justing the butt, she looked over her shoulder at her reflection in the mirror and burst out laughing. This was better than she hoped. The T-shirt hung down just enough to cover the top of the rubber crack, and the jeans fit tightly halfway down. She turned in a circle for the full effect, then she tucked the shirt inside the jeans in the front so the pillow wouldn't show. Next, she slipped on the jacket. It was too short in the back, giving a full view. Still giggling she strapped on the last item, a tool belt. Making it snug would ensure that her jeans stayed put. She hurried back downstairs. When she got to the bottom step, she strolled across the room. Boggs turned to watch and smiled. Toni then lumbered past her and bent over slightly at an attempt to retrieve something from the shelf.

Boggs couldn't contain herself. "That . . . is . . . hysterical!" She gasped in between laughs as tears streamed down her face. "Oh, my God. That looks so real. Did you see yourself?"

Unable to keep a straight face, she nodded vigorously. "Upstairs in the mirror. Isn't it a hoot? Take a few pictures of me, okay?" She handed her the camera. "My folks want to see the final product."

Boggs took the camera, took several shots, then said, "Now how about a nice shot in front of the fridge?" She chuckled.

Toni complied and struck several poses, each one more exaggerated than the one before. She gestured for the camera and grabbed Boggs's hat from the nearby table.

"Okay, gumshoe," she said, "couple of mug shots for the authorities, please."

Boggs seemed slightly embarrassed but donned the hat and posed. She even pulled back the trenchcoat enough to reveal her shoulder holster. Toni was momentarily taken aback when she realized it held a real gun. Well, of course she carried a gun . . . duh. *Don't be naïve*, Toni told herself. And of course that's why Boggs always wore a jacket. Toni grinned and took the picture. A woman with a gun—sexy.

Toni shook the thought from her head and came back to reality. "I think we'll have the best costumes."

"Well, I don't know about me," Boggs replied, "but you've certainly got a winner." She turned a seemingly critical eye toward Toni's costume. "I don't know, Toni. Don't you think your pants are a little out of style? They look a little nineteen seventies, if you know what I mean."

Toni laughed then said as seriously as she could, "Thank you very much, Ms. Cutting Edge. Kindly refrain from making any further *cracks* about my outfit." With that, she turned and reached for her glass of wine.

"Can you sit?" Boggs asked.

Toni shrugged. "I guess I better give it a try." With a plop she landed on the couch. "Hey. Not too bad. It's not as uncomfortable as I had imagined."

"But can you get up?"

Toni struggled a bit but was able to extricate herself from the couch. She turned her back toward Boggs. "Does my butt look okay? Did my jeans stay in place?"

Boggs surveyed the area. "Looks good to me. But, how are you going to manage at the haunted house? It is usually pretty tight in those places."

"Oh, I'm bringing a change of clothes. I figured I'd change before we go. You don't think Sam and Betty will mind, do you?"

"Oh, no. Not at all. Most people begin peeling off their costumes after about an hour. Especially the ones who wear masks." Boggs looked at her watch. "I guess we could head out if you want. It's about a twenty-minute drive from here."

Toni agreed and picked up the plate from the coffee table. Boggs followed her to the kitchen carrying the wineglasses. Toni put the plate in the fridge and nearly bumped into Boggs when she turned around. Their eyes met and the electricity was back in full force. Damn it, Toni thought.

"Um, oh, thanks . . ." she stammered as she took the glasses from Boggs.

Boggs seemed to immediately sense Toni's nervousness. She gazed at Toni again and smiled as if she'd decided to think about this for a few minutes, as if it could be fun.

Toni, regaining her composure, pushed past Boggs with her large stomach.

"Looks like there's a full moon out tonight."

"Boy, you really crack yourself up, don't you?"

"If you don't mind, Slim, I think I'll drive, I know where Sam lives. Anyway, my vehicle can handle wide loads."

Toni grabbed her wallet and keys, then reached for her bag near the door. The process of bending over caused Boggs to start laughing again. Toni, still bent over, backed up toward Boggs. "Beep, beep, beep," she chimed. "Wide load, watch out." She laughed. "Since I'm obviously such a sight to behold, maybe I should hire you to be my bodyguard for the night. Or at least clear a path for my butt."

Boggs readily agreed. "Sure, Slim, be happy to accommodate you. It's the least I can do after you went to all that trouble fixing the hors d'oeuvres."

Toni said good-bye to Mr. Rupert, who had been napping on the couch, and the two women headed out the door.

When Toni and Boggs reached the party, Sam and Betty greeted the new arrivals with their typical haunting hellos, but Boggs noticed an underlying distress immediately. After introducing Toni to Betty, she confronted Sam. "What's wrong?"

He hesitated a moment, then stepped out on the porch with Toni and Boggs. He looked back at Betty, who smiled and nodded, then retreated inside with the other guests.

"Judge Haley has been murdered." Sam gave a detailed account of what he knew so far. At the conclusion he looked at the ground.

Boggs was astonished. "I can't believe that son of a bitch walked out of Metro last week. Some pissant screwed up and now Judge Haley's paid the price." She took a deep breath. She noticed that Sam was still looking at the ground. It looked as though he was taking this personally. Boggs put her arm around him. "I know it's rough," she said softly. "We'll get him."

Sam looked up and smiled. "You're right. Frank will find him. Let's go inside. We have a party to go to."

Once inside, Sam bellowed over the sounds of animated conversation. "I think most everybody's here. Anyone else who shows up is on their own. First of all, Morticia and I would like to welcome you all to our haunted . . . er, I mean hallowed home."

A few groans could be heard and Betty rolled her eyes.

"Next, introductions. Names to go with costumes. If you want to know what someone does for a living, their favorite music or their availability, you're on your own. Here we go. There will be a quiz later. Buffalo Bill here on my left is normally addressed as Dave. Calamity Jane is, well, Jane. The Clintons over by the chair are actually Dick and Monica. The head on a platter is Anne. Nice entree, by the way. Mr. Peanut is Billy. Tammy and Joan are the M&Ms. I believe Joan is the peanut one. Oscar is dressed as . . . well, I'm not quite sure. A nerdy investment banker? Anyway, he's next to Delores, who is a hairdresser on acid. Next is Toni, a.k.a. 'Slim' the refrigerator repairman, and Boggs is something new this year, an *undercover* gumshoe. Sandy is the chef with a cleaver in his head and Andy is the banana with a cleaver in his head, or as he refers to himself, a banana split. And last but not least, Vicky is the sumo wrestler. Be careful of her near food."

Betty took over. "Thank you, Gomez. Now, everyone help yourself to plenty of food and drink. We'll start a couple of games soon for anyone who is interested. Our transportation will arrive around nine to take us to the haunted house. As always, don't worry if you overindulge. We have designated drivers for your trip home. Most of all, enjoy!"

The group traipsed into the kitchen, filling their plates before wandering back to the family room. Toni was in line next to Vicky, the sumo wrestler. "So," she asked. "What's your dieting secret?"

They giggled and Toni poked Vicky's sumo wrestler stomach with her finger. It looked like a giant bodysuit stuffed to the max.

"Well," Vicky whispered confidentially, "I try to limit myself to only ten dozen Twinkies after each meal and snack only on marshmallow cream. I see you're starting a little dieting yourself." She laughed. "And if I'm not being too forward, I just love your butt."

"Thank you very large, no pun intended." Toni piled Smokie Joes and cheese on her plate. "Do you think these will hurt my figure?"

"Oh, not at all." Vicky shook her head. "Anyway, it's a party, might as well shoot the moon."

Toni grinned and rolled her eyes. "Well, I suppose I'll be the *butt* of many jokes tonight." Several people around her laughed and nodded. With a full plate in one hand and a glass of wine in the other, she headed back to the family room. She spotted an empty chair near the sliding glass door, but once she was in front of it she realized she had a slight problem. Holding something in both hands and attempting to plop down in a low, overstuffed chair spelled disaster. She didn't see Boggs and there wasn't a table nearby so she stood there, momentarily perplexed.

Just then Betty appeared at her side. "Having a bit of a logistics problem, Slim?"

Toni, slightly embarrassed, nodded. Betty took the plate and glass and motioned for Toni to sit, which she did with a thud. The chair looked far more padded than it actually was. She reached for the plate and balanced it on her leg, then took the glass of wine. "Thank you," she said. "And thanks so much for inviting me to your party. I'm glad I finally got to meet you. Sam talks about you so often, and he's been wonderful to me at work. He has really welcomed me."

Betty smiled broadly. "That's Sam all right." She pulled a chair over next to Toni and sat down. "He's talked about you, too. He thinks you're an asset to the department. It's probably been a little hectic for you. I mean, you started a new job and then all this business with Crown. I know it's been getting to Sam and he's not even working the case. He'd probably like to be in the thick of it, but I think he's also glad it's Boggs. He thinks the world of her, you know, and so do I."

Toni smiled ever so slightly and nodded.

"Well, Toni," she said. "Again, thanks for coming and I hope you have lots of fun tonight. I'm going to start the games." With that, Betty got up and headed to the center of the room. "Attention wild people," she called. "We are now going to attempt to play charades. The rules are simple, unless you've already had too many drinks. We'll have two teams, one on each side of the room. All the answers have something to do with the wonderful

Halloween season. No talking if you're up, but anything else goes. Ready?"

Cheers erupted. Toni assumed this was an annual event and pretty fun, judging by everyone's reactions. She searched the room for Boggs, who suddenly appeared out of nowhere and sat down next to her.

"I guess we're on the same side, Slim," she said with a wink.

It did not go unnoticed by Toni. Hmm. That wasn't a quick "I'm in your corner" wink, she thought. That was a deliberate—long—wink. *Here we go again.* She took a long swallow of wine. Well, maybe she'd play along and try to match her tit for tat. She laughed out loud at the thought.

"What's so funny?" Boggs asked.

"Just me," Toni replied. "I just decided that I'm going to let loose and have a gay old time tonight." She kept a straight face and turned her attention to Sam, who was stirring up slips of paper in a plastic pumpkin. Boggs was grinning.

Vicky wandered over with a bottle of beer tucked in her sumo thong, a plate in one hand and dragging a folding chair with the other. "Mind if I join you, Slim and Ms. Private Dick?"

Boggs laughed and helped her position the chair next to hers. "Need help navigating your butt to its target?"

"Yes, thank you very much."

Toni sensed these two knew each other quite well. Before she could ask, Vicky spoke.

"My name is Vicky, in case you missed it in Sam's intro. I should have introduced myself when we were in the food line. I've known Boggs here for several years, so I'm not being obnoxious without good cause. I've earned the right to call her any number of unflattering names."

Toni liked Vicky's style. "I'm Toni. So how do you know each other. Friday night wrestling matches?"

Vicky laughed. "I like your attitude. Boggs was right. You are different from most attorneys, no offense."

"None taken. In fact, I take that as a compliment."

"Well, to answer your question, I met Boggs about five years ago. I was considering shooting her but decided against it. Too much paperwork, you know." By this time, Vicky was leaning forward so she could speak to Toni. Boggs was sitting between them, but Vicky completely ignored her. "I'm on the Fairfield police force, in background investigations now, but then I was a patrol officer. We got an anonymous call about a drug deal about to go down at a local bar. All we knew was it supposedly involved a white female and a Hispanic male. When we went into the bar there were only a few people inside. No Hispanic males and this nut was the only female. My partner, a neo-Nazi who has thankfully moved on, screams at her to 'assume the position,' which she does. I must say it was rather amusing. Anyway, when she 'assumes,' my partner Adolph sees what he think is a bulge and yells, 'Gun.' I, of course, immediately draw down on her. Adolph is screaming obscenities and Boggs doesn't say a word. Finally, I tell my enlightened partner to cover me while I frisk and cuff her. Something didn't seem right. I had never had a perp so calm. As I begin to frisk her, she calmly tells me who she is and that her badge is in her back pocket, which of course it is. She then tells me the 'bulge' is actually a walkman and that her weapon is secured in her ankle holster. I totally cracked up. It took about five minutes to convince Adolph, but Boggs was such a good sport. We've been friends ever since." She paused and took a sip of beer. "So, Toni, what's it like working hand in hand with the infamous Boggs?"

Before Toni could answer, Boggs leaned forward and waved her hand in the air. "Hello. I'm sitting right here. Vicky, must you always talk to people as though I'm not in the room?"

Vicky shook her head and gestured as if shooing a fly. She leaned over Boggs's lap and got a conspiring look in her eyes. "Any good dirt on Boggs?"

Toni was up for the fun. "Well," she said slowly, "I've got a plan that's bound to work. I'm going to get her all liquored up and then challenge her to a game of truth or dare. I'm bound to get some juicy stuff from that. I'll record everything and give you a copy, okay?"

They all laughed but were interrupted when Sam announced,

"Let the game begin." There was giggling and outright laughter as the opposing team tried to figure out the ridiculous gestures by the "head on a platter." Finally someone guessed "carving pumpkins" and the head took a bow. Sam walked to their side of the room and held up the plastic pumpkin.

"I'll go," Boggs volunteered. This was followed by a few groans and much applause. Apparently, Boggs was somewhat creative at this game. She took a slip of paper and went to the center of the room. She read the slip, thought for a moment and grinned. Then she went into a dramatic silent portrayal of a dog howling.

"Howling!" Joan the peanut M & M shouted. "A dog howling."

Boggs gestured that she was half right.

"Werewolf howling," someone else yelled.

Boggs nodded vigorously. Then, without warning, she ran over to Toni, took her plate and glass and handed them to Vicky. She yanked Toni from her chair, pulled her to the center of the room and turned her toward the fireplace, bending her over slightly. Toni was stunned, to say the least. She glanced over her shoulder as Boggs again acted out her howling and pointed to Toni's butt.

There was silence for a brief moment, then someone called out, "Werewolf howling at the moon!" This was followed by loud cheers and laughter. Boggs took a deep bow and then pointed again to Toni's butt. Cheers again erupted.

The banana split shouted from the back of the room. "But that's not fair . . ."

Laughter and groans could be heard in response to his choice of words.

Sam held up his hand and made the official call. "Okay, props can be used, just no talking by the players. The rules are final. No ifs, ands or buts!" Again there was laughter. "Since we are now tied, prizes for all." Everyone cheered some more. Sam took a bowl of "prizes" and began tossing them to the crowd. Toni caught a plastic pumpkin ring. Boggs snagged a Milky Way bar and Vicky grabbed some Sweet Tarts. Someone got up from the other side of the room and drew a slip of paper from the plastic pumpkin. The game resumed and Boggs and Toni returned to their seats.

"Nice teamwork," Vicky said wryly. She handed Toni her plate and glass. "Maybe you two should go on the road." She ignored Boggs and addressed Toni. "So, next subject. Are you changing before we go tonight?"

"Absolutely," Toni said. "I'm afraid I'd get stuck if I didn't and then I'd have a bunch of strange people groping my butt. As a rule I don't mind strange people, but I'd prefer to pick them myself."

Vicky nodded. "That's exactly how I feel. Obviously we're both sitting with a strange one here, but that's okay. I'm going to change, for obvious reasons, before we go, but I have a feeling Boggs will remain in character. Can you stand it? If not, we can always lose her in the haunted house."

Toni thought for a moment and looked Boggs over with a discriminating eye. "I suppose we could put up with her for just one night. It's not like we'll be seen or anything. I understand that these places are pretty dark. I mean, I could stand it. How about you?"

Vicky rolled her eyes. "I guess it's okay with me. It's not like it's a date or anything."

There was a split second when Toni saw a look in Vicky's eyes, as though she might have betrayed a confidence. Boggs smiled ever so slightly. Vicky continued quickly, clearly hoping Toni hadn't noticed. She had.

"Any-who . . . let's all go in the same van, okay? I think the idea of a haunted house is great. Sam and Betty really outdid themselves this time."

After several more rounds of charades, each getting sillier, and several more "prizes" awarded to the group, Betty announced that it was time to get ready for the big event. Vicky motioned for Toni to follow her and they both grabbed their bags and headed down the hall.

"Betty said we could change in the back. There's an extra bedroom and a bathroom. Take your pick," Vicky said.

Toni opted for the bathroom and began peeling off her extra layers. She took the old pair of overalls from her bag and pulled them on over her shorts and T-shirt. Done. She packed her rubber

127

butt into her bag, careful not to crush it. While bending over her bag, she heard voices coming from the heating vent. Being an ever-curious soul, she leaned closer.

Vicky was saying, "I guess I almost blew it, huh? I figured you had told her, especially since you two had come here together. I'm really sorry. Me and my big mouth. Do you think she caught on to that 'date' crack?"

Toni heard a mumbled response. She pressed her ear closer to the vent.

"And how are you so sure? Did she tell you?" Vicky asked.

Toni heard Boggs's voice this time and literally smashed her ear into the vent.

"No, she didn't tell me, but I know. I talked to Dan last night and he told me that the guy she's always hanging out with is as gay as they come."

"Oh, geez, Boggs. You must be in lust, because you're not thinking with your head. What the hell does that prove? Remember Kelly from vice? She hangs out with Tim all the time. Even goes to the clubs with him sometimes, but she's as straight as an arrow. What are you thinking? Any other 'evidence,' Ms. Private Eye?"

There was a long silence. Finally Boggs said, "Damn. How stupid could I be? I guess I just wanted it to be true, so I convinced myself. Brilliant detective work. I better just cool my jets. But still . . ."

"What now?" Vicky asked. "And help me out of this thing, will you? Here, pull on the arm."

Toni heard some rustling around and then Boggs said, "It's just that I thought I felt something with her. I don't know how to explain it, but . . . I don't know."

Toni's eyes got wide and she felt her face flush. There was a funny feeling in her stomach and it wasn't the wine. Dear God. Had Boggs felt it too? *I wasn't the only one to feel it.* The electricity. *Could she actually be as attracted to me as I am to her?* Toni continued to eavesdrop.

"Maybe it's just a physical thing, Boggs. I mean, hell, she's not bad to look at, at least I don't think so. Here, pull the other arm so I can get the pillows out."

"Of course she's gorgeous," Boggs said. "But that's not what I'm talking about. I felt something deeper. You could just feel the electricity between us. It was fantastic. Maybe it was just in my own head. For now, I'm going to be Ms. Perfect Manners. No more flirting."

Toni was stunned. "Oh, my God. Oh, my God," she kept murmuring to herself.

Vicky said, "Well, I don't care one way or another. I think she's a total blast. We're going to have a ton of fun tonight. Okay, I'm ready. Let's go."

Toni waited a couple seconds after hearing the two leave the room. She took a quick look in the mirror and noticed her ear was bright red. Oh, the price one paid for confirmation.

Back in the living room, the crowd was gathering in the kitchen and on the front porch, preparing to go.

Betty was shouting above the voices, "The vans are outside and ready to go. You can leave your stuff here. They know we're coming, so as soon as everybody has arrived, we'll be ushered in and given the VIP tour."

Smiling, Toni walked up to Boggs and Vicky and grabbed their arms. "Ready for some fun, girls?"

# CHAPTER 14

Officer Patty Green was back on patrol. She and Steve had canvassed Judge Haley's neighborhood but gotten no leads. No one saw or heard anything unusual. After informing Frank, she resumed her normal routine. The unusually slow night had given her way too much time to think about the crime scene, and the way Judge Haley looked. The image of Mr. Haley stuck in her head. How horrible it must have been for him to find his wife like that.

Patty glanced at her watch. Only a couple more hours left on her shift. The night dragged on. As soon as that thought crossed her mind, she got a call from dispatch. It never failed. Once she told herself how slow it was, she always got a call. Murphy's law.

The dispatcher gave her the address of a citizen at his residence. Report of a possible prowler. Name was Ralph Fredrickson.

Patty rolled her eyes. She had taken many a report from Ralph. Most of the time they were about one of his neighbors. She was only a couple of blocks away. "Ten-four. Put me out at that address."

When she pulled up in front of the house, Ralph was on the

front porch waiting. She grabbed her clipboard and a blank report form and got out of the patrol car.

"Good evening, Mr. Fredrickson. What can I do for you tonight?"

Ralph was his usual animated self. He began talking a mile a minute.

Patty let him go on for a bit and then stopped him. "Okay. Let's start at the beginning. When did this happen?"

Ralph took a deep breath and retold the story that he said he had told Anne Mulhoney the night before. When he got to the end, he shook his head. "See, I told this to Ms. Mulhoney, but I figured she wouldn't do anything about it. I know she's awfully busy with this killer out on the loose, but I feel kinda protective. We have to take care of our own neighbors, don't you know. She probably thought it was no big deal, but I worry about things. I just wanted to make it official."

Normally Patty would have taken the report and left, but tonight had been slow, and he was the neighbor of Ms. Mulhoney. And Judge Haley had been killed, probably last night, not too far from here.

"Why don't you show me where the man jumped the fence?" Patty said.

Ralph nodded and explained that although he didn't see it, the Simpson girl had pointed to the general area. He walked across the street with Patty. She shone her flashlight along the top of the fence, expecting to find nothing, of course. About midway along the fence, she spotted something. Upon closer inspection it looked like a torn piece of fabric. There was a dark stain on both the fabric and the fence. She went back to her car and retrieved a small plastic bag. Carefully she covered the area with the bag.

"Which side of the house did the girls see him come from?" she asked.

Ralph pointed to the west side. He was clearly excited to see that Patty was taking this seriously. He started to follow her.

"Mr. Fredrickson. Could you please stay here and make sure no one touches this plastic bag?"

Ralph eagerly agreed and stood like a guard next to the fence. Patty laughed to herself and set out for the side of the house. Near one of the windows, she noticed one clear footprint. Although the sill was a little high, an adult would clearly be able to look inside. She went back around to the front and rang the bell.

Anne's husband, Bill, answered the door.

"Good evening, Mr. Mulhoney. My name is Officer Patty Green. I was wondering if I could talk to you and your wife for a moment."

Bill nodded and ushered her in. "Honey," he called. "It's not Ralph. It's a police officer."

Anne came to the front hall and smiled. "Patty, right? Metro? What can I do for you?"

"Well," Patty said. "Your neighbor Mr. Fredrickson called in a report. He said he told you about this last night?"

Anne nodded and rolled her eyes. She gave Bill a quick synopsis.

"Normally I would have just taken the report and not bothered you," Patty went on. "But it looks like there's blood and some fabric on your fence. There's also a clear footprint by your side window. I wondered if you had heard anything last night . . . or if perhaps Mr. Mulhoney had been outside near the window recently and left a print."

Bill shook his head. He looked concerned. Very concerned.

Anne smiled as if trying to act nonchalant. "I don't think it's any big deal. Probably one of the teenaged boys in the neighborhood looking for a friend and got the wrong house." She sounded almost convincing.

Because Anne was the prosecuting attorney, Patty decided it would be okay to tell her about Judge Haley, in case she didn't already know. "Ms. Mulhoney, you may be right. I'm feeling just a little overcautious tonight. I was at Judge Haley's house earlier." There was no reaction from Anne, indicating she didn't know. "Judge Haley was killed. It probably happened last night. It looks like the same MO."

Anne's jaw dropped. She didn't say a word but fell against Bill as if her knees had gone weak. "Last night? Killed?" she said. It wasn't a question. It was a statement of disbelief. Patty saw a momentary glimpse of fear in Anne's eyes before she regained her familiar air of control and confidence. Anne apparently didn't really think there was a connection between her house and Dexter Crown, but she didn't want to take any chances. She looked at Patty and nodded. "Do what you need to do, Officer Green," she said.

Patty smiled and went back outside, calling dispatch on her radio. She asked for a crime scene unit to meet her at this address, then returned to the fence. Ralph was still standing guard.

"We really appreciate your help in this, Mr. Fredrickson. A unit is going to come and take a closer look." Ralph was beaming. "Could you tell me the name of the neighbor girl that saw the man?"

Ralph gave her the information, along with a few added comments. Patty took down what she needed then asked Ralph to go back to his porch. To keep him busy, and out of the way, she asked him to keep an eye on the neighborhood while the unit worked. If he noticed anything unusual, he was to write it down and she would talk to him before she left. Ralph looked as if he felt truly appreciated and almost ran back to his "station." Patty smiled to herself. *It's all in how you deal with people.*

The crime scene unit arrived within ten minutes and Patty filled them in. While they were working, she went to talk to the Simpson girl. It only took a few minutes to get the statement. Nicki Simpson had seen the guy for only a second or two. He was "an old guy, at least thirty," and was wearing a dark jogging suit. The only thing that stuck in her mind was his trying to be a stud and jump over the fence, but he stumbled. Nicki laughed and rolled her eyes. Patty took down the names of the other girls in the car and thanked her. The techs were making a plaster cast of the footprint when Patty returned and Sergeant Cooper arrived shortly thereafter.

"What do you have, Green?" she asked.

Patty filled her in on what she knew so far.

"Do you think there's a connection to Crown?" the sergeant asked.

"I don't know, Sarge. It doesn't seem likely, but I thought we should at least preserve the evidence. Judge Haley doesn't live very far from here, and according to the girl, this was no teenaged boy trying to sneak a peek."

Sergeant Cooper nodded as if she approved of Patty's thoroughness and her way of thinking. She told Patty about the blood at the murder scene. "If there is a connection, we should know by Monday. Maybe the son of a bitch is finally starting to make mistakes. Write up what you have and leave it on my desk." With that, Sergeant Cooper left.

Patty finished her report just as the unit guys were packing up their equipment. She waved good-bye and headed over to see Ralph, who was still standing on his porch with the pad in his hand. He had written down the license plate of every car that had gone by and proudly handed his "report" to Patty. She thanked him for his diligence and told him she would contact him if she needed his help again. Ralph was still grinning as she drove away.

Patty considered how fate might possibly be playing a role in this whole thing—if there was a connection, that is. If Ralph had called this in last night or earlier today, she wouldn't have given it a second thought. She never would have dreamed of calling in a crime scene unit. They would know by Monday. Patty sighed and headed back to the station. Her shift was over.

The men in the crime scene unit pulled up to the lab and began unloading the evidence. Jack, the rookie tech, had taken the fabric sample and the blood sample from the fence. His supervisor had observed him carefully and complimented him on both his technique and diligence. Jack knew the supervisor hadn't thought this was an important case, so he'd let the rookie do the complete job.

"Go ahead and log everything in and lock it up," his boss ordered. "I'll see you tomorrow. Good job tonight, Jack."

Jack was excited. This was his first job completely on his own and he loved what he did. Most cops preferred chasing the bad guys, but he loved the technical side of law enforcement. He took the evidence to the lab and was surprised to see the cream of the crop still at work there. He knew they had worked another Crown scene, but figured they had long since gone home. Not only did this team do the scenes, but they were also trained in analyzing some of the evidence. Jack stood quietly in the lab, watching them work.

"Hey, kid," called Bannon. "Whatchu got?"

Jack was thrilled. They were talking to him as though he were one of them. He quickly described the scene and how there might be a connection.

Bannon called him over to the lab table. "We've got a blood type on ours here," he explained, a note of skepticism in this voice. He motioned for Jack to pull up a stool.

Enthralled, Jack ignored the idea that Bannon wasn't serious about the connection theory. Jack had big ideas of working closely with this team and being able to one day solve an important murder case.

Bannon glanced at him. "How about if I show you how things are done here." He explained how this specific blood had been distinguished from the rest due to the splatter.

Jack listened attentively.

"We know this blood came from our guy because it's type A and we know that Judge Haley's blood type is B. If we didn't know that Crown was the bastard, this would be invaluable for the prosecuting attorney at trial," Bannon explained. "Since I'm sitting right here, why don't you and I go ahead and test what you have."

Jack nodded and carefully brought the evidence bags over to the table, hoping Bannon noticed the care and technique that he'd used in processing the evidence. A few moments later, Bannon complimented him. Jack beamed. While Bannon detailed the procedure, Jack kept mental notes. It took no time for the results to become apparent.

"Well," Bannon exclaimed, "this is pretty interesting. It looks like we've got type A here. That's not the most common type, you know."

"You think it was him?" Jack asked.

Bannon seemed more than a little intrigued. "Y'know, this whole Crown case has been a puzzle. There hasn't been any good hard evidence." The other two techs huddled over the lab table and Bannon filled them in. The three techs talked things over for a couple minutes, then Bannon looked at Jack. "Well, kid, what do you think about all this?"

Jack thought for a moment, a little nervous about sharing his ideas with these experienced guys. "Well," he began hesitantly, "if it was Crown at Ms. Mulhoney's house, that could explain why he was bleeding at the judge's house."

Bannon and the other guys nodded. This was the absolute highlight of Jack's career—at least so far.

"I think you're right, kid. I think I'll go ahead and send these samples to the lab upstairs and have them do a DNA test. I'll mark it in connection with the judge's case. This has got me curious. If that bastard was at Mulhoney's house, maybe that means he's going after her next." He looked back at Jack. "I'll let you know what the results are, how's that?"

Jack grinned. He watched Bannon package everything and send it to the lab. Before taking off, Jack heard Bannon call Detective Parker and leave a message on his machine. He'd also called Anne Mulhoney personally, explained what they'd found out and told her to be careful. It sounded as if he thought a lot of her and probably couldn't stand the thought of anything bad happening to her. Jack felt the same way.

Anne Mulhoney put down the phone, feeling a little weak. This whole thing was getting to her. She was still in shock about Judge Haley. How could she be gone? How could those jerks at the jail have let Crown just walk away? God, she hated incompetence. Why hadn't Frank found that bastard?

Bill walked over and put his arms around her. "Who was that, honey?" he asked.

She filled him in but tried to tone down her concern.

He shook his head. "Finding the same blood type is too much of a coincidence." He picked up the phone. "I'm calling the police chief. What if that nut is after you? I want a twenty-four-hour guard here."

"Don't be ridiculous, sweetheart. He's not after me. Besides, you're here."

Bill shook his head again. "I'd just feel better if—oh, I don't know."

The phone rang again. This time Bill reached for it. He murmured, "Yes, I agree" a few times and Anne mouthed, "Who is it?" but he ignored her and continued to listen.

After a few minutes he hung up. "That was Captain Billings. He told me the media has already gotten the story, even about our house. He said the reporters usually monitor police scanners. I guess our address was given out over the radio about the guy last night."

Disgusted, she shook her head. All this would create more fear in the public and make the police look like fools. "Well, what else did he say? Why didn't you let me talk to him?"

"Because you would have told him no and not given me the full story," he said matter-of-factly. "At this point he's concerned about anyone connected with the case—the women, at least. He's going to assign someone to you, starting tomorrow. I guess he figured it would be okay tonight since I'm here."

"Oh, Bill, this is ridiculous. They should be out on the street looking for Crown, not here babysitting me."

"Listen, honey, I know you like to do things your own way, but this would make me feel better. At least I know you'll be safe when I have to work late. It should only be for a few days." He was pleading.

Anne sighed. She would hate this, but a part of her did feel a little bit relieved. This guy was nuts. Plus, Bill usually worked late at his dental office at least two nights a week. Finally, she nodded and Bill hugged her tight.

"You know, maybe you're right," she said. "But I'm not the one who was in the courtroom. That was our new attorney. As far as I know she lives alone."

Suddenly Anne was worried. She got out the phone book and looked for Toni's name. Not listed. Damn. She thought for a moment, then quickly dialed Dorothy, their all-knowing secretary, who answered on the second ring.

"Sorry to bother you so late," Anne apologized. She gave her the lowdown and expressed her concern.

"I've got everyone's home number right here in my book," Dorothy replied.

Within moments Anne had the unlisted number and was again dialing the phone. She was greeted by an answering machine. Damn it! After the beep, Anne left a professional message telling Toni to call her immediately at home, regardless of the hour. After hanging up she frowned at Bill.

"Track her down, honey. You won't rest until you do."

She nodded and called back Captain Billings. She needed to know who knew what and how much information was being given out. She also voiced concern about Toni's safety. He told her that Detective Parker was in charge of this and would let him know. He would also have the desk sergeant send a patrol car to Toni's place.

Still feeling vaguely unsatisfied, she hung up the phone. She pulled out her address book and called Sam. Another answering machine. Next she tried Boggs. Answering machine. She pounded her fist on the table, startling Bill.

"Isn't anyone home anymore?" she yelled. The stress and frustration was finally working its way out. Then she remembered Sam's Halloween party. They had declined to go this year because they were supposed to be away for the weekend. "Sam's party," she said.

Bill nodded. "What about cell phones? Doesn't everyone have them?"

Anne smiled and nodded. Usually it was she who remained calm and collected. She looked in her book again and called Sam's cell. As chief investigator, he would be able to track Toni down or find someone who could.

Sam answered on the fourth ring. It sounded like he was in a bar. The connection was bad and there was a lot of strange noise in the background. She found herself screaming into the receiver. Sam, acknowledging this was something important, told Anne to hold on for a second.

When he returned to the phone, Anne told him about the possible connection between a prowler at her home and Judge Haley. "The chief is assigning an officer to me and to Toni, just to make sure. I tried to call her at home, but she wasn't there. Can you track her down?"

"I can do better than that," Sam answered. "She's right here."

"I'm really concerned," she said. "Can you make sure she's not alone tonight? We'll have some kind of schedule worked out for tomorrow, but tonight can you take care of this?"

"Absolutely. Boggs is with her now and so is Vicky Carter from Metro."

"Thank you. I feel somewhat responsible—I gave her this case, you know," she said. "I'll talk to you tomorrow."


Sam hung up the phone. His body seemed to shake involuntarily. This was hitting a little too close to home. He took a minute to regain his composure, then called Captain Billings. He set things up for tonight and went back to his guests. He told Betty and then pulled Boggs, Toni and Vicky aside. He told them he didn't think it was safe to be at the haunted house tonight. It would be too hard with people in masks and the house itself being in almost total darkness. Boggs and Vicky agreed.

139

After hearing the news, Toni stared at him in disbelief. "Ms. Mulhoney really thinks I could be in danger?" she asked.

Sam nodded. "It's really just a precaution, but it's better to be safe, Toni. I'm sure Vicky will be more than happy to babysit you, especially since she'll be on the clock." He tried to make it sound like no big deal. Vicky and Boggs apparently recognized his technique and followed suit.

"What a deal for me, Toni," Vicky said. "Now I can get some much needed overtime. I'm trying to save up for a new car and this will be perfect. It'll be like an old-fashioned slumber party."

"Hey, this means we can charge all our meals to the department. I vote for eating out at the best restaurants in town," Boggs said, as if hoping Toni would fall for the act and regard this as just standard practice, although Toni knew better than to take scarce department resources for granted.

Playing along, Toni laughed with the rest of them. No big deal. "Okay, girls, let the fun begin."

Vicky went back inside the house to get her bag and Toni's. The rest of the guests were herded into the vans by Sam and Betty.

Toni whispered into Boggs's ear. "I guess you really are my bodyguard tonight." She was standing so close to Boggs she could feel her body heat. She looked into Boggs's eyes and felt her knees get a little weak.

She thought about the conversation she overheard at the party. She thought about whispering in Boggs's ear and how it made her feel. Then she thought about Judge Haley, and how quickly life could be taken away. She remembered the loneliness she felt when she was with her friends . . . and the emptiness she'd experienced in the last few years. It occurred to her that she had never felt so alive, or laughed so hard as she had in the last few weeks. Life was short. Life was incredibly precious. Maybe it was the wine she drank at the party. Or maybe it was the fact that she might be the next target for a serial killer. Whatever the reason, Toni decided that she wanted to live her life to the fullest. With all those thoughts and emotions rushing through her in less than a minute, she made a decision. She leaned forward to whisper in Boggs's ear once again. Boggs, clearly more than a little paranoid, pulled back ever so slightly.

Toni recognized the small shift and instantly knew what Boggs was thinking. Boggs had felt the deep connection, too, but was attempting to deny and conceal it. It was at that moment Toni knew she was making the right decision. She trusted Boggs. She felt some uncanny bond with her. And now, she was trusting her life to this woman.

"I know about you Boggs," she whispered.

Boggs leaned back, a startled look in her eyes.

Toni took a half-step forward and gently placed her hand on Boggs's arm. "It's okay," she said with a wink and a teasing smile. "I believe we belong to the same club."

Boggs raised her eyebrows and tilted her head slightly.

Toni confessed, "I heard you talking to Vicky in the bedroom at Sam's."

Boggs seemed to turn several shades of red, although it was tough to tell in the dark night. She started to speak, but all that came out was a stammer.

Toni shut her up completely by saying, "I feel something, too."

Boggs was grinning from ear to ear when Vicky returned with the bags.

"So," she asked. "Did I miss anything?"

Toni shrugged. "Just the usual chitchat. We solved the ozone problem and thought up a cure for the common cold. We were just about ready to discuss some really important issues when thankfully you appeared." She graciously took her bag from Vicky.

"Good," Vicky replied. "I'd hate to think I missed anything earthshattering. Now, let's move on to those important issues. What's our plan here? We'll need food, coffee and footed p.j.'s for later. I can offer my luxurious apartment for our party, if there are no complaints."

"Well," Toni answered. "if no one minds a mess, I'd like to go back to my place. I don't like to leave Mr. Rupert alone all night."

Boggs and Vicky agreed and the plan was set. Vicky would swing by her place and pick up supplies. Boggs and Toni would go over to Boggs's apartment for a change of clothes and then meet at Toni's. Toni gave Vicky her address and was about to give directions when Vicky waved her off.

"I used to patrol that area back in the good old days. See you there."


Boggs and Toni got in the car. "First of all," Boggs said with a grin, "I'm so glad we made it past that first huge hurdle. I can't begin to tell you what I've been going through in the last few weeks."

Toni laughed. "Me, too. Jeez!"

"Okay. We'll talk about that for hours on end at some point, I'm sure. But until this other issue gets straightened out, I doubt if we'll be alone. I mean, Vicky is cool with this, obviously, but others are definitely not."

Toni interrupted her. "I know the drill. Law school hasn't exactly moved away from the good ol' boys' network."

Boggs nodded. She still hadn't started the car. She looked in the rearview mirror. Everyone had left. The sexual tension in the air was thick as butter. Nervous, she glanced at Toni. She'd wanted to kiss her from the moment she'd seen her. This was her chance. Why was she feeling so apprehensive? It wasn't as though she'd never kissed a woman. Hell. She'd kissed more than her share—and in more risky places. Still, she felt like a teenager.

Toni broke the silence. "I guess we better get going or Vicky will beat us there."

"I guess so," Boggs said. But she didn't move.

Toni turned to face her. That did it.

Boggs reached out to touch Toni's cheek. It was so soft. Toni smiled in return. She gently slipped her hand behind Toni's neck and felt her hair slide between her fingers. She pulled her closer. They were inches apart now. Boggs could feel her breath and smell her light perfume. She drank it all in before leaning closer. Their lips met and Boggs heard Toni moan ever so slightly. The kiss was tentative and light. She pulled back and looked into Toni's eyes. They took her breath away and lit a fire inside her. She kissed her again. And again, harder this time. Their tongues met and Boggs hungered for more. Much more.

This time Toni pulled back. "If we stay here any longer," she said, breathing hard, "we'll get arrested."

Boggs laughed. "I know you're right, but that doesn't mean I want to stop. How about we pick up later—where we left off?"

Toni smiled and winked. "Try to stop me."

Boggs started the car. She remembered what brought them to this point and the gravity of the situation Toni was in. "Tonight isn't going to be what I'd like it to be. I mean, I might not be myself, exactly. I'll be in more of a bodyguard mode, I suppose. I just, well, I wish it could be different. I didn't want you to think, I mean, well—"

"Boggs, I understand. This isn't exactly what I would have wanted for our first date, but protocol is protocol. Let's just try to make the best of it. From what I've seen of Vicky, that shouldn't be too hard."

Boggs laughed. "That's true. Vicky is lots of fun. And she's good, so don't worry. You're in good hands, Toni."

# CHAPTER 15

Boggs parked in front of her apartment building. "We're here," she announced. "Come on in and I'll give you the nickel tour. Please excuse the dust and mess. My maid has the year off."

She hopped out of the car and quickly scanned the area. Everything looked normal. She was glad she had on her shoulder holster instead of the ankle holster. It afforded a much faster access. She unlocked her door, flipped on the light and glanced around. Satisfied, she waved Toni inside, then shut and locked the door behind her. Toni looked almost startled.

"No. I'm not locking you in. Just routine safety procedures. Not a bad idea, though," she said with a wink.

Toni shook her head and smiled. Boggs gave her a quick tour and then left her in front of the fish tank while she changed her clothes. She thought about what to wear for the first time in a long time. She wanted to be comfortable and had decided she wanted to keep the shoulder holster. It gave her a better feeling of control because she was constantly aware of its presence. In this situation, she didn't want to lose sight of the potential danger, and just being with Toni could make her forget her own name. With that in mind, she pulled on a pair of old jeans and a tank top. She refastened the holster and slipped her gun inside. She grabbed a denim workshirt from her closet and put that on. She glanced in her mirror. The shirt was big enough to gain easy access but still completely covered the holster. She took her gym bag from the closet and emptied out the clothes, leaving the shampoo and toiletries inside. Then she picked out a change of clothes for tomorrow and headed back to Toni, who seemed to be mesmerized by the fish.

"I'm ready for the slumber party," she said, holding her bag up for inspection.

Toni didn't even look up. She pointed to the tank, careful not to touch the glass. "What's this one?" she asked. "He looks like a miniature Jaws. And this guy is hysterical. I didn't know you could have frogs in a fish tank. He swims for a few seconds, then just stops. It's like he's posing for a picture. I love this."

"Yeah, he's my favorite," Boggs said, then went on to give a quick description of all the fish. "We better hit the road. Vicky will be getting to your place any moment now."

She did another quick scan before allowing Toni to walk outside. She was on a mission and taking it very seriously, but she tried not to be too obvious for Toni's sake.

On the drive to Toni's apartment, Boggs talked about her fish and attempted to answer all of Toni's questions about each one. Meanwhile she constantly monitored her mirrors, looking for anything out of the ordinary. When they arrived at the parking lot she turned off the engine.

"Let's wait here for Vicky," she said. When she pulled up a little later, Boggs unlocked the door and went in first. Vicky was right behind her. She turned on the light and motioned for Toni to remain at the threshold. With an expertise gained from years of experience, the two swept the area, their guns unholstered. After the main floor was clear, Toni was ushered inside and the door was locked. Toni remained by the door while Boggs and Vicky headed upstairs.

"We're having company tonight, boy," Toni explained to Mr. Rupert, who had been lounging on the couch. "It seems my boss is a little concerned for my safety."

It wasn't until they'd arrived at her place that Toni realized the true seriousness of the situation. She knew enough about police tactics to sense that Boggs had waited for her "partner" to arrive. Toni felt like one of those protected witnesses in a mobster movie and shuddered involuntarily.

Mr. Rupert seemed a bit confused, as if he sensed her nervousness and that made him uncomfortable.

When Boggs and Vicky came back downstairs and were laughing, Toni let out a breath, relieved. At that moment Mr. Rupert decided he too would need to protect Toni. Filled with determination, he sat up straight and tall. He didn't even flinch when Vicky said, "My God, he's huge."

Toni introduced her to Mr. Rupert. "He's not huge, just big-boned. Anyway, make yourselves at home." She went into the kitchen. "Anyone like something to drink? I've got coffee, water and some diet Mountain Dew. Sorry I'm not more prepared."

"Coffee sounds good to me," Boggs said.

"Me, too," Vicky agreed. "And let's break out some food and get comfy."

Toni retrieved some cheese from the fridge. She had just finished with the coffee and turned on the pot when Vicky joined her in the kitchen with her own bag of goodies. She had obviously stopped by the deli. She asked for a couple plates and bowls, then kicked Toni out of the kitchen. Toni took her plates to the living room and then noticed the light flashing on her answering machine. The first message was from Jake, asking her to call and give him the scoop on the party. The next was from Linda, wanting to know if she was going to the flag football game tomorrow, and the last was a message from Anne Mulhoney. "I guess I don't need to call her now that I have my very own bodyguards. She must have tried me before she got ahold of Sam," Toni said, half to herself. Boggs nodded.

Vicky made several trips during this time into the living room and soon the entire coffee table was full of food.

Toni could hear the last gurgles of the coffeepot and started to get up, but she was waved off by Vicky. "I've got it, Toni. How do you like your coffee?"

"If it's okay with you guys, I'd like a splash of Kahlua and milk in mine," she answered.

Vicky grinned. "Sure. I'm a great bartender. Boggs, you still like a little milk?"

"Yes, please."

Vicky returned with three steaming mugs of coffee. She surveyed the table. "Quite the spread, don't you think? I doubt we'll go hungry in the next few hours."

The table contained an assortment of deli meats, crackers, bread, potato salad, fresh veggies with onion dip, fried chicken, a Wisconsin cheddar and a box of Hostess Cupcakes. The women dug into the food as though they hadn't eaten in days. There was some idle chitchat, but for the first ten minutes they all ate.

"I suppose this whole situation is fairly commonplace to you two," Toni said. "But this is a whole new experience for me. I don't mind telling you I'm a little nervous. Even more so because we're not talking about it."

Boggs took a sip of her coffee. "Well, from the practical side, we're here to protect you. Anne's concerned that maybe Crown wants to get even with everybody involved in this case. Since you're the attorney of record, and you were the one in the courtroom, he might try for you. As you know, the women he killed before and now Judge Haley were all alone at the time. There was no forced entry, so either they let him in or he got in before they got home. We've swept your entire place and he's not here. Since there's no way any of us are going to let him in, you should be in pretty good shape. But we're definitely not taking any chances. That's why Vicky got assigned to the overnight shift."

Vicky said, "We're doing everything by the book, so that's why it seems so dramatic. No one is going to let you answer the door or go out by yourself. Metro also has units patrolling the area. It shouldn't be long before we nab him."

"The whole thing just seems so unreal to me," Toni said. "I mean, he confessed, then he just walks out of the jail. It just doesn't seem to fit. I don't know. Something just bothers me about the whole thing."

"I never even saw the guy." Vicky shrugged. "I just know what I heard on TV and the murmurs around the station. I figure he's crazier than shit and just got lucky." She glanced over at Boggs. "What do you know? Aren't you the investigator?"

Boggs nodded. "Yeah, but I didn't do hardly anything on this case. When Frank brought him in and got the confession, there wasn't a whole lot left to do. As far as we were concerned, the guy was going to plead and that would be the end of that. In fact, I don't think there was any hard evidence, and no one to interview. The only paper I ever got was that fax."

Toni remembered. "That was just a psych assessment from a few years back. I read it and he definitely fits the profile. Borderline Personality Disorder and a real problem with women."

"You understand all that psychobabble?" Vicky asked.

"Basically," she replied. "Before I went to law school I was a psychotherapist. Y'know, something didn't sit right when I read the report, but either I was interrupted or I decided it didn't matter. I've got it upstairs." She headed toward the stairs. Boggs was right behind her. Toni looked at her.

Boggs grinned. "We're not even going to let you go to the bathroom by yourself until this is over. It's just one of the perks of working at Metro."

Up in her bedroom, Toni retrieved the file from her desk and caught Boggs staring at her. Her cheeks burned and she averted her eyes. "I've got it," she stammered. She felt the excitement of being alone in her bedroom with Boggs. For a moment she recalled the dream she had after seeing Boggs for the first time. She suddenly felt warm all over and for the second time that night her knees were weak.

Boggs turned to leave but Toni caught her arm. She knew Vicky was downstairs but right now she didn't care. She leaned in and kissed Boggs softly on the ear. Then on her neck and finally on her lips. The kiss was light and sensual. Boggs put her arms around her and pulled her closer.

"I want so much more," Toni whispered. "But not now. Not with Vicky downstairs." She pulled away and headed back to the living room.

Boggs blinked several times as though she couldn't find any words. She followed Toni to the living room.

Vicky was propped up in the corner of the couch, chewing on a carrot stick. Toni cleared a corner of the coffee table and set down the file. While she reread the fax, Boggs cleared a few of the plates and refilled everyone's coffee mug.

Vicky let out an audible sigh and fanned herself. "Maybe it's just me and the coffee, but is anyone else warm?"

"Oh, that's the furnace again," replied Toni. "We've had problems with it the last week or so." It came on even though the temperature was set at 65. Maintenance was supposed to have it fixed a few days ago. They tried, but it didn't work. "Earlier this week it was like a sauna in here. We can open the windows if you want."

Vicky looked at Boggs, who shook her head.

"That's okay," Vicky answered. "I'll just change into a T-shirt." She retrieved her bag and headed upstairs.

Toni continued to read and kicked off her shoes and socks. A few more minutes passed. Then she found it. "Here. This was what was bugging me. In the diagnosis." She pointed to the page and waved Boggs over. Vicky joined them. "See? Right here. Acrophobia."

Boggs and Vicky looked at each other and shrugged.

"He's afraid of heights. But to have it diagnosed, it means more than just a little nervous. It means a *real* fear. This guy would probably have a panic attack if he were up high. Having this diagnosis means that it interferes with normal functioning. I mean, I'm not crazy about high places, but it doesn't interfere with my life. I can go up to the top story of a building and look out without freaking out completely. Does that make sense?"

Vicky nodded. "But why is this such a big deal? So the guy is a crazy son of a bitch who also doesn't like high places. What's so odd about that?"

Toni was about to respond when Boggs blurted out, "The third murder. He got out through the window. She lived on the fourth floor."

"Exactly," Toni said. "A guy like this would have freaked out if he had to leave through the window. It doesn't make sense." She scratched her head and looked at Boggs. "Do you think there could have been a mistake and he really left through the front door?"

"I don't think so. Our crime unit is the best. I can't see them making a mistake that big."

"Maybe the guy isn't as bad now as he was when the shrink looked at him," Vicky suggested.

"I suppose if he got treatment, but that doesn't seem likely. Phobias are pretty tough to overcome on your own, and Crown doesn't seem like the kind of guy to read self-improvement books. Anyway, maybe I'm just looking for something to get a handle on this guy since he may be lurking around the corner. I mean, we've got his confession on tape. All we need to do is find him before he kills someone else."

Boggs tried to reassure her. "I'm sure Frank will find him."

Vicky agreed. "Frank is good. He's a bastard, but he's good." She began fanning herself again. "Jeez . . . when is that furnace going to stop? Do you have a twenty-four hour maintenance number we could call?"

"It's on the fridge. Maybe if you call they'll actually do something about this."

Boggs had been pacing around the living room when she suddenly stopped cold. "Hey. Didn't the first victim have a maintenance malfunction? The security or something?"

"Helen Carter," Toni said. "The security system in her building had been malfunctioning for a few days. Otherwise, he would have never gotten in and out without anyone seeing him. Talk about dumb luck."

"Just wondering. I mean, don't you think it's unusual that your furnace is having a problem that they can't seem to fix?"

"Not until just now." Toni looked around the room. "Now I'm more than a little paranoid. Maybe Crown is a lot more clever and devious than anyone thought. Maybe that's how he got into their homes, by pretending to be a maintenance worker." She was up and pacing around now. "Just think. I would have let in a maintenance guy in a minute, especially since this has been going on a while and I'm roasting in here. Maybe that's what happened." She looked at Boggs. "Do you remember if the others had problems with their buildings or anything?"

Boggs shook her head. "I don't recall anything else, but that's not to say there wasn't. I don't think anyone was looking in that direction." She glanced around the room. "Do you have some paper? Since we're brainstorming here, let's keep a list of things we want to check out."

Vicky hung up the phone and returned to the living room. "The guy said they've tried to fix it twice, but it doesn't seem to take. He said there's probably something wrong with the thermostat inside. He'll try to get someone here within a couple hours." She grinned. "I told him it was an emergency and I may have mentioned something about being a cop, otherwise we'd have to suffer with this crap all night."

Boggs filled Vicky in on their latest theory. She agreed that they would need to be careful. The constant hum of the furnace made Toni jumpy, but she felt safe with Vicky and Boggs in the room with her.

"Back in a flash," Vicky said, and Toni noticed for the first time that she was wearing a pancake holster in the back of her shorts.

"Hey. Where are you going?"

151

Vicky turned and smiled. "Just a little detour to the powder room."

Toni was embarrassed and she was scared. She had two armed professionals guarding her in her own home and she was quizzing one of them about going to the bathroom. Jeez! This was beginning to get to her, and to top it off, the place was turning into a sauna again. She looked down at her coffee mug. "Maybe I should switch to something cold. Do you want a soda or some ice water, Boggs?"

"Ice water would be nice. It is getting a tad bit sticky in here." Boggs opened the dining room window about an inch. Just enough to let a slight breeze come in.

In the kitchen, Mr. Rupert was lying on the cool floor next to his water bowl. Toni reached down to scratch his head. She got out a couple of glasses and filled them with ice. Then she took one cube and put it in Mr. Rupert's bowl. He promptly got up and stuck his paw in the water, pushing the cube around. She shook her head and laughed, then filled the glasses. Back in the living room, she saw Boggs standing by the dining room table, looking at the blank wall. Toni stopped dead in her tracks. Boggs had removed her workshirt and was standing there in just her skintight white tank top and jeans. Her shoulder holster was clearly visible. She was looking at the sexiest woman she had ever seen.

Boggs turned toward her and pointed to the wall. "What's supposed to be hanging here?" she asked. "I noticed it the first time I came over. There used to be something here, right?"

Toni just stared. Holy cow. Was this a fantasy or what?

Boggs spoke again, but Toni didn't hear a word. All she knew was that Boggs was coming toward her. Toni managed to let some strange sound escape her mouth. Her knees again felt a little weak. This was beginning to be a pattern. Boggs reached her side just as Vicky came back.

"Toni, are you okay?" Boggs asked.

Vicky was on alert. "What's wrong. Did something happen?" Her hand automatically reached for her gun.

"I don't know. I was asking her a question and she just stared at me. Didn't seem to hear a word I said."

"Is she in shock?"

"No, I'm not in shock," Toni said. "And I can hear you." She rolled her eyes.

Both Vicky and Boggs let out a sigh.

Boggs put her hand on Toni's shoulder. "What happened? You looked like you were on another planet. Do you need to sit down?"

Toni was too embarrassed to say what she had been thinking. "Well, I was just remembering something." She noticed the concerned look on their faces. "No, it didn't have anything to do with Crown or anything. It was just, it was a dream . . . kinda, I guess. I'm okay. It's no big deal." She was really embarrassed now.

Boggs grinned. "Sit down anyway." She ushered Toni to the couch, taking the water from her. "I was asking you what's supposed to be hanging on the wall over there."

Vicky immediately went over to inspect the wall. "Hey, you're right. There was a picture hanging here. What happened to it?"

Toni laughed and went to the closet. "I took it down the first night you came over."

They looked at her and shrugged. Toni was still giggling. If nothing else, it helped to break the sexual arousal she was feeling. She retrieved the picture from the closet and hung it in its place.

Vicky stepped back to admire it. "I think it's gorgeous. Why on earth would you put it in the closet?"

Boggs sat down in the center of the L-shaped couch, so Toni chose the end nearest Boggs, far enough away but close enough to be able to reach out and touch her.

"I hadn't met Boggs yet," Toni explained, mainly to Vicky. "Sam had told me that an investigator would bring my fax over here. All I knew was that the investigator's name was Boggs. The only other thing I knew was that this Boggs person was referred to as a hard-nosed investigator."

Vicky was now seated at the other end of the couch. Toni pulled her knees up in front of her and continued to tell the story to Vicky, who was now thoroughly enjoying the scoop.

"Anyway, I thought it would be some old guy wanting to charm me with war stories. I looked around the living room and noticed a few items that might 'give me away,' shall I say?"

Both Vicky and Boggs nodded in understanding.

"So," Toni went on, "I took a few books off the shelf and then noticed the picture hanging there. I was just putting it in the closet when the doorbell rang."

Boggs laughed. "The closet . . . how appropriate!"

All three laughed. Vicky scooted closer to the center of the couch and leaned forward in a conspiratorial way. "What happened when the two of you met?" She looked at Boggs. "Did you know who she was?"

"Not really, no," Boggs said. She told Vicky about the elevator mishap. "I did begin to wonder why it took her so long to open the door. Then she asked who it was, and I thought I recognized her voice. It took me a minute to put the two together."

Toni smiled. "The reason it took me so long was because I looked out the peephole first."

Vicky interrupted. "And the sight of her made you think twice about letting her in?"

"No, no. I thought that she . . . um, well, no. I was just surprised," Toni said.

They were all laughing when the doorbell rang. Toni froze in place. Vicky and Boggs immediately shot up.

Boggs motioned for Vicky to go to one side of the door, while Boggs looked out the peephole. Toni watched as Vicky pulled her gun from its holster. Boggs's gun was in her hand, pointed to the floor behind her right leg. She took a deep breath and asked who was there.

"Quickie Maintenance, ma'am," replied the man. "I'm here about the furnace."

Boggs opened the door, keeping her right hand hidden behind her body. She stepped back to allowed him inside. Vicky was on the other side of him, her gun also behind her back. He was carrying a tool box. Even though he wasn't Crown, they obviously were taking no chances.

"Sir," Boggs said, "would you mind setting your tool box on the floor and stepping over to this table."

He looked confused. Vicky produced her badge with her left hand and spoke in a confident and professional manner. You'd never have known she was practically on the floor laughing only seconds before, Toni thought.

"Metro police. Please, sir, this is just a routine precaution," she said, pointing to the table.

The man gently set his box on the floor and walked slowly to the table. Boggs nodded to Vicky and brought her gun into full view of the man.

Vicky holstered her gun. "Sir, for your safety and ours, I'm going to pat you down for weapons." He nodded and Vicky did a quick check. "Okay, sir. Thank you. Now, if you don't mind, I'm going to have to check your tool box here."

While still under Boggs's cover, Vicky looked through the box and appeared satisfied that it contained only the type of tools needed. She then nodded to Boggs, who reholstered her weapon. Toni hadn't moved during this time.

Vicky turned to the man. "I'm sorry about that, sir," she said. "We've had some trouble in this area and we're just being careful."

He nodded but remained standing where he was. He continued to look at Boggs, perhaps afraid she'd pull out her gun again.

After a moment, Boggs said, "So, you're here to fix the furnace?"

He nodded again but didn't speak. Apparently he was still in shock. Grinning, Vicky led him to the furnace, which was located next to the washer and dryer in the kitchen. Boggs stood in the doorway to the kitchen like a sentinel.

It only took five minutes for him to replace the thermostat. Vicky thanked him and escorted him to the front door. After he left she locked up behind him. Vicky and Boggs turned to look at Toni.

"Are you okay?" Boggs asked.

Toni smiled weakly. "Yeah, I guess it's pretty bad when the maintenance man can scare the crap out of you." She laughed. "I bet this was a first for him. It's not every day you get frisked on your way to fix a furnace." Even though she was joking, she was still scared.

Boggs put her hand on her shoulder. "I know it's a little scary, but it's just routine. Vicky and I aren't going to let anything happen here."

Toni nodded and smiled slightly. "It's just that I feel like there's nothing I can do but sit here like a stump. At least you two get to point guns at people and frisk them."

Boggs seemed to understand her helplessness. She picked up the pad of paper she'd been writing on earlier and handed it to her. "You'll feel better if you do something. Let's see if we can come up with some more things that don't add up or that we want to check on. Maybe we can get a handle on this guy."

Toni gladly took the pad and began making notes, beginning with acrophobia. After a moment, she looked up. "Okay, what's different about this case? Sometimes that helps me to find a pattern, like trying to distinguish cases when I'm writing a brief. If we find some kind of pattern, maybe that'll help Frank find this bastard."

"Since we're just kicking around ideas," Boggs said, "and none of this will leave the room, something's been bugging me. Why is it taking Frank so long to find this guy? He bragged about cracking this case and being able to read Crown like a book. That's how he got the guy to confess so quick. Now he can't find one lead on him? Doesn't that sound odd to you guys?"

Vicky thought for a moment. "Well, Frank is a real bragger, that's for sure. But I saw him a couple days ago and I thought he looked like shit. His pants were all wrinkled and it looked like he hadn't slept in days. Is there something else going on with him?"

Both Boggs and Toni shrugged.

"Not that I know of," Toni said. "I don't like him, but I will say that this whole case has taken a toll on almost everyone. People around my office are kinda off in their own worlds. It's as though everyone is trying to keep busy and out of sight. Everyone seems drained, except Anne. She seems pretty good. Of course, she's incredibly busy with all those meetings. Paul's taking over her load and you can tell it's wearing on him. He looked awful last week. And he was even vaguer than usual about what he wanted me to do. He just seemed, well, not right. Not like he was a year ago. Maybe he's just preoccupied by all the extra work, I guess. Maybe that's all there is to it."

Boggs frowned. "I don't know. Maybe it's this case and all the media hype, but I kinda agree with you. A lot of people aren't acting like themselves. Probably I'm just looking at everyone too hard, but I don't like coincidences. Frank has been a mess lately. He's even been bitchy to Sam, and they're usually pretty friendly." She paused. "Then last Wednesday one of those clone attorneys bumped into me in the hall and dropped the file he was carrying."

Not sure what that meant, Toni looked at her with a raised eyebrow.

"Clone guy. You know. Looks like he stepped out of a law school catalog? I think his name is David something or other the third."

Toni nodded. "Oh, I know the guy." She grinned. "He's definitely a cookie-cutter lawyer."

"Anyway," Boggs continued, "he just glared at me. He didn't apologize or anything. I mean usually he says something to me in the halls, but this time he didn't. It was just out of character. Even Paul—he's usually friendly, but Thursday when I took him my report he didn't even look up from his desk. He usually reads it while I'm standing there and he always wants to talk about the case. And he was sweating. I've never seen him sweat before, even on the hottest day of summer. Anne must be really piling it on him, because he looked like he slept at his desk the night before. People just seem to be out of sorts lately. In fact, this is the first time Sam forgot to make a bet with me for tomorrow's football game. Of course, I suppose with the party and all . . ."

Vicky had been listening quietly, but now she seemed animated. "Okay, let's list all we know about Crown." She took the notepad from Toni and started writing. "Maybe this guy does have a pattern that Frank hasn't seen. I mean, he picked him up fairly quickly. He probably didn't even get that far into his profile. Maybe that's why he's having a tough time finding him again. The first time was dumb luck and now he has to do all the legwork."

Toni chimed in, "Crown, well, he's a dropout and he's never held a job longer than a few weeks. He detested his mother and referred to her as a whore. He's afraid of heights. The only other thing I can think of is that his videotaped confession was completely monotone. It was as though there was no emotion. I think that's weird because you'd think in a guy like this, there would be a lot of anger and frustration . . . and intelligence."

"I agree," Boggs said. "I don't know a lot about this kind of guy, but I've read about serial killers before. They always seem to be smart."

"That's right," Toni said. "Look at Ted Bundy. He was charming and intelligent. A law student. No one who knew him had a clue, except for his girlfriend."

"Okay," Vicky said. "This is some good stuff. Now what about the murders?"

"All the women were very powerful and intelligent." Toni tried to push the thought of Judge Haley from her mind and just concentrate on the facts. "All of them lived alone except for Judge Haley. I wonder where her husband was that night? Crown must have known she was alone. That was his pattern."

"Maybe he didn't know she was married," Vicky offered.

"No," Boggs said. "That would be out of character. It sounds like Crown knew enough about his victims to know when they would be home. Anyway, everyone in the city knows that Judge Haley is married to Mr. Newspaper himself."

Toni nodded. It was no secret. "Hey," she said. "Here's a quirk. Why did she let Crown inside? She knows what he looks like. Why wouldn't she call the police?"

"Good thought." Boggs popped a cracker in her mouth. "Maybe he was already inside. Or maybe she called some type of repair guy." She thought a second, then shook her head. "No, that wouldn't make any sense. It was nighttime and how would Crown know if she called anyway? That's not it."

Toni had been drumming her fingers on her knee. She was frowning.

"What's going on in your brain there, girl?" Vicky asked.

Toni grinned. "Oh, it's stupid. I was just remembering this book I read a couple years ago. It's nothing."

"Go ahead," Boggs said. "What were you thinking?"

"Well this cop was looking for the bad guy. The usual stuff, but it turned out there's this copycat killer."

"And you think this could be the case here," Vicky said.

"Not really. But it would answer the question as to why Frank is having such a hard time finding this guy. I guess it's really sorta Hollywood, but I was just reminded of the book when we were talking."

Boggs scratched her head. "It's a possibility. Maybe Crown is dead. I can't imagine Judge Haley would let him inside, that's for sure. I wonder if there were any signs of a break-in or anything else out of character for this one."

"I guess we'll know more when the reports are in," Vicky said. "I can nose around a little at the station. See who was first on scene. Maybe someone will tell me something."

Toni yawned. Boggs looked at Vicky and nodded ever so slightly.

"Why don't you try to get a little sleep," Boggs suggested. "I think that's enough brainstorming for one night. We can do more tomorrow. One of us will take the first shift and keep things under control down here."

Toni started to protest but realized that all the adrenaline had taken a toll on her. She started to gather the remaining plates from the coffee table.

"I'll take care of all this, Toni," Vicky offered. "I'm still pretty wide awake, so I'll take the first shift." She glanced at her watch. "I can watch reruns of *I Love Lucy*."

Boggs looked at her watch also. "Come and get me at five. Three hours should be enough for me. Come on, Toni, let's get you in bed," she said with a wink.

Toni grinned slightly. It seemed like all of the sudden she was more tired than she had been in her entire life. She headed up the stairs with Mr. Rupert by her side and Boggs close behind.

Toni grabbed a T-shirt from her closet and went in the bathroom. Mr. Rupert followed her. Boggs sat down in the small overstuffed chair in the corner of the room. She moved it slightly so that she would have a clear view of the hall. When Toni came out of the bathroom, Boggs was in the chair with her feet propped up. Her gun was still resting in her shoulder holster.

"Do you plan on sleeping like that," Toni asked.

"Yes, in fact I do," Boggs said. "I think I'll be very comfy, thank you."

Toni shook her head. "There's more than enough room for you in my bed."

Boggs smiled. "Well, now there's an offer. No, seriously . . . I'd doze in this chair. If I got in your bed I don't think I'd want to be sleeping. And anyway, if I actually did go to sleep, I'd probably sleep too hard and it would be tough to wake up quickly if needed."

Toni didn't even put up a fight. She nodded and crawled into bed. She pulled the covers up and tossed Boggs the extra pillow. "Here you go. Oh, there's an extra throw blanket on the floor there."

Boggs thanked her and arranged the pillow and blanket on the chair. Her feet were propped up on the desk chair. Toni could hear her settle in and she felt safe. Smiling, she closed her eyes and tried to get a little sleep.

# CHAPTER 16

Standing outside a small cabin about 50 miles south of Fairfield, the man looked up to the sky. The moon gave enough light for him to complete this task without a flashlight. He had taken his jacket off and rolled up his sleeves. He was covered in sweat, but it was something he had to do. He was almost finished. He'd been at this nearly three hours.

He surveyed the area. It looked good. The woodpile was just as it had been before he began. Just a few more and no one would ever guess what lay underneath.

He placed the last few logs on the top of the pile. He reviewed every step in his mind, making certain he had done everything correctly. First, he had moved the logs, one by one, to another pile about 15 feet away. He was careful about putting the logs in a leafy area. He didn't want anyone to notice that the pile had been moved. Then he'd retrieved a shovel from inside the cabin. Even though this was not his cabin, he knew there would be a shovel inside and there was. Digging was the hardest task. It wasn't just the backbreaking job of shoveling dirt, it was the purpose of the digging. This was not a task that he enjoyed, but he knew it must be done. It was a part of the big plan. He was even sorry that it had to come to this, but he'd always known it would. As he had continued to dig, he took comfort in knowing it was all for the greater good.

The hole he dug was not as deep as he would have liked, but he had hit rock. Barely four feet deep and only about three feet wide and six feet long, it was big enough, though. He had climbed out and dusted himself off, pleased with his effort.

Satisfied, he rested for a moment, leaning against a tree. "I knew you would like it up here. It's very pretty. You can see the lake there, just past those trees," he said. "Yes, this is a good place for you. You've done a really good job, Dexie. I'll finish here. We both knew I'd be the one who would have to finish—it's my destiny, you know? Just like we always talked about. I won't forget all you've done. You rest easy now, okay?"

Earlier that night he had asked Dexter to stand on the canvas so he could show him how he was able to kill the women so easily. Dexter never even questioned the request. Just as he hadn't questioned him when he told him what to say to the police. Or to leave the holding cell when another man's name was called. Dexter had never questioned him. Dexie trusted him completely. The sight of the knife didn't even bother him.

Slicing Dexter's throat caused no emotional reaction in the man and that surprised him. He thought he might feel a little sad, but it was just another task. Only the thought of the burial made him a little uneasy. He himself didn't like confined spaces.

He took a deep breath and continued working. The heavy canvas served as a shroud for Dexter. He pulled the edges inward and then carried the body to the hole. With absolutely no ceremony, he dropped Dexter in. He then retrieved the shovel and replaced the dirt. After packing the dirt as best he could, he began the task of replacing the woodpile.

With every log back in place, he stepped back to admire his work. Perfect. No one would ever know. He picked up the shovel and went back inside the cabin. He laughed to himself. The owners had secured their cabin with only the one small lock on the door. Its resistance was less than the average bathroom door. Even a child could get inside. He laughed again at how stupid most people were. He looked around the inside of the cabin, making sure he hadn't disturbed anything. Of course he hadn't. He relocked the front door on his way out. He would be home before the sun broke the horizon. Before anyone noticed he was gone too long. Everyone was working on the case. He was no exception.

While driving back toward the city, he worked on the next step of the grand plan. He had berated himself earlier that night when he learned about that police bitch who found a possible connection between Judge Haley and Anne Mulhoney. After thinking about it for a while, however, he decided it would only confuse the police and that made him happy. Even his mistakes were brilliant. He hummed a nondescript tune all the way back home.

# CHAPTER 17

Boggs was dozing in the chair when the whisper of her name brought her wide awake. Her hand automatically went to her gun as she scanned the room. All her life the whisper of her name would bring her out of a dead sleep, although she could sleep soundly through thunderstorms, telephones and loud music. She exhaled a sigh of relief when she saw Vicky standing in the hall, motioning to a cup of coffee in her hand. Boggs nodded and joined her in the hallway.

"I just made a fresh pot," Vicky whispered. "I think it would be okay if we let her sleep alone for a few minutes. Come on downstairs."

Boggs agreed. She took a quick look back at Toni, who was sleeping soundly. Mr. Rupert blinked at her. She waved to Mr. Rupert and then tiptoed down the stairs. "How was your night?"

"Just spiffy. Thank you for asking. I watched a little late-night TV. Nothing too exciting. Although I did watch an infomercial about these fabulous cooking pans that also chop, dice and puree. You can fix an entire gourmet meal in just a fraction of the time. I almost ordered a set."

Boggs laughed. Vicky never cooked.

"Anyway, I called Sarge and asked who was on 'Toni' duty today. I found out it's Patty Green, and she was the first on scene at Judge Haley's. Guess she wants the overtime. She should be here in a couple hours, so I'm going to hang around until then so we can pick her brain. Oh, and I volunteered both of us for bodyguard duty, too. For the next few days I have midnights and you have evenings. While she's at work the sergeant isn't going to have anybody assigned."

"Good. I think she'd be more comfortable with people she knows," Boggs said. "And Patty's really nice."

"Oh, you are so correct. Gee, I bet you never even considered that you want to spend every second with her." Vicky laughed. "So fill me in. When did you figure out you liked each other?"

"Well, it didn't really come out like that. When you went to get the bags last night she told me she overheard us at Sam's."

Vicky grimaced. "Sorry. I was probably talking too loud."

"No. It turned out great. We had a small 'moment' before we drove over here. If this Crown shit hadn't been going down—well, you know." She remembered Toni's kiss. "Anyway, as soon as all this is over . . ."

Vicky was grinning. "What the hell were you doing sleeping in that chair?"

"I was doing my job," Boggs said, feigning indignation. "And with you within earshot? No way. Anyway, she was sound asleep in two minutes." She poured herself a cup of coffee and went to the fridge for some milk. "Jeez. There's still enough food in here to feed an army. Were you PMSing when you went to the store last night, or what?"

"Very funny. No, I just thought it would be nice to have some food for last night and today. I figured this thing might take a few days."

Boggs sipped her coffee. "Yeah, you're right. That was pretty smart of you. I guess that's why you make the big bucks."

"Well, I wouldn't go that far, but I've done the witness protection thing before. Some of the people are so keyed up and nervous they want to eat all the time. I found it easier to have a huge variety in the fridge instead of going out for food every half-hour. So, how do you think Toni is holding up?"

Boggs shrugged. "I guess she's doing pretty good, considering. I don't think she really believes he's after her. I think she's pretty well convinced herself he's only after very powerful women."

Vicky agreed. "I think the deal with the maintenance guy kinda threw her for a loop, but she doesn't really believe she's in danger. That's going to be the hard part, because she's likely to take more chances and not even realize that she's left herself open."

The two women continued to sip their coffee, lost in their own thoughts. After a few minutes, Toni appeared with Mr. Rupert. "Good morning. Any coffee left?"

Boggs poured her a cup while Toni fed Mr. Rupert his breakfast. The women sat on the couch while Mr. Rupert inhaled his food.

"You know something?" Toni said. "I realize we were throwing a lot of ideas out last night, but I've got a strange feeling about this whole thing. I know it's supposed to be an open-and-shut case, but something doesn't feel right."

Vicky nodded. "I know what you mean. The more we talked last night, the more it didn't add up. It wasn't anything in particular, just a gut feeling. Almost like the murders were too perfect. Does that make any sense?"

"You know," Toni said, "I remember looking at the crime scene photos and thinking, these photos are good, almost too good. Perfect to show a jury."

They looked at one other.

"You mean you think the murders were staged?" Vicky asked.

Toni shook her head. "No, not exactly. Just that the photos were too perfect. The lighting, the angle, everything. The way the body was lying. It's just plain strange."

Boggs hadn't considered that before. "Maybe it's also because all the photos were taken by the same team . . . and they're the best." She thought about this. Usually photos were pretty crappy. Only the major cases got the number one unit.

"You're right," Toni said. "There could be tons of great crime photos, but the majority of the cases plead and never go to trial. I guess none of us spends too much time looking at photos when we know we aren't going to use them." She got up and took the coffee mugs into the kitchen for a refill. She came out of the kitchen shaking her head.

"What?" Vicky asked.

"It's like you said. Everything is too perfect. Or maybe it's just because we're pissed off that we had the guy and we let him go. I mean, he gets into the homes of these women, who are by no means stupid. He's able to kill them and leave no evidence behind. Then, we catch the guy and he makes a full confession on videotape, waiving his Miranda rights. On some fluke he walks right out of jail and disappears. A week later he waltzes into the judge's home and kills her. Either this guy is a total genius or he's the luckiest son of a bitch on earth."

"No shit," Vicky said. "And one of my questions is, how did Crown know to answer to the other guy's name in the holding cell? Where was that other guy?"

"He had passed out," answered Toni. "He's a regular down in the drunk tank. Comes in almost every weekend, kinda like Otis from the Andy Griffith show. But how did Crown know that? And by Monday morning, wouldn't you think that Otis the drunk would be sober enough? He wouldn't still be passed out, would he?"

Boggs shook her head. "He should've been fine, especially if this is a regular occurrence for the guy. Does anyone know if they checked him out? Maybe he was paid to do this or something."

"Hey, that's a thought," Toni said. "In the meeting that morning in Anne's office, the jail guy said they were going to check on him, medically. He was taken to the clinic, I guess. Maybe Crown did pay him off. You know, offer him a few bottles extra if he didn't get up when his name was called. But don't you think that's a pretty risky plan? This is the same guy who's been able to get into all these homes without detection. I wouldn't put my money on a drunk for an escape plan."

Boggs agreed. "I think Crown is a lot more clever than that. I'd put my money on drugging the guy. That way he'd know for sure the guy wouldn't wake up."

"But how would Crown get ahold of drugs in the jail?" Toni asked.

Boggs and Vicky both laughed.

"The guys in there can get almost anything they want," Vicky said. "It's amazing. Every once in a while they'll crack down, but it always goes back to the way it was. I guess someone shells out a lot of money and that's hard for some of the guards to resist."

"Well, that's another mission for a later date," Toni announced. "So, it's possible that Crown drugged Otis so he could just walk out. He'd have to make sure that no one would recognize him. By some coincidence that day, the desk sergeant wasn't the one who let everyone out. It was a couple of rookies who'd never seen Crown. At least that was the info I got from that meeting. Again we have another coincidence."

Vicky put her two cents in. "Hey, maybe it is a conspiracy, you know? Maybe someone wanted Crown to get out so he'd kill more women. Maybe it was someone in law enforcement who didn't mind seeing women getting killed."

Boggs had been jotting down some notes on the pad of paper from last night. "I don't think the conspiracy plot is very likely, but I'm writing it down. It would take a lot of planning and cooperation. I'd think by now someone would have talked, but who knows? I can think of a few of the good old boys who would love nothing more than to get rid of the women in law enforcement, but I don't know if they'd stoop to killing."

"I guess that's a little too drastic," Vicky said. "But at this point, I think any idea we come up with is worth thinking about. I'm with you guys, this whole thing stinks."

"And since we don't know anything for sure, just our own hunches, I suggest we keep our little list to ourselves," Boggs said.

Toni and Vicky agreed.

"I'm pretty sure that if someone else is involved in this, it almost has to be a man," Toni continued. "I mean, it seems clear that this person does not care for women. Or at least women in powerful positions."

Boggs smirked. "It's got to be another man. And frankly, in my opinion, at this point everyone has become a suspect—"

"Absolutely," Vicky interrupted. "In fact, I was thinking about Toni's idea—a copycat guy. He was the best friend of the cop, so he knew the inside scoop. Only in this case, maybe the best friend is a cop. That would mean that there's a really good chance that one of us knows the other guy."

"If we continue with this theory," Boggs said, "we'd better trust only us until or unless we can rule someone out."

"That makes sense to me," Vicky said. "Toni, I forgot to tell you. Patty Green's coming over later. I know her and she's a good cop. Although I don't suggest we tell her what we're thinking, I don't think we'll have any problems there."

Toni took a deep breath. "This doesn't seem real."

Vicky continued, "I'm on midnights, so I'll show up around eleven or so every night. Maybe earlier, then we can brainstorm a little. During the day, at least while you're at work, you'll be on your own. I don't think you'll be in any danger inside Metro. But to be on the safe side, keep to yourself, okay?"

Boggs laid out the rest of the plan.

"Sounds good to me," Toni said. "Let's have breakfast."

As Toni went to the kitchen to fix some food, Boggs wondered if she would indeed be safe inside Metro.

The man stepped out of the shower and toweled off. He'd been home less than 30 minutes. He'd decided to shower and start his day as he would any other Sunday. He would dress and go out for a big cup of latte and pick up his usual Sunday papers, the *New York Times* and *Fairfield Daily*. He knew that if he willed his mind to do something, it would obey. All he had to do was to tell himself that he had just gotten up from a restful night of sleep. He would then be able to make it another 15 hours or so before going to bed.

After dressing, he thought perhaps he'd treat himself to a little something extra for the day. He went to his closet and dug in the pocket of his jacket. He pulled out a small plastic bottle marked *aspirin*. He shook out two tiny pills. Speed. He loved speed. It made his thinking even sharper. Pleased with himself, he snapped the lid shut and slid it back into the pocket before heading out the door.

It was a fairly brisk morning, but he chose to sit at an outside table at the small bagel shop. Only one other table was occupied. He gave his order to the cute young waitress and opened the *Daily*. He was surprised to see the headline. Instead of a feature article about the serial killer on the loose, the headline announced, "Airlines Threaten Strike."

He scanned the rest of the front page. Nothing about him. Page two. Nothing. He was beginning to get angry. How could a possible airline strike be more important than his work? Who cared about the damn airlines? He was making the big plan possible for all. He was fulfilling destiny. He could not understand the stupidity and simplicity of most people. When the waitress brought his espresso, he merely huffed at her.

Maybe the story was in the Metro section of the paper, he thought. He quickly turned to that section. Nothing. Then he checked the editorials. Surely there would be something about the complete incompetency of the entire police department. Nothing. He shook his head in frustration. How could this be happening? How could there be nothing in the paper about him? The common people needed to know. They needed to be aware of his incredible accomplishments, even if they did not yet understand their significance. He sat at his table, sipped his coffee and stared blankly at the street. The waitress reappeared a few minutes later.

He felt like screaming at her. She was unaware. She had no idea that she was within inches of greatness. He longed to tell her, to tell everyone, but it wasn't time. He took a deep breath in order to calm himself and ordered another latte. This time he added an order of a raspberry scone.

Feeling somewhat calmer, he looked through the newspaper. In the police blotter he found the article he was looking for. The headline was small. In just three short paragraphs the story was told. Judge Haley was killed. The chief of police was concerned for the prosecuting attorneys who were involved in this case and had assigned extra police to patrol the city.

His rage grew. There were no details. Nothing about his brilliance. He began to hear the voices again. In his agitated state, he accidently knocked his coffee to the ground. He quickly looked around. No one saw. The cup hadn't broken. He took a moment to refocus, then casually picked up the cup. Within seconds a calmness overcame him. He knew his destiny. His confidence soared. His power grew. When the waitress finally returned to his table with his check, he smiled broadly and handed her a twenty-dollar bill. He even told her to keep the change. She thanked him several times. He smiled to himself and left. One day, he thought, that girl would realize how lucky she was to have waited on him. The great one. He decided to go to his office and get some work done. He had more plans to make.

# CHAPTER 18

Sunday went by quickly for Toni. Patty had arrived as scheduled and both Boggs and Vicky had gone home to sleep. Toni chatted with Patty for an hour or so but found it difficult to stay awake. She dozed off and on for the rest of the day while she and Patty sat on the couch watching football. The doorbell jolted her awake at nearly 6:30. It was Boggs and Vicky. Patty stood to leave.

"How'd it go?" Vicky asked.

Patty grinned. "Well, except for the first hour or so, she slept like a log."

Toni was embarrassed. "Sorry. I was more tired than I thought."

Good-byes were exchanged. Boggs locked and bolted the door while Toni went into the kitchen to make coffee. After filling their cups she returned to the couch and sat next to Mr. Rupert. Boggs retrieved their pad of paper from the bookcase.

"Okay," Vicky began. "This whole thing has been driving me nuts. I think that someone is definitely helping Crown. Someone on the inside. I think that's how Crown knows how to do things."

"Well," Toni said, "I think that he had to have help getting out of jail. And there's just something about him that doesn't add up. Maybe it was the confession. I don't know."

Boggs was taking notes. "I'm still thinking there might have been something about that maintenance man angle. Toni, do you have the file here? Maybe we could look at the police reports."

Toni nodded and went to get it. "Let's divide it up into the first three murders," she said as she began pulling papers from the file.

Boggs and Vicky began reading the police reports and autopsies. After about 20 minutes they began filling one other in on the details. It didn't take long to discover what the victims had in common. All were white women in their early 40s. They held influential and high-profile jobs and lived quite comfortably. Each one died as a result of her throat being slit by a sharp knife, probably a switchblade. The bones in the right hand were crushed, probably by squeezing, and a pair of her own panties stuffed into her mouth. They hadn't been sexually assaulted. Aside from those details, there seemed to be no other common characteristics.

As for the differences, two of the women lived in apartments, one in a house. In only one report was there a maintenance problem. All three practiced different religions and none belonged to the same country club, business association or gym. One was a Democrat, one a Republican and one a Libertarian. All three went to different colleges. One was married, one divorced and one single. There was no indication that the women knew one another at all.

Toni shook her head. "It seems like they were targeted because they were powerful and outspoken. I think he hated powerful women and maybe thinks women should stay at home. He also has that issue with his mother, you know. He referred to her as a whore, according to the psych report. I'll bet that's where the panties come into play."

Vicky nodded. "Okay. He's going along killing powerful women because they piss him off, right? He thinks women should be barefoot and pregnant. Then Frank finds him and he confesses to the whole thing. Then someone helps him get out of jail and he kills

173

the judge. Why? Because she had the power to put him in prison for life?"

"Maybe," Toni said. "It would make sense to kill a female judge because she's powerful. At least Judge Haley was. And she was hearing his case. But here's what doesn't add up. When he gets arrested, Crown confesses. He just says that he killed them, but there was no emotion in his voice. Don't you think if he hated women so much he'd have said something? Again, look at the psych report. He calls his mother a whore. I'd think he would've said something like 'yeah, I killed those bitches.'"

"Exactly," Boggs said. "The way the psych report read, this guy justified hitting women because they deserved it, or they started it. Why wouldn't he do the exact same thing when Frank interviewed him?"

They sat in silence for several minutes.

"You know," Toni said, "even if this guy is a total genius, and he's just playing everyone for a fool, how would he know that he'd be able to walk out of jail? If he was taunting us with the confession—'Yeah, I did it. What are you going to do about it?'—then he would somehow have to know he was going to walk. He didn't do anything nuts, so I don't think he was looking to get an insanity plea going."

"That would mean," Boggs said, "that Crown knew when he was arrested that he'd be walking out the door. How could someone know that unless he had some connections with law enforcement. If Crown does have a connection, then he could easily assume he'd walk away."

Vicky sighed. "That means we're looking for an accomplice within our midst. Let's make a list of everyone, and I mean everyone, who could have the ability to do this."

"I think we should stick to the men," Toni said. "It's got to be someone who has the same beliefs about women. We just might not know how deep those beliefs are."

After about twenty minutes the list was as complete as they could make it.

"Okay," Boggs said. "Here's what we have so far. The jail guys, including the desk sergeant and the two rookie boys. Also the night shift at the jail and the guard who took Crown from regular lockup to the holding cell. Then we have all the high-ranking cops who could possibly pull strings. That means lieutenant and higher. Next we have detectives, which includes Mr. Personality, Frank. I think we should also add attorneys."

Vicky agreed. "I don't know this cookie-cutter guy, but the prosecuting attorneys do have some influence."

As Boggs wrote down the names, Toni began thinking how long this list had become and how impossible it all seemed. "Since we're adding almost the entire male population here, what about the investigators?"

Boggs tilted her head to the side for a moment, as if considering the possibility. "I guess you're right. Investigators would be able to pull some strings. And we've got a new one, Peter. I don't really know much about him. Sam has had him working a fraud case. He's been buried in paperwork for weeks. Or at least I think he has." She sighed. "This is a big list here. Now the question is, how do we eliminate anyone? If there's an accomplice, there'd easily be alibis for all the murders."

Toni thought for a moment. "Let's try to factor in the information we have from Judge Haley's murder," she suggested. "Maybe we'll get something else to go on."

After a few minutes of discussion, they decided that Judge Haley fit the common profile and seemed to have no other connection to the other victims. The only question was how Crown got into the judge's house.

"I don't think she would willingly let Crown inside," Toni said. "She knew what he looked like and knew he was on the loose. In fact, I don't see Judge Haley as the type of person who would open her door to anyone she didn't know."

"But she might open the door to someone like a delivery guy," Vicky said. "Maybe Crown puts on a flower delivery jacket and baseball cap. People look right past a person's face and look at the flowers."

"I could go for a theory like that," Boggs said. "But it would have to be some other type of delivery, otherwise they would have found flowers or at least some kind of trace evidence. What about UPS or something?"

Toni shook her head. "No, I don't think so. They all have those trucks and uniforms. Harder to pull off. What about a pizza delivery guy? All he'd need is some type of car, a baseball cap and a square red bag. Even if you didn't order a pizza you'd probably open the door and tell them you didn't order."

Boggs and Vicky pondered that for a while before Boggs began shaking her head. "Nope. You might open the door, but you wouldn't let the guy inside, even if you had ordered the pizza. I don't know about you guys, but I just take the pizza from the guy right there. He never even crosses the threshhold. Here, we've got no struggle, and the bodies were all well inside the front door. Somehow, Crown is getting all the way inside the house without them getting suspicious. By the time they figure it out, if they ever do, they're only seconds away from death."

"Well," Toni said, "that takes us right back to square one. The other ones may have let Crown inside for whatever reason, but we agree that there's no way Judge Haley did."

"What about the copycat theory?" Vicky asked. "Maybe Crown didn't kill the judge. Maybe it was someone who wanted her dead and found this to be a perfect opportunity. Everyone would just assume it was Crown and never look for anyone else. That could explain why she let this guy in."

Toni thought about it for a minute. "Well, that might explain letting the guy inside. It would have to be someone who'd either worked on the case or is close to someone who did. The details about the panties and the type of knife have never been released to the press. If we're looking at a copycat, then maybe we can use our list to eliminate people. They might have an alibi for the other murders, but not for Judge Haley. How do we go about asking where these guys were on Friday night without arousing suspicion?"

"I can maybe eliminate some of the cops by checking their schedules," Vicky suggested.

"Hey," Boggs said. "What if the guy was a cop and was on duty at the time? Judge Haley would surely let a cop in the house and he'd have an alibi. He would be 'working.'"

"That makes sense to me," Toni agreed. "That would also explain how he'd know about details of the other murders."

Vicky nodded. "Okay. I'll only scratch someone off the list if he was at the jail Friday night or I can put him at some other location with witnesses. This is going to be tough. But I think I like the idea of this guy being a cop. I mean, I don't like the whole thing, but at least this gives us an angle."

"What about everyone else?" Toni asked. "What do we do with the rest of the list?"

"I've got an idea," Boggs said. "Let's see if we can get people to tell us on their own. You know how that works, Vicky. You say something like 'Were you at blah blah Friday night?' A lot of times they'll say, 'No, I was at the mall' or something. If they don't say where they were right off, I always say, 'Are you sure? I swear I saw someone who looked just like you.' Then they usually tell you where they were. It's a quick way to cross a few names off the list, or at least see if they have an alibi. The most important thing, though, is to see how they react when you ask. Watch and see if they seem nervous, or look at you funny. That's the real key here."

Toni and Vicky agreed and they split up the list of names. Vicky took all the cops. Boggs took the investigators and detectives and Toni was left with the attorneys.

At this point, Toni felt they had pretty much exhausted the subject until they had more information. She yawned.

Vicky looked at her watch. "Well, girls, I'm officially on the clock. Rest assured that I am alert and will have no problem standing guard through the night."

Toni wondered if that meant Boggs would leave, hoping she wouldn't.

"Well," Boggs said, "I was thinking that I might crash here

tonight." She was looking at the floor, deliberately not making any eye contact. "It would save me the trouble of driving all the way past Metro to go home and then back again in the morning."

Vicky snickered. "That makes total sense to me, Boggs."

Toni immediately jumped in. "I'd really appreciate it if you'd stay, Boggs. I think I'd feel better knowing there are two of you here tonight. Especially if we continue on the theory that we know the guy who killed Judge Haley. I mean, it could be anyone."

Vicky nodded. "She has a good point, Boggs. I think you should stay." This time Vicky was serious.

Boggs smiled and pointed needlessly to her bag on the floor. "I brought over a couple changes of clothes just in case." She winked at Vicky. "It's always good to be prepared."

Toni smiled. "I'm going upstairs then. Give me a couple minutes, Boggs, then the bathroom is all yours."

When she heard Boggs reach the top of the stairs, Toni motioned for her to come inside. She had changed into a long red nightshirt that fell a little below her knees. Three buttons at the top were purposely left undone. Boggs stopped about a foot away.

Toni pulled her close, wrapping her arms around Boggs's waist. Boggs dropped her bag and held her. They remained that way for several moments, just holding on.

"I'm scared," Toni whispered.

Boggs caressed her hair. "It'll be okay. I swear."

Toni squeezed her tightly, then stepped back. "I'm sorry. I guess this is just so overwhelming. I've never been in a situation like this." She wiped a tear from her eye. "I'll let you change."

She was sitting on her bed, leaning against the headboard when Boggs came in wearing shorts and a T-shirt. She put her bag on the floor.

Toni motioned for her to sit beside her. "Sorry about that, Boggs. Too many emotions, I guess."

"Don't worry about it," Boggs said. "I think you're holding up pretty good."

Toni smiled. "I think I've got it together now. At least for the moment. But there's this other thing." She put her hand on Boggs's leg and moved it slightly upward. "When I'm not thinking about Crown, I'm thinking about you. About being in the car with you. The feel of your kiss, your hands. That image is burned in my brain. When I think about it, I'm there again, feeling everything." Her hand moved slightly. She dropped her gaze. "I want to kiss you again." She took a deep breath. "But I want more. And I want it now, but with all this other stuff going on and with Vicky downstairs . . ." Her voice trailed off.

Boggs leaned closer. "Me, too."

"Just one kiss, okay?" Toni said. "Then let's just hold each other and try to sleep."

"Okay," Boggs said. "I feel the same way. I want to be able to take my time. One kiss."

Toni pulled Boggs closer and brushed her lips against hers. She kissed Boggs softly. One kiss. But one wasn't enough. The second kiss was a little more passionate and the third more so. Toni felt her body reacting and she knew if she didn't stop now, she wouldn't. She made herself pull away. She was breathing hard. "We've got to stop," she said.

"I know," Boggs said. "But I don't want to." They kissed one more time. "But you're right. We'll get there. Soon, I hope."

Toni leaned back against the headboard again. "This is the right thing," she said, more to convince herself than Boggs. "It'll only be a few days, right?"

Boggs grinned. "Less than that if I have anything to do with it. This is hard. Let's try to get some sleep."

They crawled under the covers and Boggs cradled Toni in her arms. Neither spoke. It took a while, but both eventually slept.

# CHAPTER 19

The morning started off as normal as possible for Toni. Aside from waking up with a woman in her bed and one downstairs, it was just like any other morning. She went downstairs to make coffee, but it was already made. In fact, Vicky had even fed Mr. Rupert. Toni gladly accepted a steaming hot mug and plugged back upstairs for a shower. A half-hour later she returned to the living room. She was dressed and ready for work.

"Okay," Vicky said as she was leaving. "We all know our missions. Remember to be subtle. I'll see you guys back here around ten tonight."

Toni retrieved her briefcase and some fried rice from the fridge before she and Boggs also headed out the door.

After settling in at her desk, Toni found this Monday morning to be like any other. There were a couple short court appearances, motions to file and numerous phone calls to make.

Around one Toni headed into the lunchroom to reheat her rice.

She was waiting for the microwave to beep when she felt a presence behind her. She turned quickly to find David Wellington III, the cookie-cutter guy, standing right behind her. She had been introduced to him when she started but hadn't spoken to him since. Although she had seen him in the courtroom and in the halls, he never seemed very friendly. In fact, she thought he was a snob.

"Hello, David," she said, trying to act casual. "Waiting for the microwave?"

Of course it wasn't the most intelligent thing she'd ever said. He was standing there with an unpopped bag of microwave popcorn in his hand. He smiled slightly. The microwave beeped and Toni removed her rice.

"There you go," she said. "It's all yours." She knew she needed to ask him about Friday night, but she was a little nervous. This was not her cup of tea, but she gave it a shot. "Oh, David," she asked with a smile, "were you by chance at Duffy's Bar Friday night?"

He looked at her with surprise, as if she were flirting with him. He blushed slightly. "Um, no," he said. "I haven't been there since law school."

"Really?" Toni said. She was getting the hang of this. "I swear I saw you there."

"Um, no. I was at the Westdale High football game. My little brother plays," he added.

"Gosh," Toni said, probably a little too enthusiastically. "You must have a double. I was going to go over and say hi, but then you left. Or your twin left, I mean." She turned to go back to her office. With her rice in one hand she waved to David with the other. "See you later."

She was pretty pleased with herself. It was just like Boggs said. Most people will gladly tell you where they were and what they were doing. She felt that David was being truthful, although it would be tough to prove he was at the game. She crossed him off her list. She was still mentally patting herself on the back when she literally bumped into Paul Capelli and nearly spilled her rice. He was still filling in for Anne Mulhoney. He'd been reading something on his yellow legal pad and never looked up. He merely grumbled something and continued on. Toni noticed he was limping slightly. She also realized there was no way in hell she'd ask him about Friday night.

Toni was sitting at her desk, reading some motions and eating her fried rice when she was startled by a knock on her opened door. "Well, hi, Betty," she said. "You startled me."

"Oh, I'm sorry, Toni," Betty said. "Did I catch you at a bad time?"

"Not at all. Come on in. I was just eating my lunch and catching up on some backlog. What brings you down here?"

Betty smiled. "Well, I brought some lunch for Sam. Usually he goes out with Boggs on Mondays, but with all this activity going on, I guess they're keeping close to the office. I just thought I'd pop in and see how you were doing."

"Okay, I guess," Toni said. "This whole thing is so strange. I feel like I'm in the witness protection program. I sure will be happy when he's back behind bars."

"So will I," Betty said. "I just wanted to let you know I was thinking about you. And I'll send some prayers your way."

Toni thanked her. Betty smiled and waved good-bye. Toni walked her to the outer door of her office.

Before leaving, Betty turned around and hugged her. "Take good care of yourself, Toni. And be careful."

She felt deeply touched by Betty's concern. She wondered for a moment if Betty knew more than she was saying and that Toni was in more danger than she realized. She went over the events of the past few days in her mind. After a minute or so she realized she was standing near the doorway, totally zoned out. She wondered if anyone had seen her standing there, staring off into space. Slightly embarrassed, she returned to her office.

⤬

The man had seen the two women standing at the doorway. Before Betty left, he thought he heard her say to be careful. She didn't see him, but it wouldn't have mattered. He would have acted normal and she wouldn't have thought anything about it. After she left, he noticed that Toni stood there a while. She looked disturbed and deep in thought. He wondered for a moment if she had seen him there in the hall, but he didn't think so. Still, he wanted to be cautious. Everything must appear to be normal. Even though he could easily come up with an answer as to why he was just standing there, it wasn't a normal pattern for him. He watched her go back into her office. He didn't particularly dislike her, but he wasn't as obsessed with her as he was with the others. She was young and single. Maybe she was just "being a lawyer" until she found a man to marry. He smiled. He liked being able to have a positive outlook on things. As he walked through the corridors of Metro, he felt his pride and confidence soar. Here he was . . . and no one knew how close to his greatness they were. He then went about his day. The next lesson for the rest of the world was close and he had lots of work to do.


Later that afternoon, Toni was summoned to Anne's office. She grabbed her notebook and hurried down the hall. Even though Anne had never given her a reason to panic, Toni was always apprehensive in front of her boss. After all, she was a new attorney and had a lot to learn. She stood in front of Dorothy's desk.

"How are you, Toni," Dorothy asked. "Things okay?"

"Everything's fine," Toni said. "Just the usual stuff in the day of an assistant prosecuting attorney." She laughed.

Dorothy smiled. "Go on in," she said. "Anne's waiting for you."

Toni knocked lightly on the door and heard Anne beckon her inside. "You wanted to see me?" she asked. She immediately berated herself for asking such a question. Of course she wanted to see her.

"Yes," said Anne. "Sit down. I wanted to know how you're doing. It's pretty nerve-wracking to have a bodyguard."

"Everything is fine," Toni said. "Although the whole situation is scary, I feel very comfortable with Boggs and Vicky." Toni wanted to say more, to talk about her suspicions, but she knew the time wasn't right. Besides, they really didn't know anything. "Is there anything new on Crown?" she asked instead.

"No good leads as of this morning," Anne replied. "Frank is still checking places. We did get the blood results back this morning. The blood on my fence matched the blood at Judge Haley's. I guess that confirms the same person was at both places. We never tested Crown because there was no blood at the other crime scenes. Once we get him back in custody we'll ask for a warrant to get a sample from him."

Toni could see the involuntary shudder in Anne. The thought of someone stalking her had clearly reached her core. She sat there quietly, apparently lost in her own thoughts. Toni broke the silence. "Did we ever get any medical results from the guy at the jail? The man who was drunk and they couldn't wake up?"

Anne's focus was now back on the case. "Mr. Collins? Oh, yes. Last Friday," she said. "He had a significant amount of a drug called thioridazine in his system, which is a tranquilizer, as I understand it. It looks like someone, probably Crown, must have slipped him the stuff early that morning, because the doctor said it would have been impossible for him to have taken it the night before. Too much alcohol. He would have been out, or maybe worse. The desk sergeant who worked that night said the guy was singing until about two a.m. A pretty typical happy drunk. In fact he had to tell him to be quiet several times." She rearranged a few papers on her desk, then sighed. She seemed exhausted. It was the first time Toni had noticed and she desperately wanted to reach out. "You know, Toni, Crown may be a lot smarter than we thought. Please be careful."

"I will," Toni promised.

"Let me know if your caseload gets too chaotic," Anne said.

"And don't worry about doing your weekly status report for a while. It's not a priority right now. I'll let Paul know so he doesn't expect it."

Toni nodded. Anne reached for a file, so Toni stood up to leave. As Toni opened the door, Anne said, "Oh, yes. Where is my head today. There's a memorial service for Judge Haley Friday at two thirty. The courthouse will be closed for the afternoon, so feel free to attend."

Toni thanked her for the information and headed back to her office. Her mind was in a spin. Being stalked. Crown disappearing. An accomplice? Judge Haley's memorial service Friday. Having a bodyguard assigned. With all this going on, she still had to do her job. Add that to the excitement she had about being with Boggs in the near future and Toni felt almost completely overwhelmed.


The man had seen Toni go into Anne's office. She wasn't inside too long. He was able to see Anne's outer office from his vantage point. He stood near one of the vending machines, holding official-looking documents. No one even noticed him. He kept up the appearance of examining the papers but he watched Toni as she left the outer office and went down the hall. She seemed concerned and possibly upset. Why had Anne called her in and what had Anne told her? He began to fume just thinking about Anne in her high and mighty job. Plan. He must go and make plans.

He returned to his office and disregarded the work he had neatly stacked on the corner of his desk. He was fixated on the flashing red light on his phone. A message. It could be from a hundred different people. He hated it when people left those damn "voice mail" messages. Then it was up to him to call them back. He liked things the way they used to be. If someone wanted to talk to you they had to keep trying. The light continued to flash, almost mocking him. Part of him longed to ignore it, but he hated loose ends and unanswered questions more than the flashing light. He picked up the receiver and punched in his code.

The first two messages were unimportant. He immediately deleted those. Next, he heard Anne's voice. Why would she leave him a message?

"Hello, Anne Mulhoney here. I just wanted to make sure you knew that Judge Haley's memorial service is Friday at two thirty. Also, the blood tests are back and it appears the blood found at my house is a match for the blood found at Judge Haley's. If you want to talk about what's going on, come by my office."

The message ended. He didn't move. He felt his heart begin to race. A bead of sweat formed on his upper lip. He blinked several times before he realized that the automated voice on the phone was repeating itself. "If you'd like to hear this message again, press two. If you would like to delete this message, press four. If you would like to save this message, press seven. For the next message, press eight. If you would like to hear this message again, press two. If you would like to delete this message . . ."

He stared at the phone. What number to hear this again? He waited. Number two. He pressed number two and held his breath. He again heard Anne's voice. After the message he pressed seven to save, then slowly replaced the receiver.

He was up now, pacing in front of his desk. He glanced at his open door and then shut it. He took a deep breath and returned to his desk. He straightened the stacks of paper on his desk. Why did Anne leave this message about the blood? Did she know something? Was she trying to show her superiority by flaunting information? Of course he knew about the blood. He paced some more.

He then closed his eyes and carefully reviewed the events of Friday night. As he remembered walking to his preview, he was filled with excitement. Soon his preview would become the feature presentation. He tried to calm himself down and concentrate on the events, without so much emotion. The fence. He had been startled by the car full of laughing girls. The cut on his leg. He automatically reached down to touch the wound. It was still tender and slightly swollen. Then he remembered the blood-soaked sock when he got home. He hadn't realized until later that he had left blood at both places. Now they had the results and knew that it came from the same person.

The voice inside him screamed obscenities and called him names. How could he be so stupid? Not only did the carload of girls see him, but he left blood at both places.

He tried to calm himself down and quell the inner voice. It took a few moments, then his thinking began to clear. They assumed the blood belonged to Crown. There was no reason to connect anything to him, and by the time the world understood his mission, it would be too late. He smiled.

A few more minutes passed and he continued to be pleased with himself. Then the thought of Anne leaving that message returned. He hated the way she acted, as though she knew more than everyone else. Now she had left this message, flaunting her authority. He didn't like the sound of this or of her. She was next. Soon. He reached in his pocket and retrieved his *aspirin* bottle. Two small pills would help him think more clearly. After a few moments he decided the phone message meant nothing to him.


Anne Mulhoney sat at her desk and tried to concentrate. It seemed inordinately difficult. Along with her caseload, she was also responsible for running the office, handling the media and playing politics. She hated the political side of her job, but it was a given. She glanced at her appointment book. She had held more press conferences in the last few weeks than she had all year. This Crown case was a nightmare, on more than one level.

She was determined to at least clear off her desk in hopes of gaining some sense of control. She began with her in box and sorted the papers into a pile for Dorothy to file, a pile that needed some type of response and a trash pile. Her frustration grew. There were several memos from various attorneys complaining about the new investigator, Peter. He apparently was too busy to handle routine requests from them. Great. All she needed was an investigator with an attitude. She made a note on her to-do list to call Sam and have a chat with him. Normally he was really good about dividing the work among the investigators. The next disturbing bit of information was the weekly assignment sheet. Since she had been dealing with the media a lot lately, she had given the task of assigning cases to Paul. Normally she wouldn't have given it another thought after that, but the assignments didn't look right. On first glance they seemed evenly distributed, but upon further study she noticed that the big cases, like murder or aggravated robbery, were all assigned to the men. The female attorneys had been given only misdemeanor cases and minor property crimes.

Why would he do this? She wondered. Cases were to be assigned according to the experience of the lawyer and on no other basis. What was he thinking? He'd even assigned an embezzlement case to David Wellington, who had absolutely no clue about that type of crime. Elizabeth was far more experienced and actually liked paper cases. Anne tried to look for an explanation for Paul's system but could find none. She added a note to her list to call Paul. After about an hour she had gone through all her paperwork and called Dorothy into her office. Dorothy appeared before Anne hung up the phone.

Anne grinned. She could always count on Dorothy. "What took you so long?" She laughed.

Dorothy made some remark about having to finish typing several letters.

"Could you file these for me?" Anne asked. "And also, could you call Sam and Paul and ask them to come and see me? David Wellington too. Oh, I suppose I should talk to Frank as well. I need to see what the status on Crown is this afternoon."

Dorothy nodded. "Is there any time in particular, or just whenever they can come?"

"Well, I'd like to see them before I leave today if they're available."

Dorothy buzzed Anne a few minutes later. "Paul will be down in a few minutes. He has court in forty-five minutes. David will be

188

here in a half-hour and Sam will be down in an hour. I told Frank to come in an hour and a half."

Anne thanked her and looked down at her desk. It was relatively clean. She pulled a legal pad from her drawer and began jotting down some notes.

The man sat at his desk in shock. Anne had summoned him to her office. That bitch. Who did she think she was? She acted like she was the queen of the palace calling for her servants. His blood boiled. He should just do it now. Why wait? The thought of being polite and kind made him sick. The voices inside his head made it very hard to concentrate, and that's when he made mistakes. The voices were pushing him, screaming at him. He needed to think. He was tired. He reached inside his jacket and retrieved two more tiny pills and swallowed them without water. He closed his eyes for just a moment and willed himself to calm down.

He knew it would be next to impossible to teach Anne her lesson in her home, as he had done with the rest. Not with body-guards day and night. Unless . . . hmm. He smiled. Perfect. He would set the stage in her office. In her big fancy office. The place she had no right to be. To show the world that she didn't deserve that office or the responsibilities it held. Yes. This would be per-fect. No one would be expecting this. It could be his best ever. He grinned. Just a few minor details to iron out and he would be ready. With renewed hope he prepared to meet Anne.

Anne sat at her desk and looked at her notes. It was after 5:00 and Frank had just left. She had an uneasy feeling but couldn't really say why. She looked at her notes again.

Paul had apologized about the assignment sheet and explained that David had expressed an interest in white-collar crime. He told her that he had been so swamped this past week that he literally assigned the cases by just going down the list of attorneys, without regard to their experience. Each new case was delegated to the next name on the list. He had apologized again and promised to rectify the situation. After he had left, Anne noticed that, in fact, the assignments did follow the alphabetical list of attorneys and that by some coincidence, the women had been given the minor cases. Still, Paul just didn't seem to be himself. He'd seemed distracted, or something.

David Wellington III had arrived next. He was skittish, but she wrote that off to being a fairly new attorney summoned to the boss's office. She explained to him that she was removing him from the embezzlement case but would allow him to second chair with Elizabeth. This would give him the exposure and experience that would enable him to possibly do the next one alone. He seemed slightly annoyed but mostly distracted. When Anne had asked him how things were going otherwise, he grinned broadly and announced that everything was fine. To Anne, this seemed way out of character.

After talking to these two, she was ready to confide in someone about the unusual behavior. When Sam walked in her office, her first instinct was to talk to him. That thought quickly disappeared when he sat down. His eyes looked a little glassy and he didn't seem to be focused. Anne wondered briefly if he was drunk. She quickly explained the situation about Peter, and Sam merely nodded. After she finished, Sam rose to leave and announced that he would take care of it immediately. At the last minute he turned to her and smiled. For a moment she saw a glimpse of the old Sam, but then it was gone.

By the time Frank left, Anne was fairly well convinced that everyone was having major attitude problems or she had lost her mind. Frank had displayed his usual arrogance, but it seemed to have a sharper edge than normal. He also looked like he had a few too many cups of coffee. Anne noticed his hands were a little shaky. She was still trying to digest all this when Dorothy knocked and entered.

"I'm getting ready to head home," Dorothy said. "Is there anything else you need tonight?"

"No, but thanks," Anne said, still troubled. She must have had a disconcerted look on her face because Dorothy walked over to one of the chairs and sat down.

"What's wrong, Anne?" she asked.

Anne looked up and smiled. She trusted Dorothy and knew she could read people like a book. "This might sound nuts," she began, "but did you notice anything different about the people I talked to this afternoon?"

"Different in what way?" Dorothy asked.

"I'm not really sure. It just seemed like everyone was, well, not themselves . . . or something."

Dorothy nodded her head slowly. "Do you really want my opinion?"

"Please," Anne implored. "I have a bad feeling and I'm not sure if it's something I'm missing here, or if it's just me and I'm losing my mind."

"Well," Dorothy said as she made herself a little more comfortable. "I've been at that desk for many years now. And I've watched folks come and go. Some decent and some a little underhanded, if you ask me. But I will say that all the people here now seem to be pretty good at their jobs."

Anne just looked at her. This was not what she had in mind when she asked for her opinion.

Dorothy gave her a soothing smile. "Now, as to the people you saw today, let's see. Frank is Frank. He reminds me of the men who worked here twenty-five years ago, but not quite as polite. He has that good ol' boy mentality. He's been a little more short-tempered the last few weeks. Sam? Very personable. I like him. He seems to care. He was very much on edge today. When he came in this afternoon he looked frustrated. Very frustrated. Who else? Oh, that David boy. He's not right. He's like a lost puppy who refuses to admit that he doesn't know up from down. I'm sure he's good on the legal side of things, but that boy has no social skills. And then there's Paul. Well, he and I go back many years. He has always been very kind to me . . . and very professional. He always seems to do the right thing, and I understand he's one of the best in the courtroom. I have no reason for this, but I don't like him. Never have. Today was no different." She took a deep breath and leaned back in her chair. She smiled, mostly to herself it seemed, as if she appreciated Anne's asking. "It's not you, Anne," she concluded. "I think there's a lot of stress in the office the last few weeks and everyone seems to express it in different ways. You just happened to get a large dose of it today."

"Thanks, Dorothy," Anne said. "I was beginning to wonder. I thought maybe I was overreacting. I really appreciate your candor."

Dorothy was clearly pleased. She again asked if there was anything she could do for Anne, who just shook her head.

"Have a really good evening, Dorothy. I'll see you in the morning."

Anne remained at her desk and stared at her notes. Dorothy was probably right. Everyone had been tense these past couple weeks. She smiled. She remembered when she was in law school. During finals everyone was incredibly stressed. Some of the students would eat junk food all day and carry their books from one fast food place to another. Others would be camped out at the library from morning to night. Still others found that cleaning everything in sight worked for them. They always had the cleanest apartments during finals. For Anne, lifting weights was her stress reliever. She realized that she had been doing an extra set every morning for the past few weeks. That must be what's going on, she thought. Everyone was dealing with the situation in different ways.

Satisfied that she had a handle on the situation, she decided to finish up some work. If she could get one more pile out of the way, she would feel much better. She glanced at her watch. It was 5:45. She called Bill and told him she would be working late. He sounded worried, but she promised to call him when she left the office. She also reminded him that she had an escort home.

"Just be extra careful, honey," he said.

"I will. It won't be too long. Only an hour or so. I just want to get this out of the way."

After hanging up from Bill, Anne paged the officer assigned to her in the afternoons. He called back immediately.

"Johnny?" she asked. "This is Anne Mulhoney. I'm going to work in my office for another hour or so. Go ahead and do whatever you need to do. I've got your pager number, so I'll beep you when I'm ready to go."

# CHAPTER 20

Toni glanced at her watch. It was after 5:30 and she knew Boggs would appear any minute now. She'd only seen her briefly twice in the hall today. She had been in a hurry both times, so they merely smiled at each other.

Toni packed up her briefcase and straightened her desk. She was anxious to get out of the office today. The stress level seemed to have risen as the day progressed and her visit from Betty kept popping up in her mind. Her paranoia skyrocketed every time she thought about it. As if to confirm that fact, she nearly jumped out of her chair at the sound of Boggs's voice.

"Oh, my God," she said. "You scared the shit out of me."

Boggs was immediately apologetic. "I'm sorry. I should have knocked. Are you okay?"

"Yes, just paranoid. Sorry. I hope you're ready to hit the road, because I can't wait to get out of here and out of these damn panty-hose."

Boggs grinned. "Absolutely." She went a little closer. "And I'd love to get you out of those pantyhose."

Toni smiled. "Be patient. Okay, I'm ready. I just have to drop this report off at Anne's office and then we can head out." Even though Anne had told her not to worry about the report, she felt good completing it.


The man was so excited he could hardly contain himself. This was better than he had ever hoped for. He'd heard Anne's conversation with Dorothy and her two phone calls. He could hardly believe his luck.

He had been hiding in his secret place. It was a former men's bathroom located right next to Anne's office. It had two doors, one on an outside hallway and the other in Anne's office. Apparently, one of the previous prosecutors had ordered it locked because not only could the bathroom patrons hear him, he could clearly hear them. Most people weren't even aware that it was there, and there was no longer a sign on the outer door. The door inside Anne's office was partly obscured by a coatrack. He had found the locked door one weekend months ago when he was in the office. Intrigued, he located a key from one of the old janitors. He quickly realized the potential of this hideaway. After hearing Anne's plans for the evening, he hurried back to his office.

Once in his office he made a showing of preparing to leave for home. He said good night to almost everyone he saw and carried his coat on his arm. Just before he reached the elevators, he turned and entered the stairwell, as was his normal custom. He never did like riding the elevators, especially if there were other people inside. He stood just inside the stairway and listened. When he heard the elevator door close he proceeded up two flights of stairs. He knew that floor would be deserted this time of night. He quickly walked to the back set of stairs and went down to his floor. The back stairway was located only a few feet from his office.

He was ready. The thought was almost too much for him and

he again willed himself to calm down. He took a deep breath. He still had plenty of time. He checked his pocket and felt the cold, hard steel of his knife. It was well oiled. It was razor sharp. But still, he had to check. He knew that his ability to double-check details was one of the reasons he was great. He slowly pulled the knife from his pocket. He could feel himself salivate and he ran his tongue over his lips. The knife caught the light from above and glistened. He tingled with excitement. Then with a practiced hand he sprung the knife open. Perfect. Slowly and with loving care he returned it to his pocket.

He went over the details one more time in his head. The voices were helping him now as he envisioned the entire thing. There would be some deviations in this one, but still it would be an act of perfection. He would not be able to retrieve pretty panties for this one, so he would have to use what she had on. He also realized he wouldn't have to wear gloves. He had been in her office only hours ago, so his prints would naturally be there.

He continued to play out the scene in his mind, becoming more excited as the moment approached. He had decided on the ruse to use for this one. He would ask her if he could borrow a few dollars, saying that he forgot his wallet. She would, of course, agree and go over to her filing cabinet. Everyone knew that Anne kept her purse in the filing cabinet. Once her back was to him, he would be able to fulfill his destiny. He would then put on his coat and calmly leave. He never got any blood on himself. He was taller than his victims and always attacked from behind. After the quick slash, he'd watch as the blood spurted from their neck away from him before they fell to the ground. But even if he did get blood on him this time, his coat would cover it. He knew there would be no one at his house when he got home. Perfect. He would be able to relive the moment over and over. Life was good.

He peeked out his office door before going to Anne's office. There was no one in sight and he expected to see no one. If trouble somehow arose, he would be able to utilize his secret place. He had unlocked the inner door earlier. He knocked lightly on Anne's door and entered.

Anne looked up from her desk as if mildly surprised to see him again.

"What are you still doing here?" she asked. "Working late?"

He nodded. Then he smiled. "Just a little. I wanted to clear up a few things." His hand was inside his pocket. The feel of the cold metal made him giddy. His heart was pounding. He tried to compose himself, but heard his voice crack slightly when he spoke. "Actually, I have a huge favor to ask of you," he said, convincingly to his ear. "I was wondering if I could borrow a few dollars. I left my wallet at home. It would really get me out of a jam."

Anne smiled. She always did like a problem that could easily be fixed, he thought. She rose from her desk and crossed the office. As she opened the file drawer and pulled out her purse, he was behind her. He pulled the knife from his pocket and flipped it open. This was as perfect as he knew it would be. In a flash the knife was on her throat. Then he thought he heard voices in the hall. The sound stopped his movement for just a moment. Anne turned her head slightly before the knife made contact. He'd begun to move away as the knife sliced through her skin. People were coming. After he let her fall to the floor, he heard the voices again, this time louder. He looked down at Anne and realized that he would not be able to finish. At least not right now. He panicked for only a split second then scurried to the door behind the coatrack and slipped inside. The door had just softly clicked shut when he heard a knock on Anne's door. Then he heard the door open and Boggs yell for Toni to call 911.

There was no time to spare. He unlocked the outer door of the bathroom and quietly let himself out, relocking the door behind him. He reached the stairwell without seeing anyone and descended to the parking garage. He was two blocks away in his car when he saw the ambulance. He pulled off to the side of the road, just like everyone else. Then he smiled so wide it made his face hurt. They were too late. The great one had struck again. Even though he was unable to complete the lesson for Anne, just the fact that he performed it in her office, inside the Metro building, while she'd had bodyguards assigned, was enough to make him proud. Very proud. He went home, happy and content. He couldn't wait for the call informing him of Anne's horrible death.

Back at Metro, Boggs was kneeling next to Anne's body, applying pressure to the wound as best she could without cutting off her air supply. Anne was barely alive.

Joe, one of the Metro guards carrying a first-aid kit, rushed in with Toni on his heels. Since Toni had called 911, the cops were everywhere.

The guard pulled a large bandage from his first-aid pack and said to Boggs, "Here. Put this on the wound. It'll cover a bigger area."

Boggs complied. It seemed like a lot of blood was lost in that brief moment that she released her hand.

Joe felt for a pulse. "She's still with us."

Boggs looked to the door, anxious for the medics to arrive. She knew every minute was crucial. She looked at Toni. "Lean down and put your ear near her mouth and nose. Her breathing is so shallow, it'll be hard to tell if she quits."

Toni leaned down as she was told. "She's barely breathing."

The medics finally appeared. Joe, Boggs and Toni moved away, watching as the crew went to work in a frantic effort to save Anne's life. In no time, an IV was in place and they were wheeling her out of the office. They just stared.

"Now all we can do is say a few prayers," Joe whispered.

Boggs nodded and looked down at her hands, covered in wet blood. Joe wiped off as much as he could with some paper towels, for which Boggs was grateful.

By now the police had taken over and the crime scene unit had arrived. Boggs noticed it was the number one team and she shivered inside. This was the same team who'd worked all the other Crown murders. She closed her eyes for a moment and prayed Anne wouldn't be number five.

"Let's go out in the hall," Toni said, looking a little pale.

Patty was there blocking off the office with crime scene tape. "Are you okay?"

They nodded.

"Do you want me to have one of the guys drive you home?" she asked.

Boggs took a deep breath and let it out slowly. "No," she answered. "I think I'm okay to drive. It'll just take a little while for me to recover."

"You look like you're both in a bit of a shock," Patty said softly. "Is Vicky still working the night shift?"

When Boggs nodded, she offered to call Vicky at home and fill her in on the situation.

Vicky insisted on coming by Metro to drive them home. Patty seemed geared up for an argument, but Boggs only shrugged. What could she say? She was too drained to argue. Patty left Toni and Boggs sitting in the outer office while she finished her work.

After containing the area, Patty returned to Toni and Boggs.

"I need to take initial statements from you," she said and sat down at Dorothy's desk. "You first, Boggs."

Toni went into the hall and Patty pulled a chair next to the desk.

Boggs sighed as she sat down. "I didn't see a thing, Patty. I can't believe this. I didn't see anyone. We were walking down the hall, just talking, and I thought I heard something fall. Then I just headed to her office. No one came out. There was no one in there but her. I can't believe this."

Patty wrote down what Boggs said then put her arm around her. "It's okay, Boggs. Let me talk to Toni for a second."

Boggs went to get Toni. Her color had improved but she was still in shock. While she gave her statement, Boggs took a long drink from the water fountain.

Vicky arrived at Metro within 20 minutes. She looked like she had just gotten out of the shower and thrown on some old clothes. Boggs was never so grateful to see someone. Vicky spoke to Patty for a few minutes then herded Toni and Boggs to her car. The drive to Toni's apartment was quiet.

By the time they got there, Boggs had pulled herself together. She and Vicky did a sweep of the apartment and sighed in relief when no one was found.

"Toni, go upstairs and put on some comfy clothes," Vicky instructed. "Boggs, you need to change, too. And you might want to wash up a little," she said after eyeing her hands.

Both Boggs and Toni complied. By the time they returned to the living room, Vicky had fed Mr. Rupert and poured three glasses of iced tea. Everyone sat on the couch, including Mr. Rupert, who yowled.

"I guess he wants me to tell him what's going on," Toni said. She scratched his head and he curled up next to her and began to purr.

Toni described her day to the last detail, including conversations she'd had with David, Anne and Betty. Boggs let her ramble on, knowing she needed this release. Vicky had retrieved the notebook from the shelf and was taking some notes.

"Well, I talked to Peter, the new investigator. He's kind of a jerk." Boggs rolled her eyes, wishing she didn't have to work with guys like that. "Anyway, he said he was at his mom's house. I guess it must have been the thing to do Friday night because Sam was at his mother's for most of the evening also. I didn't press too hard with him. He was really distracted today. I saw him hanging around the soda machine earlier, just standing there."

Boggs shook her head, trying to get a clearer picture of things. She continued with her information and then described the scene in Anne's office to Vicky.

"So neither of you saw anybody?" Vicky asked.

"Nope," Boggs said, taking a sip of the sweet tea.

"No one," Toni said. "Boggs got there first and was inside while I was still in the outer office. There was no one in there but me."

Vicky ran a hand through her hair. "It doesn't make sense. If what drew your attention was the sound, where was the killer? There's no way he could have gotten past you. People just don't vanish into thin air."

"Maybe the sound came from a different office and we just assumed it was in Anne's office," Toni suggested.

"I guess that's a possibility," Boggs said. "Let's see. Who has an office near there. Anne's is on the corner, then there's Elizabeth's and then the library, right?"

"The vending machines are next to the library," Toni mused. "But isn't there another office in the middle?"

Vicky ripped a piece of paper from the notebook and began to make a sketch. "It's like this, isn't it?" she asked.

Boggs and Toni looked over the crude drawing. Boggs fleshed it out as best she could.

Toni pointed to one of the offices. "I think this is actually two offices here, but one isn't used. To be honest with you, I can't really remember."

"This is ridiculous," Boggs said. "I've been working here for how long? And I can't even draw a decent sketch? Damn it. I wish we had an accurate floor plan. At least then I could figure out my bearings."

"It sure would be easier," Vicky agreed. "Not that it's going to answer any questions, but at least we'd get a better idea. Maybe the sound traveled. The hall was empty except for you two."

They sat in silence. Boggs was trying to figure out some sort of scenario that would make sense. Vicky grabbed her cell phone from its holder on her waistband. Toni looked puzzled.

"It's on vibrate," Vicky explained.

Boggs listened to the one-sided conversation, trying to piece together what was being said. She and Toni were both on the edge of the couch staring at Vicky as she spoke.

"What about the cameras at Metro? Who's looking at the tapes? Okay. Are you staying at the hospital? Will you let me know the second you hear anything? Great. Thanks, Patty. Yes, I'll tell her. Do you know who it is? Fred? Okay. He's good. Thanks again. 'Bye."

"Well?" she and Toni asked at the same time.

"She said that Anne's still alive. She's in stable but serious condition. Her carotid artery was nicked and there was some damage to her vocal chords. The ER doc said he couldn't believe she was alive. It must have been because you were there so quick and put pressure on it immediately. She's in recovery now. Anyway, they won't know more until later." Vicky took a deep breath and sighed. "Frank's in the waiting room. I guess he's been there since he got the call. The captain asked if he wanted someone else to take watch, but Frank insisted that he be the one who stayed. Frank also wanted to know if Anne said anything to Toni, but Patty told him no. Let's see. What else. Oh, they got the tapes from the cameras at Metro. The main entrance, the garage and the judge's entrance. The captain himself is looking at the tapes."

Boggs shook her head. "They aren't going to see Crown."

"Well," Vicky continued, "the captain wants to be involved on the ground level now. He's an okay guy and a good cop. I worked with him before he got the promotion. He's sending a uniform to sit outside here. Fred Koffman. You know him, don't you, Boggs?"

"Yeah," she replied. "He's good."

"That's what I told Patty. He should be here in about thirty minutes. He'll ring the doorbell when he gets here. He's also bringing over a walkie for us."

The sound of the phone ringing made everyone jump. Then they giggled.

"Are we a little uptight or what?" Toni said.

Laughing seemed to ease the panic just a little bit, Boggs thought.

Toni answered the phone and mouthed "Captain Billings" to Vicky and Boggs.

Vicky cocked her head to one side and immediately grabbed the phone from Toni. "This is Detective Carter. Identify yourself, please." After a moment, she nodded to the others.

Boggs listened intently to the one-sided conversation. She could feel her heart pounding. Seeing Anne on her office floor had rattled her, to be sure, and now she was in full protect mode. After what seemed like eternity, Vicky hung up the phone. "Well," Boggs said. "What's going on?"

Vicky took a long drink of her tea. "He agreed that someone on the inside is helping Crown. That's why he's sending Fred over tonight. He has orders only to answer to the captain, so it's pretty clear that he doesn't trust anyone. Also, he's watching the Metro videotapes himself. Oh, and he's sending over the blueprints of Metro. I told him we wanted them."

Boggs had a feeling there was more. "What else?"

"And apparently everyone is under the impression that Anne might have said something to Toni," Vicky said.

"I just leaned down to listen for her breathing," Toni explained.

Boggs was concerned. If "everyone" thought that, then the killer must think that too. "Don't worry about it, Toni," she said as confidently as she could. She reached over and stroked Toni's arm.

Toni suddenly shivered.

"Are you okay?" Boggs asked.

"No," Toni said, her voice just above a whisper. "If people are wondering if Anne talked before the medics took her away, then the killer could think that Anne said something to me while I was leaning over her. That means he would have to get rid of me next." Toni's eyes were as big as saucers.

Boggs scooted closer to her. "We know, Toni. It's going to be okay. We know that and the captain knows that. We've got everything under control. You won't be out of our sight until this bastard is caught."

"That's right, Toni," Vicky said.

Toni nodded slightly, then got another look of desperation on her face. "What about Anne?" she asked. "If there's any chance she'll pull through, the guy has to get to her. She could identify him in a minute."

"That's why the captain has one of his men over there," Vicky said. "I guess he doesn't trust Frank at the moment. Neither do we." The phone rang again. This time Vicky answered it.

"Sam," she said, handing the phone to Boggs.

Boggs listened and after a few minutes the conversation ended.

"That was certainly weird," Boggs said. "He first wanted to know how we're doing. Then he asked if Anne said anything to

203

Toni. Next, he wanted to know if I needed him to take over as bodyguard for a while, just to give me a break or something. Very strange." Boggs struggled to figure out a reason for his uncharacteristic behavior.

"Do you think it could be him?" Vicky asked.

Boggs thought for a moment. She liked Sam, but . . . "On any other occasion I'd say no way, but he has been acting strange lately. I don't know. I guess at this point we can't rule out anyone. We need to be almost overly cautious."

"I have a hard time believing it could be him," Toni said. "But I'm with you. I'm not trusting another living soul until we know for sure."

The phone rang again. Toni answered and mouthed "Paul." The conversation lasted less than a minute.

"You thought Sam's call was weird, this was weirder. He wanted to know if my bodyguards were still here and then if Anne said anything to me. That was it. He never even asked if I was okay."

"I don't trust him either," Boggs said, to which they all agreed.

Toni glanced at her watch just as the doorbell rang. Boggs motioned for her to remain seated as she and Vicky went to the door.

"It's Fred," she said. "Boggs, I think we still need to be on the safe side, okay?"

Boggs nodded. She stepped away from the door and drew her weapon. Vicky opened the door and motioned for Fred to come inside and then shut the door behind him. He immediately saw Boggs and froze. "Nothing personal, Fred," she said with a smile.

He smiled in return. "Captain Billings told me to answer only to him and to you all, of course. The walkie and blueprints are in my bag there."

Vicky retrieved the items.

"Thanks, Fred," Boggs said. "We really appreciate this."

"I want to catch that son of a bitch, too," he said, motioning to the door.

Boggs nodded and he went toward the door.

"Hey," Toni said. "Why don't you give him one of the dining room chairs?"

Vicky opened the front door and shooed Fred outside. Then she reached for one of the chairs and handed it to him. Before closing the door she winked at him. "Thanks for being such a good sport, Fred," she said.

"Anytime, Detective. And you can count on me. The captain does."

Once the door was locked, Boggs holstered her gun. She wished she had on her shoulder holster instead of the pancake holster she wore for work. It was in the small of her back and it took just a moment longer to get to her gun. Nothing she could do about that now, she thought.

The women returned to the couch. Vicky set the walkie-talkie on the floor while Boggs pulled the blueprints from their container and Toni cleared some space on the coffee table. They looked at the drawings for a while before finding the second-floor plan.

"Here we go," Vicky said. She pointed to Anne's office. The halls of Metro formed a large rectangle, with a kind of courtyard in the center. Anne's office was located on the southeast outside corner. The offices on the outside were usually large and assigned according to seniority, but there were always exceptions. The inner offices, those facing the courtyard, were smaller. The blueprint only showed the dimensions.

"I don't think the captain would mind if we wrote on this," Toni said. "They're copies. Let's mark all the offices we know." She retrieved a red, felt tip pen from the kitchen drawer and handed it to Vicky, who promptly wrote "Anne" on the corner office. Toni and Boggs pointed to their own offices and gave the names of those around them. Slowly they pieced together all names that went to the offices. They also identified where the vending machines were located on that floor and the copy machines, just in case.

After it was completed, Boggs shook her head. "I guess it's possible the guy just ran out, then something, or Anne, fell. If that's so, then he could have headed down the other hallway and we would have never seen him. By going the opposite direction, he could have gone into his own office, if he works here—or anyone's office, for that matter, or headed for the stairs."

"Maybe Anne was hurt and she was trying to get to her purse for some reason," Toni suggested "That would have given him maybe a minute or so."

"I don't know," Boggs said. "She was cut pretty bad. I don't think she would have been able to get to the filing cabinet."

Vicky looked at her, puzzled. "How do you know she went to the filing cabinet," she asked.

"Everyone knows that's where Anne keeps her purse," Boggs said.

Vicky thought for a moment. "Then maybe he knew that too," she reasoned. "We all agree that Anne knew the guy, right?"

Toni and Boggs nodded.

"Okay," Vicky continued. "Suppose the guy gets Anne to go for her purse—maybe they're planning to walk out together or something. When Anne gets to the filing cabinet, he strikes. Like all the others, he always comes from behind."

"That would explain why she was by the filing cabinet with her purse on the floor," Boggs said. "But if the sound we heard was Anne falling, or at least her purse, why didn't we see him leave the office?"

Vicky scratched her head. "I guess we're back to square one."

Toni had been curled up on the corner of the couch, petting Mr. Rupert. She leaned forward and began looking more closely at the blueprints. "Hey," she said a few minutes later. "What's this? It looks like there's a bathroom next to Anne's office."

Boggs examined the plans trying to envision Anne's office.

"It looks like a closet to me," Vicky said.

"No," Toni said. "It's a bathroom. Or at least it used to be. Look at the pipe configuration."

Vicky looked at her in disbelief. "Pipe what?" she asked.

"Pipe configuration," Toni repeated. "Jake is an architect. He used to show me all his drawings and stuff when we were in under-grad. I guess some of it stuck with me. Here, look." She pointed out the pipes and the two doors to the bathroom. "See. This one goes right into Anne's office."

"I don't remember ever seeing a door in there," Boggs said.

Toni began sketching in the furniture in Anne's office. After drawing the desk, chairs, filing cabinet and huge plants, she sat back and said, "Well, the door is to the left of Anne's desk. Surely I would have noticed it, but I can't remember ever seeing it before. Maybe it's been covered over."

"I know they did some remodeling a few years back," Vicky offered.

"That's right," Boggs added. "They divided some of the larger offices into smaller ones and put in a new computer room."

Toni sighed. "Well, I guess that's a dead end."

They sat in silence for a while.

"How about some food?" Boggs suggested. She was hungry and thought maybe a break would help them sort this out.

Toni got up. "What kind?"

"Doesn't matter," Boggs answered.

They went in the kitchen and dumped several of the half-empty cartons into a large bowl and popped it in the microwave. Toni grabbed some of the deli food and got out some crackers and cheese. Boggs collected plates and utensils. Over dinner, the conversation turned to food and what each considered the best kind of leftovers.

Suddenly, Toni yelled out. "Coatrack."

"What?" Boggs and Vicky said in unison.

"Coatrack," Toni repeated. "That's what's behind Anne's desk. A coatrack. It must block the door. Of course. The door is still there, but the coatrack blocks your view."

"That means the guy could have gotten out that way," Boggs said, "assuming the door hasn't been sealed shut." She looked at the plans again. "He could have gone through that door, and once we were inside her office, he could have gone out the door into the hall. We would have never seen him." She was excited now. This made sense.

Vicky grabbed her cell phone and called Captain Billings. She briefly described what they had figured out from the plans. He said he'd send the crime scene unit back there immediately. Vicky was smiling when she hung up the phone and passed on the information to the others.

"Well," Toni said as she ate a cracker. "At least now I feel like we're doing something constructive instead of sitting on our butts."

Boggs felt the same way. At least now they had a sense of direction.

# CHAPTER 21

The man was worried now. Very worried. Anne wasn't dead. As he sat there, he couldn't believe it. How could she have survived? Did she say anything? Everyone he asked told him she hadn't regained consciousness, but how could he be sure?

He heard the voices inside his head again. They were so loud he could barely hear himself think. "Idiot! You never could do anything right. At least your brother never pretended to know anything. You'll never amount to a pile of shit. I knew the minute you were born you'd be a piece of shit, and you never fail to live up to that."

He shook his head, trying desperately to get rid of her voice. He hated her voice. He looked at his hands and they were trembling ever so slightly. A few tiny white pills had always helped before. When was the last time he took some? He couldn't remember. On some level he knew he shouldn't take too many, but he also knew how much they helped him concentrate. Without thinking about it anymore, he quickly swallowed five more pills.

It seemed as though only seconds had passed, but he couldn't be sure. All he knew was that the sound of her voice had waned and was replaced by another. "Kill them both. Kill them all. It's time for the world to know your true destiny. Then they will all understand. Just kill them now. Do it now."

He took a deep breath and smiled. He began to feel the confidence and strength well up inside him. Plan. He must plan. Several minutes passed. His mind was racing, but he couldn't seem to formulate a cohesive plan. He shook his head and tried to slow his mind down. His thoughts were just random blurbs. He tried to listen more carefully to the voices. "Kill the bitch. Finish the job." "Your destiny is being fulfilled." "They know it's you. Kill all of them." "They're laughing at you."

He could stand it no longer. He had to walk. He had to think. He stood up and headed for the door. He circled the entire block once before he felt himself get into a rhythm. For a brief time he believed his mind had cleared. He knew it didn't matter if they knew it was him or not. In fact, he was anxious for the publicity now. They would all be amazed at his brilliance.

He grinned. He could see it all now. He would be in front of the camera, interviewed by the best. Maybe *60 Minutes*, or *Dateline*. After he explained his mission, they would be in awe of him. Cheering crowds would greet him at every appearance he made. Yes, it was time to finish this job. He knew they would understand, but he had to finish what he'd started. Then he would finally let them in on all of it.

As he rounded the block again, he noticed a van drive by. Hadn't that same van driven past before? Was he being followed? Why would anyone follow him? No one suspected him. Not the great one. He kept strolling, careful not to vary his pace. Out of the corner of his eye he saw an old man on the other side of the street, meandering with his dog in the opposite direction. He was sure the old man was staring at him even though he seemed to be looking straight ahead. Another van drove by. It was a different color, but he knew it was the same van as before. Somehow they had changed its color. He was more than a little nervous now.

A few feet farther down the sidewalk he heard something that made him gasp. Laughter. Two women were laughing. They were standing near a car and laughing. He knew without any doubt that they were laughing at him. Mocking his presence on this earth. The sound made his ears hurt. He tried to walk faster but the sound kept coming. They were laughing at him because he screwed up again. Anne was still alive. She was out of surgery now and she was laughing at him. He could picture the whole thing. She was sitting on the edge of her hospital bed laughing. There were nurses all around her, laughing. The doctors were all laughing. His hands automatically went to cover his ears. It didn't help. He could still hear the laughter. His eyes darted from side to side as he continued down the walk. Everything was very clear to him. He knew everyone knew, and they were all laughing. The people on the bus. The young man on the motorcycle. The old lady in the Dodge Dart. Some covered it up better than others, but they were all laughing. His mind was racing. He tried to replay the performance in Anne's office, thinking it would give him some comfort. It didn't. As soon as he remembered those two women interrupting him, his face burned with anger. It was their fault that everyone was sneering at him now. It was their fault. He imagined them sitting together laughing at how they ruined everything for him. They were laughing at him, calling him names. He kept walking, but now he was headed back to his car.

He slid into the front seat and quickly shut the door. It was dark outside and he didn't want the interior light to give him away. Once inside the laughter wasn't as loud. He looked in the rearview mirror to check for people behind him.

He continued to look out all the windows and check the mirrors. His gaze darted back and forth. He made sure all the doors were locked. Then he checked again. He could still hear the laughter, but he realized that the people were at least fifty feet away from him. Suddenly he grinned. He had developed extraordinary hearing. Amazing! His mind was so powerful that he could hear people over great distances. His mind was clearer now than it had ever been. The tiny white pills were working. He dug into his pocket and downed a few more.

He sat in his car for what seemed like an hour, but was by the dashboard clock less than ten minutes. He needed to make sure that no one saw him. When the laughter got too loud, he ducked down in the front seat. After the sound faded, he would peer out the windows again.

During this time he formulated his new plan. First, he needed to silence the laughter of those two bitches who interfered with his last performance. They were the ones who caused him to force his hand. Although he was still very much in control, this had changed the time frame for his proclamation to the world. His teeth began to grind as he thought of those two whores. They must be taught a lesson. How dare they interfere with his grand work? He dug through his briefcase, which he had left in the car. Somewhere in there he kept a list of names and addresses of everyone who worked at Metro, his co-workers. In less than a minute he had located Toni's address and was driving toward her apartment.

He knew that Toni was with Boggs and Vicky. He also knew there was a guard posted outside her front door. Neither of those things caused him any concern. He'd find a way. He had to. It was his destiny.

He drove past Toni's apartment. Not too fast and not too slow. He didn't want to bring any attention to himself. He saw the police officer sitting in a chair. He also noted that Toni lived in a two-story townhouse. He was pleased with his keen ability to pick up details. He pulled into the parking lot of Hardee's, just a block away. He surveyed the surroundings for several minutes, making sure no one followed him. The people here weren't laughing at him. They were amazed by his greatness. He had to be careful. He didn't want to be mobbed by admiring fans. Not now. He willed them to stay away. He had to close his eyes tightly for several minutes in order to accomplish this, and that was dangerous. When he opened his eyes, it had worked. The people were staying away from him, letting him work. He knew it was hard for them, hard to stay away from greatness, but they obeyed his will.

He got out of his car and went to the trunk. He checked the

people again. They were still giving him leeway. He breathed a sigh of relief. From the trunk he retrieved a medium-sized gym bag. He quickly closed the trunk and got back inside his car. He locked the doors. Then he double-checked the locks. He slowly unzipped the bag. Inside there was a dark blue running suit and baseball cap, along with an extra pair of running shoes and several sets of latex gloves. In the bottom of the bag lay a plastic box, the kind normally used to hold fishing tackle. He pulled it out and set the bag on the front seat. This was his emergency kit. It contained everything he thought he might possibly need. He had taken great pains to put it together. Each item was placed lovingly inside. He had even made a list of the contents and glued it inside the lid. He was looking for one item in particular. He began pulling unneeded items from the box and stacking them one by one in the lid. Duct tape. Scissors. Screwdriver. Hammer. Wire. Balsa wood. Molding clay. Superglue. Bobby pins. Clamp. Piece of rubber hose. Rope. Razor blades. Ballpoint pen. Paper clips.

Finally, at the very bottom of the box, he found what he wanted, a glass cutter, the kind that professional burglars used. A small black suction cup held the glass in place while you cut a circular hole a little larger than a man's fist. He had "borrowed" this tool from the property room at the police department and practiced using it several times, but this would be the first time he used it in his work. He placed it on the dash of his car and then diligently replaced the other items inside the box. He then put the box back inside the gym bag and zipped it shut.

He was almost ready now. He pulled his knife from his pocket. The feel of the cold steel made him giggle. He pictured everything. He knew it would be perfect. He flipped open his knife to make sure but was instantly horrified. The knife, his beautiful, wonderful knife. There was still blood on it. Those bitches had made him stop in the middle of his work and he hadn't cleaned his knife. Anger boiled inside him. He was gripping the knife so hard that his knuckles were white. How could they have done that to him? What had he ever done to them? A single tear ran down his cheek. His vision was blurry and he couldn't think. He continued to grip his knife. Slowly he pulled a handkerchief from his pocket and tried to rub off the dried blood. It didn't work. He spit into his handkerchief and rubbed again. Slowly the dried blood disappeared and he began to calm down. He polished the blade until it shone. When he returned the knife to his pocket he was more determined than ever. He started his car and drove to Toni's apartment.

# CHAPTER 22

The crime scene unit returned to Anne's office ten minutes after receiving the call from Captain Billings. He'd asked them to fingerprint the closed-off bathroom. Bannon had been suspicious of the Crown murders after the second one. The scene was just too clean for the average Joe to have committed these murders. After sneaking a peek at Crown at his preliminary hearing, he was convinced this guy didn't have the know-how, but there was little Bannon could do. The phone call from the captain confirmed his worst nightmare—someone else was doing the killing or at least helping Crown. The captain must have thought so too, or he wouldn't have specifically mentioned looking for fingerprints. The only reason to look for prints would be if they didn't belong to Crown.

Bannon and his team first photographed the door on Anne's side of the bathroom and then began dusting for prints. He wasn't surprised to find some on the door handle. He was extra careful about transferring these prints.

"No telling how long those've been there," said one of the other technicians.

Bannon nodded. When he was finished, he motioned for his team to proceed inside the bathroom. The door wasn't locked. Inside the bathroom it smelled musty. It was obvious it hadn't been cleaned in a long time. Aside from some paper towels crumpled on the floor in a corner, it looked as though it hadn't been used in ages.

Bannon headed immediately to the outside door that led out to the hallway. The rest of the team covered the interior which included three stalls and urinals. He was able to recover fingerprints on the door handle, but on the doorframe he hit pay dirt. There was one print, partially in blood. He couldn't believe it. He checked the doorknob and found it locked. He mentioned this to his team and then proceeded to the outside hallway via Anne's office. At this point he didn't want to unlock the door himself. Once out in the hall, Bannon took more prints from the door. He packaged all of them and went back into Anne's office.

"You guys find anything interesting?" he said.

"Nope," said one of the techs. "Everything in here is covered with a thick layer of dust. Nothing looks like it's been disturbed for quite a while. You want us to give it the full treatment?"

Bannon didn't even hesitate. "No," he said. "Let's just get this back to the lab. I don't think anything happened in there."

They packed their equipment and headed back to the lab. Bannon sent the rest of his team home. Since he was handling the prints, there was nothing more they could do. He prepared the prints and scanned them into the computer. Then he typed in Crown's name for a comparison. As the computer did its job, Bannon called the captain to fill him in.

"You know, Captain," he cautioned. "These fingerprints could have been there a long time . . . or a week. There's no way to tell if they were left tonight. The bloody print, though, was definitely our guy."

"I understand," replied the captain. "How long before we get a name?"

"Our first answer just came up," said Bannon. "They're not Crown's."

There was a moment of silence. Bannon was already typing in the next comparison request. He could hear the captain sigh over the phone.

"Put in a check for everyone who works at Metro," said the captain. "And Bannon, I don't want anyone to know the results but me, understand?"

"Yes, sir," Bannon said. "I'm one step ahead of you. The results should be up any second."

The two men waited in silence as the computer checked the scanned prints against everyone who currently worked at Metro and those who had worked there in the last ten years. That included every secretary, janitor, judge, attorney, investigator and police officer. It didn't matter if they had worked there twenty years or two weeks, part-time. Everyone had to be fingerprinted to work at Metro. The wait seemed interminable. Finally, a match was found. A perfect match.

"Son of a bitch!" Bannon said. When he told the captain, his response was the same.

"Until we know it's him for sure," he instructed, "don't let this go any further."


The man pulled into the parking lot of Toni's apartment. He was very excited. This was a new type of lesson he was about to teach. He checked his knife again. It was perfect. He looked out the windows. No one. He admired his hands. They were the tools of his greatness. He noticed for the first time that he hadn't changed his clothes from work. He took off his jacket but left on his tie. No, he wasn't pleased with this look. It wasn't right. He looked in the backseat and grabbed his lightweight windbreaker. Then he took off his tie. Perfect. That would give him the right appearance for tonight. It would also conceal his cutter and give him greater mobility than his suit jacket. Satisfied, he checked the windows again. Then his knife. While caressing his knife he felt his small bottle of pills. Grinning, he pulled it from his pocket and shook five into his palm. He checked the windows again before swallowing them. Now he was ready.

He got out of his car and walked toward the apartment. The cool breeze blew against his damp skin. His upper lip was covered with sweat and his eyes continued to dart back and forth. He was smiling when he approached Fred. He wasn't sure Fred knew who he was, although he thought everyone knew him. Just to be safe, he produced his credentials immediately. Fred looked at them and nodded.

"I just wanted to come by and check on you," he said. "I know it's a tough and lonely job. Is there anything I can get for you? There's a Hardee's up the street, maybe a burger or some coffee?"

"No, thanks," Fred said. "I'm good."

The man leaned against the building. "I hope we catch the son of a bitch soon," he said. He was waiting for an opportunity, and he got one.

Fred nodded and pulled a cigarette from his uniform pocket. The man seized this wonderful opportunity. "I've got a light," he said as he reached into his pocket and stepped toward Fred. The man was on him before Fred could even move. The knife plunged into his chest, and then in his side, and last in his stomach. He had tried to get up from the chair, he tried to reach for his gun, but he wasn't able to complete either task. He slumped forward and slid down the chair.

The man grinned. Then he giggled. He looked around and saw no one. He was so talented. He paused for a moment to soak in his own greatness. Then he carefully cleaned his wonderful knife and returned it to his pocket. Next he pulled Fred back up on his chair. It took some doing, but he managed it very well. He was careful to pull Fred from the back so he wouldn't get any blood on himself. Once positioned, the man thought Fred looked perfectly normal. He took Fred's gun and tossed it in the bushes. He even considered putting a cigarette in his mouth, but decided against it. He didn't care for cigarettes. The smell upset his stomach.

His plan was working perfectly, as he knew it would. He walked to the side of the apartment and looked up at Toni's bedroom window. That was his point of entry. There was a small ledge surrounding the second story. It wasn't very wide, but it would be big enough to hold him while he cut the glass. Now all he had to do was get up there. He glanced around. He saw someone in the parking lot getting into a car. He concentrated hard. Very hard. The woman didn't even look over his way. She simply got in her car and left. He smiled. He was still able to will others to stay away.

He saw a drainpipe going up the side of the building. He knew that someone of his talents and capabilities would have no problem climbing it to the ledge. He walked to the drainpipe and touched it. Then he willed it to become his own personal ladder. He giggled to himself. There was absolutely nothing he couldn't do. Next he checked his knife. He wanted to make sure. Just the feel of it in his pocket thrilled him. He flipped it open and it caught the light from the streetlamp across the road. It was beautiful. He stared at his knife for several minutes. Before returning it to his pocket, he noticed the phone line that ran across the outside wall. As almost an afterthought, he cut the line.

He climbed up the drainpipe with no trouble at all. It would have been difficult for most, but he could do anything. In a flash he was standing on the ledge. He quickly scooted to the window and peered inside. He seemed to have no trouble balancing himself on the eight-inch ledge. He didn't even think about it. He could see that there was no one inside the bedroom. He got out his trusty cutter. He didn't even attempt to open the window. He knew it would be locked. He attached the suction cup and began to cut. It was easy. Too easy. In less than two minutes he had cut out a circle near the lock. He reached inside and slid the single lever to the open position and gently raised the window. He climbed inside and pulled the window back down. He grinned.

He looked around the room and shook his head. The furnishings were so common, so bland. His mind took in everything all at once. He was amazed at how he could instantly know everything about this room. He even knew the brand of drywall that was underneath the coats of paint. Again he reveled in his greatness before continuing with his new mission.

Toni, Boggs and Vicky had finished eating. Their conversation had turned from the recent attack on Anne to less stressful topics. Toni knew the phone would soon ring and Patty would be giving them an update, or the captain would have more information. But for right now, they were all making an effort to keep things light. The apartment was like a fortress and she felt safe.

She couldn't stop thinking about who attacked Anne. She tried to remember all she could from her past job as a psychotherapist. This was a serial killer. He would have to be very intelligent. That would rule out Frank. He was street smart but not what she would consider intelligent. And then there was the killer's upbringing. Crown's evaluation described the perfect home environment to foster a disturbed mind but he didn't seem to have what it took to kill. But who would Crown follow without question? His father? No, too old. What about a brother? Possible.

Boggs broke her train of thought. "Anyone need more tea?" she asked as she got up from the couch.

"I'll take some," Vicky said, getting up. "I've got to run to the bathroom. Fill me up, will you? Hey, Toni. Do you mind if I take a closer look at your bed? I think I'm going to get a new bedroom set with all my overtime pay."

"Be my guest," Toni said. "I got a steal on mine at Furniture City."

Toni handed her glass to Boggs. She couldn't stop thinking about the characteristics of the killer. He had to be agile because he had left through a window at one of the victim's apartments. That ruled out Sam. And it had to be someone sho wouldn't be out of place at the jail where Crown was released. That eliminated David. She closed her eyes and tried to get a clear picture of Crown in her mind. If it was Crown's brother who did the killing, then everything would make sense. Was there anyone who looked like him?

The man thought he heard someone coming up the stairs. He hoped it was Toni. He had decided he should kill her first. No. Maybe he should kill Boggs first. He couldn't decide. Then he realized it didn't matter and he laughed to himself. Both would be fun. His hands tingled as he waited in the dark. He had positioned himself at the entrance to the walk-in closet. Since the closet was between the bedroom and the bathroom, he would have easy access regardless of which room she walked into. This was perfect. He pulled the knife from his pocket and waited. It was almost too good to be true.

He heard someone reach the top of the stairs and head for the bedroom. Once she crossed the threshold she switched on the light. He watched Vicky look at Toni's waterbed. When she leaned over to get a closer look at the drawers underneath he made his move. He clamped his cold moist hand over her mouth and brought the knife toward her neck. He felt her freeze. Then her arm jerked and it caught him off-balance. His knife missed its target and instead sliced across her forearm as she tried to struggle free. His strong grip across her mouth held her there. He again had her pinned against his chest. She tried to move but he was all-powerful, all-knowing. Nothing could stop him. He needed to get rid of her so he could complete his mission. She was nothing. She meant nothing. He wished she'd stop moving.

When Vicky's arm had made contact with him, her blood oozed onto his jacket. He felt the warm sticky substance just as he positioned his knife on the side of her neck. He looked down at his arm and was instantly horrified. He stopped. There was blood on him. This should never happen. He pulled his hand away, the one with the knife. With his other hand still covering her mouth, he looked at his blood-soaked arm. Rage filled him. His hands began to shake. With one quick movement he plunged the knife into her side and then slammed her head into the corner of the wooden bedframe. She slumped to the floor unconscious, bleeding from the side and arm.

He again looked at his own arm, covered in that horrible sticky goo. His heart began beating faster and he started to hyperventilate. He ripped his windbreaker off and threw it on the floor. It landed on Vicky's face. His dress shirt was blood-soaked, so he tore that off. Wearing only a sweat-drenched T-shirt, he used a clean part of his discarded shirt to rub the blood from his skin. As the blood began to disappear, his breathing improved. He used the last clean piece of his shirt to clean his knife. Once the knife was clean, he felt much better and headed for the stairs.

He stood at the bottom of the stairs and listened. At first he couldn't hear anything but the radio. Then he heard them laughing and it made his ears hurt. He'd been right. He knew he had been able to hear them earlier that night, laughing at him, and they were still laughing. They had no right to laugh at him. He was the great one. They had no respect, but he would teach them. He would teach all of them never to laugh at him again. Once the world understood his true destiny, they would very likely make it a crime for anyone to ever laugh at him. Yes. That would be appropriate.

He looked down at his hands. They were beautiful. He held his wonderful knife. He was ready. This was his last lesson and he wanted it to be memorable. He checked his knife. Perfect. They were still laughing. It was hurting his ears. He checked his knife again. He decided to take a few more pills before finishing this work.


Patty Green was in her car with the siren wailing. She had gotten the call from Captain Billings while at the hospital. He'd filled her in on the fingerprints and told her he was unable to reach Fred on the radio. He had tried to call Toni's apartment but the phone just rang. Toni didn't answer and the answering machine didn't pick up. There had also been no answer to Vicky's cell phone and he hadn't yet tracked down the cell numbers for Boggs or Toni. Patty flew through the side streets faster than department policy allowed. She was only minutes away.

Vicky struggled to regain consciousness. She would begin to come around, then the room would go black again. She found it next to impossible to breathe. Her arm throbbed and the wetness of her own blood was everywhere. There was a huge bump on her head. She tried to listen for any sounds from him, but all she could hear was her own labored breathing.

She crawled toward the dresser and pulled open the bottom drawer. It took a lot of strength. After several attempts, she was able to pull out a few pair of hose. She dug around some more and found underwear. She knew she had to stop the bleeding. Using her one good arm, she placed two pair of underwear on her arm and tried to secure them with the hose. It didn't stop the bleeding, but it helped. She wrapped the hose around again and tried to make a tighter knot. This was next to impossible. Every time she tried to sit up straight, she would begin to black out. If only she could breathe better.

She knew the cut on her arm wasn't too bad. She put another pair of underwear on her side and tied it with a pair of hose. This was pretty useless. She couldn't get it tight enough. She was struggling to catch her breath. It was so hard to breathe but she had to get downstairs. She still had her gun in her ankle holster. Slowly, she crawled to the stairs. Several times the room started to go black and she would have to stop. She crawled down the steps backward. The sound of screaming was horrible. She tried to move faster but couldn't. She felt so weak. When she reached the bottom step, the room went black.

# CHAPTER 23

Toni was sitting on the couch, still picturing Crown in her mind. Boggs came out of the kitchen and handed her the iced tea. She remained standing with her back toward the stairs.

"What are you thinking about?" Boggs asked.

"I'm just trying to figure out who fits the mold," Toni said. "I was thinking that the guy could be Crown's brother, so I was trying to picture him and decide if anyone we knew resembled him."

Boggs seemed to be pondering this when Toni's eyes got big and she screamed, "Paul!"

At that moment Paul burst into the room. He was running straight for Boggs, screaming at the top of his lungs and gripping his knife. He was across the room before Boggs could pull her gun and he slammed her to the floor. He continued to scream words, but only "stop laughing" was intelligible to Toni. She watched in horror as Boggs struggled with him. Paul's knife sank deep into her thigh and then he yanked it downward. Boggs was pinned to the floor and Toni knew her gun was underneath her, useless at the moment. Toni ran to the front door, yelling for Fred. What she saw when she pulled the door open made her gag. Fred's head had fallen backward and his eyes were wide open. She could see he was covered in blood and very much dead. She ran toward him, though. She needed his gun. It wasn't there. Terrified, she turned back to help Boggs.

In the apartment, Boggs was still struggling with Paul and it looked like he had cut her again. This time it was her arm. Toni wasn't sure how bad, but Boggs was covered in blood. Paul was still screaming and Toni saw him raise his body to strike again. He had the knife. Toni ran toward him, screaming herself. She was only a few feet away when she saw Mr. Rupert. He was close to Paul and in an attack stance. Before Toni could reach him or Paul, Mr. Rupert leaped. Twenty pounds of angry cat landed on Paul's ankle and Mr. Rupert's teeth sank into flesh and bone. Paul screamed in pain and lashed out at the cat with his knife. But Mr. Rupert would not let go. He lashed out again. Toni screamed for Mr. Rupert and jumped in the middle. She barely felt the knife slice the back of her head.

Paul's change in position and momentary distraction was all Boggs needed. She pulled her gun from its holster behind her back, but Toni was now in the line of fire. There were sirens in the distance, but it was clear they would be too late. Boggs struggled to move, but her leg wouldn't cooperate. Her hand was covered in blood and she could barely hold the gun. Paul was blathering insanely and slashing at both Toni and Mr. Rupert. Boggs, still on the floor, rolled slightly to her left and fired. The sound was deafening. The kick of the discharge in her blood-soaked hand caused the gun to slip, but she regained control immediately.

Everything froze for a moment, then Paul fell on his back. Boggs scooted backward and leaned against the wall. With her uninjured leg she kicked Paul. He didn't move. There was a bullet hole in his chest. She assumed he was dead.

"Toni," she whispered. "Are you okay?"

Boggs remained where she was. She was bleeding pretty heavily and had pressed her palm over the wound. It hurt like a son of a bitch. She'd never been hurt this bad before.

"Toni," she called out louder.

"I'm okay," Toni said, her voice faint, "but Mr. Rupert is hurt." Just then Vicky appeared at the bottom of the steps. "Vicky," she cried out. "Are you okay?"

Vicky blinked several times. "Is he dead?" she asked. Her voice was barely a whisper and it looked like she was having trouble breathing. The side of her shirt was covered in blood.

Boggs answered, never looking away from Paul. "I think so," she said. "Are you hurt bad?"

"Just a little pooped, how about you?"

She grinned. "I'm okay."

No one moved. Boggs kept her gun trained on Paul. The sirens were closer, about two minutes out, she figured. Toni cradled Mr. Rupert in her lap. There was blood everywhere.

Patty was the first to arrive, racing inside, her gun drawn. Captain Billings came in right behind her. Patty radioed for an ambulance and went to check on Vicky.

Boggs and Toni were still sitting on the floor. Captain Billings checked Paul for signs of life. There were none, as Boggs suspected. "I think you can put that away now," he said to her. "He's dead."

She lowered her weapon and the captain took it from her as he made a quick check of her injuries. She was mostly worried about her leg. The other cuts didn't seem too bad. Patty was still with Vicky. Two ambulances arrived.

"I'm not going to the hospital," Toni announced. "Would someone take me to the animal hospital please?"

Patty grabbed a blanket from one of the medics and gently placed Mr. Rupert on it. Toni was telling her how Mr. Rupert had saved their lives.

"I'll take care of him, Toni," Patty said. She looked at the captain, who nodded. "I'm taking him right now."

Toni said she didn't want to let Mr. Rupert go without her, but when she tried to stand she became dizzy and had to sit back down. An EMT was right beside her now. She argued for a little bit, but finally agreed. Patty was out the door with Mr. Rupert before she could change her mind.

An EMT had just finished putting a pressure bandage on Boggs's leg and the medic had already taken Vicky out on a gurney. Boggs heard the siren as the ambulance rushed to the hospital. The EMT looking at Toni's injuries smiled. "Most of these aren't too deep," he told her. "But you're going to need a lot of stitches in the back of your head."

He bandaged several places on her arms and the huge gash on the back of her head. Both she and Boggs were loaded into the second ambulance and taken to the hospital.

Patty had arrived at the animal hospital within ten minutes of leaving the apartment. As she gently handed Mr. Rupert to the vet, she told him how this wonderful cat had attempted to save the lives of three people. She gave him her cell phone number. He said he'd let her know about Mr. Rupert's condition as soon as he could. She headed to the hospital.

She found a nurse in the ER and asked for any information about Vicky, Toni or Boggs. The nurse on duty was not the friendliest woman on earth and gave Patty absolutely no info. Frustrated, she paced the waiting room. After about twenty minutes, she received a call from the vet. He told her that he'd stitched up Mr. Rupert and he'd be just fine. Toni could pick him up in the morning.

Captain Billings arrived a few minutes later. Patty told him she'd gotten nowhere with the duty nurse. He smiled and pulled out his badge, fastening it on his belt. He went to the desk and started talking to the nurse. Patty couldn't hear what he was saying but it was obvious she was responding positively. Several times Patty saw her flip her hair and touch the captain's arm. After a few minutes, he motioned for Patty to join them.

"Vicky is in surgery right now," the nurse explained. "She had a collapsed lung and a deep wound on her arm." The nurse also told them that Boggs had a serious laceration on her thigh. There was a smaller cut on her arm that could be stitched down in the ER, but they would be sending Boggs up to surgery to repair the gash in her leg. She would need to be on crutches for a couple days, but hopefully no permanent damage. Toni's cuts were mostly superficial, but the one on the back of her head needed several stitches. Both Boggs and Toni were supposed to stay overnight for observation.

"Can we see them?" Patty asked.

The nurse looked at Patty and then Captain Billings. She smiled coyly at the captain. "Well, it's against policy. No one but family, but in this case I guess it'll be okay. Just a couple minutes, though."

The nurse ushered them into one of the trauma rooms. Toni was lying on her side while a doctor was working on the back of her head. Her eyes were closed.

"Toni," Patty whispered.

Toni tried to sit up but was stopped by the doctor. She looked panicked. "Is Mr. Rupert okay?"

"I just talked to the vet," Patty said, and filled Toni in on his prognosis.

Toni looked relieved. "What about Boggs? And Vicky? And how is Anne doing?"

Patty answered her as best as she could and then noticed that Toni's clothing was in a bag on the floor. It was covered in blood. "Hey," Patty said. "How about me going over to your place and getting some clothes for you? The nurse said you had to stay overnight."

Toni looked down at the gown she was wearing. "Oh, that would be great," she said. "And could you grab my keys and stuff? They should be in my briefcase by the dining room table. I'd really appreciate it. I'm surprised they even treated me without my insurance card."

"You came in by ambulance and the hospital was notified that officers were down. They probably won't bug you for insurance for another hour at least," Patty said. "I'll grab your things for you. I'm happy to be able to do something."

Patty and the captain stayed only a few more minutes before the nurse kicked them out of the room. She led them down the hall. Boggs was being wheeled out of a room as they approached. Patty walked alongside her, giving an update on Toni and Vicky. She promised to bring Boggs's bag from Toni's apartment before the nurse cut her off.

"She's got to go up to surgery now," the nurse said. "You can see her in the morning."

Patty waved to Boggs as the elevator doors closed. She looked at Captain Billings. "I'm going to head over to Toni's now, is that okay?"

"Go ahead," he said. "I'm going to stick around."


Patty arrived at the apartment to find the crime scene unit working on the area where Fred was killed. Bannon told her they had already taken photographs and blood samples from inside the apartment and prints were taken from the bedroom window. He told her it would be about an hour before he could release the scene. She saw Frank sitting in a grassy area across from the front door and she joined him there. "Hey, detective."

He looked up. "How are they?" he asked.

Patty filled him in. "How come you're still here," she asked.

"I thought I'd wait for crime scene to finish, then I'd lock up," he said.

Patty saw a gallon-sized plastic jug next to him and pointed to it.

"Oh, that stuff," he said. "I thought I'd clean up a little. That's good for blood."

Exhausted, Patty sat down next to him. This was the first time she had ever seen Frank act like a decent human being. They waited in silence until Bannon motioned them over. Silently they went inside.

The place looked like a disaster area. Aside from all the blood, the place was littered with trash from the ambulance crew. Patty found a scrub brush and paper towels in the kitchen and grabbed a trash bag from underneath the sink. Together they scrubbed the dining room carpet and picked up trash. They found a blood trail going up the stairs and another large pool of blood in the bedroom. While Patty worked on the carpet, Frank cleaned the fingerprint dust off the window and went to look for something to patch the hole.

He returned a few minutes later with cardboard and duct tape. "This should do until we can get a replacement glass," he said. It was the first time either had spoken in almost an hour.

Patty stood and stretched. You could barely see the stains. "This stuff works really good," she said. "What is it?"

"I don't know," Frank said. "My sister is a nurse and she uses it for her uniforms. I went over and borrowed it while I was waiting on Bannon." He smiled for the first time. "It does work, doesn't it?"

They retraced their steps back downstairs looking for any spots they may have missed. Patty returned the scrub brush and tied up the trash bag. "I guess that about does it," she said. "Thanks, Frank. I know Toni will really appreciate this."

Frank looked embarrassed and he merely shrugged. Without saying anything else he picked up his plastic jug and left.

Patty went back to the bedroom and gathered some clothes for Toni. She found a gym bag in the closet and put everything inside. Then she located Toni's keys and wallet and tossed those inside also. On her way out the door she grabbed Boggs's bag and headed back to the hospital.

# CHAPTER 24

Toni awoke at 7:15 the next morning, unsure of where she was. The pounding in her head and the feel of cardboard sheets, however, reminded her she was in the hospital. She tried to push herself to a sitting position but found that her lovely hospital gown remained in the middle of the bed. She was still yanking and tugging on the miniature gown when a nurse entered the room.

"How are we feeling this morning?" she asked.

"We are having trouble keeping our nightie in place," Toni said. There was no hiding the frustration and sarcasm in her voice. The nurse's smile disappeared. Toni immediately felt bad about her snotty remark. "I'm sorry," she said. "I'm just anxious to get out of here and I guess I'm a little cranky."

The nurse's smile returned. "That's okay, honey. I'm sure you can check out after morning rounds."

Toni looked around her sparse room, an empty bed next to the window, and saw a plastic bag on the table. She could see her bloody clothing inside. Next to it was her gym bag. She silently thanked Patty and then pointed to the bag. "Can I go ahead and put my clothes on?"

"Just as soon as I check your vitals," the nurse said.

"Do you know how my friends are?" Toni asked as the nurse took her blood pressure. "Boggsworth and Carter? They were brought in with me last night."

"I know the whole story, honey," the nurse said. "Your friend Vicky is doing fine now. She was in surgery a while, but I think everything is okay. Now, the other one is giving us trouble."

"Boggs?" Toni said, concerned. "What's wrong. Is she going to be okay? Is it serious? What happened?"

"Hold on there, honey." The nurse smiled. "She's giving us trouble because she's not doing what we tell her. I've already caught her trying to walk out of her room when she should be in bed. She's been trying to check up on you. They stitched her up last night, but she's supposed to stay off that leg for a few days. She keeps saying she's fine. In fact, the only way I got her to go back to her room was to promise to tell her when you were awake."

Toni laughed, which made her head ache worse. That sounded like Boggs. After the nurse finished, Toni attempted to get out of bed. She was still a little woozy and her head throbbed, but it wasn't too bad. She also had several cuts on her arms, but only two had needed stitches. The nurse helped her to the bathroom and offered to assist her in dressing. Toni refused, but immediately regretted her decision when she found herself unable to pull a sweatshirt over her head. Her left arm was stiff and sore under the bandages and dressing with one arm was nearly impossible.

"Nurse," she called from the bathroom. "Are you still here?"

"Need a little help?" she asked.

Toni laughed and gratefully accepted the nurse's assistance. In a few minutes she was back in bed, dressed in her comfy sweatshirt and jeans.

"Your breakfast should be here any time now," the nurse said. "I'll tell your friend you're awake." She smiled and left.

Minutes later Boggs appeared on crutches. Behind her was another nurse with a wheelchair. "I told you to stay off that leg," the nurse said. Reluctantly Boggs sat in the chair, but she refused to give up the crutches. The nurse accepted the compromise and wheeled Boggs farther into the room. "Now stay here," she ordered.

Boggs grinned. She maneuvered herself to the side of Toni's bed. "How ya doing?"

"I'm just peachy keen," Toni said. "I see you're causing your share of trouble."

Boggs shrugged. "I just hate being stuck in bed. Alone, that is." She winked at her. "Anyway, I'm glad you're doing okay. I just found out that Vicky has to stay in here a couple days, but she'll be fine. Want to go up to see her with me?"

Toni started to get out of bed when her nurse reappeared. "Get back in bed, honey," she said. "Both of you have to have breakfast or neither of you will get discharged today." She'd brought in two trays. She put one on Toni's table and pointed at the food. "Eat." She took the other tray and placed it on the table from the empty bed next to Toni's, removing the plastic cover from the plate. "Eat."

Both Toni and Boggs nodded. Toni took a sip of the lukewarm coffee. "Yum," she said. "This is the best coffee I've ever had." She took a bite of the cold toast. "Oooh. You've got to try the toast, Boggs. The next time I go out for breakfast, I'm coming here, for sure."

Boggs laughed and took a few bites of what appeared to be scrambled eggs. They managed to eat most of the toast and finish their juice. Toni was trying to drink more coffee when the nurse returned.

"I'm so stuffed I can't eat another bite," Toni said.

The nurse looked at their plates and shook her head. "I know it's not the best food in the world," she admitted. "But I suppose that's good enough. Now if you two can wait a couple minutes, the orderlies will take you up to your friend's room." Boggs started to protest, but the nurse cut her off. "If you don't wait, you can't go. Anyway, if you keep moving around like that, you'll open your stitches. That means they'll have to go back in and you'll be here longer."

Boggs didn't seem fazed by this news.

The nurse continued. "And if you stay longer, that means you have to eat lunch and dinner here."

That appeared to change Boggs's mind. "We'll wait right here," she said solemnly. The nurse smiled and took their breakfast trays away.

About fifteen minutes later two orderlies arrived. They looked like they were barely out of high school. One had flaming red hair and approached Toni with a wheelchair, which she refused at first but was informed that she was required to ride, just like Boggs. She was a little embarrassed, preferring to walk, but did as she was told. They were taken up to the fourth floor to Vicky's room.

Toni's stomach flopped a few times when she saw Vicky lying in that hospital bed. She was hooked up to an IV, her arm wrapped in some type of soft cast.

Vicky smiled when she saw them being wheeled in. "Geez," she said. "Talk about lazy. I see you all hired a couple of handsome guys to wheel you around all day."

The two orderlies blushed and turned to leave. The redhead stopped at the door. "Remember," he said. "You're supposed to call the nurses' station when you want to go back." The boy grinned then lowered his eyes. "I'll come back for you, okay?"

Toni agreed and smiled back at him. The boy blushed again and left the room. Toni wheeled up next to Vicky's bed, noticing that the privacy curtain was drawn between Vicky's bed and the other one. "How are you feeling?" she asked. "I mean really, how are you?"

"I'm pretty sore," Vicky admitted. "But they've given me drugs for pain and stuff, so I'm not bad. My mouth tastes like shit and it's really dry, but that's just from surgery." She pointed to her breakfast tray. "Have you guys had the food here?" she asked. "Is it horrible or what? Even the juice tastes like metal. How can they screw up juice?"

Toni and Boggs described their cardboard toast and powdered eggs. They laughed and bitched for several minutes. Toni was so grateful to be alive and thankful that none of them were hurt too bad.

Vicky was the first to broach the subject of the previous night. "I haven't pieced together any of what happened, have you?"

Boggs shook her head.

"I think I'm still in shock," Toni said. "I can see now how Judge Haley would have let Paul into her house. At that time, who would have thought it was him? It also makes sense about the jail. Paul is over there all the time. The warrant office is right next door."

Boggs and Vicky agreed.

"Do either of you know how Anne is doing?" Toni asked.

"She's holding her own," Captain Billings said from the doorway. "She's out of danger." He was balancing four large coffees. He handed one to each. "They told me you were here," he said. "I just wanted to check on you. Is there anything I can do for any of you?"

"Better food," Vicky said. "But the coffee is wonderful. Thank you."

"Nothing I can do about the food," he said. "But I do have a little bit of information you all might be interested in."

Toni wheeled around to face him.

He opened his coffee. "Frank went through Paul's desk at the office after he left your apartment last night. He found a stack of yellow legal pads filled with plans and observations about all the killings. Frank hasn't gone through them all yet, but he said there was no question in his mind that Paul had killed all of the women. Frank said the notes kept referring to 'destiny' and his 'mission.' Pretty scary stuff. There was also a supply of pills, probably speed, taken from the evidence room. Once we read the whole thing, maybe we'll have a clearer idea of what was going on inside his head." He took another sip of coffee. "I also talked to Paul's wife. She didn't seem too distraught about Paul's death, but I guess that's a whole other story. Anyway, the only pertinent information she gave me was that Paul had apparently weaned himself off his usual medication. She didn't know what kind it was but thought it was for mood swings. She didn't really know."

"Well," Toni said. "That makes sense why he deteriorated so fast. Probably some type of psychotropic med."

"That's my guess," said Captain Billings. "We'll know more once the investigation is finished. I don't think anyone knew he was taking meds in the first place. Anyway, that's all we know for now. I'll let you know when we find out more." He finished his coffee and stood to leave. "If there's anything I can do for any of you," he offered. "Just let me know." He gently touched Vicky's arm and smiled before leaving the room.

"He's a good man," Boggs said. The others agreed.

The nurse from the second floor and the two orderlies appeared at Vicky's door. "If you two want to be discharged you have to go back to your rooms for rounds," she said.

Toni and Boggs promised to visit Vicky later and went with the nurse. One hour later they were discharged. Patty was waiting for them at the entrance. "I figured you'd need a ride," she said. She was still in uniform and looked exhausted. "I hope you don't mind riding in this." She pointed to the police car parked in the loading zone.

"I wouldn't care if it was a garbage truck," Toni said. She looked at her watch. "I want to get Mr. Rupert."

"I thought so," Patty said as she helped Boggs maneuver into the front seat. "I thought we'd go there first and then your apartment. How about you, Boggs?"

"Could you take me to Metro?" she asked. "I left my car there yesterday and I'd hate to be stuck somewhere without it."

"Done deal," Patty said. "Toni, have you talked to your folks?"

"No," Toni said. "Why do you ask?"

"Well," Patty explained, "the news people have been swarming Metro and I got word before I got to the hospital that they're camped out at your apartment complex. I figured you might want to talk to your parents before they saw it on the news." She handed Toni her cell phone.

"Crap," Toni said. She stared at the phone. "I know what to say to my parents, but what about the press?"

"Call your parents first," Boggs offered. "Then call Dorothy at work. She'll know."

Toni let out a sigh. "Good idea. Thanks." She made a quick call to her parents, minimizing everything. After several protests that apparently did no good, she quit arguing and hung up. "They're going to meet me at my apartment." She rolled her eyes. Next she called Dorothy. Less than five minutes later she hung up. "Dorothy knows more about our injuries than we do," she said.

Boggs laughed. "Dorothy knows everything. What did she say?"

"She told me that Elizabeth was taking over until Anne gets back to work," Toni said. "Then I talked to Elizabeth. She told me that the chief judge had continued all my cases for a week and that I wasn't to show my face in the office until Monday. She was really sweet about everything and even asked if she could do anything for me, like run errands or something."

"She is really nice," Boggs said. "And she means what she says." She motioned for the phone. "I want to check in with Sam."

Patty was just pulling up to the animal hospital. "Do you want me to go in with you?" she offered.

"No, thanks," Toni said. "I'll be back in a minute."

At the front desk, she said, "I'm here for Mr. Rupert."

The woman behind the counter smiled. This was obviously the owner of the famous Mr. Rupert. "He's doing great," she said, warmly. "We had to shave a few spots on him, so he looks a little funny, but he'll be fine. The doctor will fill you in." She showed Toni into an exam room, mentioning that there had been more calls about this one cat that morning than all of the other animals combined. Little by little she'd gotten the full story of what happened the night before.

The doctor arrived moments later. He told her about the

stitches Mr. Rupert had required, where the cuts were located, and again informed her that several areas had to be shaved. He said that Toni had a remarkable cat. Toni grinned and asked a few questions. As soon as she began to speak, she heard the unmistakable meow from Mr. Rupert. It was almost a howl.

"That's him," she cried. "Mr. Rupert!"

One of the assistants came from the back room carrying a large cage. Mr. Rupert continued to howl for Toni. The assistant set the cage down on the floor and opened the door. He was pushing on the door before it was even unlatched. He came bursting out and ran for Toni as best he could.

Toni was initially shocked at his appearance. His entire front left paw was covered with a bandage, as was three quarters of his tail. The end of his tail, however, was as fluffy as ever. There were also several rectangle patches on his body that had been shaved. He looked like a patchwork cat. He rubbed his head against Toni's leg as she squatted down to pet her boy.

"You can take the bandages off in a couple days," the vet said. "Unless he decides to take them off earlier. Just try to keep them on as long as you can."

Toni nodded. She kept petting Mr. Rupert, not even looking up at the doctor when he talked.

"I used dissolvable stitches, so he won't have to come back for that," he said.

"Thank you very much, doctor," Toni said as she shook his hand. The assistant helped her get Mr. Rupert into a temporary carrier.

"My pleasure," he answered. "You've got one heck of a cat there."

Toni went to the front desk and looked at the bill that the woman handed her. "What's this?" she asked. There was no charge.

The assistant said, "Apparently Mr. Rupert has quite a following. Several people have called asking to pay for his care. The doctor here had already decided not to charge anything when the police officer first brought him in and told us briefly what happened. His brother is a cop. Anyway, I told everyone who called that the bill had been taken care of, but all of them insisted on at least donating some money to the clinic for its generosity."

Toni thanked her again and returned to the car with Mr. Rupert. "He's going to be fine," she said. "Now I just have to figure out what to do with the reporters. Elizabeth said I should say 'no comment' until the office releases a statement. I wish I could just avoid it all together."

"I've got an idea," Boggs said. "Why don't we drop you and Mr. Rupert off on the back side of the complex. Then Patty could drive around to the front parking area. If we sit there a couple minutes I'm sure all the reporters will come over to the cop car."

"That would be great," Toni said. "Do you think it'll work?"

"I think so," Boggs said. "It should give you enough time to get across the courtyard to your door. The reporters should be on the other side waiting for me to say something. After a couple minutes I'll give them the 'no comment' routine."

Patty agreed it might work and took the long way around the complex.

Toni got out and thanked Patty. She looked at Boggs. "Thanks. Call me when you're settled, okay?"

Boggs grinned. "Absolutely."

The plan apparently worked because Toni and Mr. Rupert made it to their front door without encountering any reporters. Once inside she carefully took him out of the carrier. After sniffing the carpet he headed for his food.

Toni looked around her apartment. There was no sign of blood. She wondered who had cleaned everything and was incredibly grateful for whomever it was. She was still standing there when the doorbell rang. She froze. Then she heard her mother's voice and immediately opened the door. Both her parents rushed in and hugged her. Her dad was carrying two huge bags and her mom had a small suitcase. Once the goods were unloaded, the three sat on the couch. Mr. Rupert jumped up and crawled on her dad's lap. Her mom gasped at the sight of him.

"We're both okay, Mom," she said. "Really." Slowly she relayed the story but left out most of the details. Her dad stopped her several times to ask questions, shaking his head upon hearing her answers. They insisted on seeing her arm and head even though her mom became a bit queasy. Satisfied she was now safe and out of danger, her mom offered to fix some lunch. She didn't even wait for a reply but simply got up and went to the kitchen.

Her dad continued to pet Mr. Rupert. "Brave as any guard dog, eh, boy?" he said. He scratched behind his ear for a few more minutes. "I think I'll take a look at that window, okay?" he said as he gently moved Mr. Rupert from his lap.

"Don't worry about it, Dad," she said. "I'm sure maintenance will take care of it for me."

"I've got my tools in the car, honey," he said. "Once I get the measurements and the glass, it'll only take me a few minutes." He grinned and went upstairs.

Her mom emerged from the kitchen with a glass of iced tea. "Did the doctor give you a prescription for the pain, sweetie?"

It wasn't until that moment that Toni realized how bad her head and arms hurt. "Yeah," she answered. "But I didn't have a chance to fill it yet."

"I'll get it for you," her dad said as he came down the stairs. "I need to get the glass. Do I have time before lunch?" He looked at Toni's mom, who nodded, and he was out the door.

After they had finished lunch and the pain medicine had kicked in, Toni dozed on the couch with Mr. Rupert. It was late afternoon when she was awakened by the sound of the phone and the smell of cookies baking. She answered the phone on the fourth ring. It was Boggs.

"Did I wake you up?" she asked.

Toni was yawning. "No," she said. "I think the sound of the phone woke me up."

Boggs laughed. "Funny. I've slept most of the afternoon, too. How are you doing?"

"I can't believe how sore and tired I am," Toni said. "My folks are still here and Mom is baking cookies. Dad fixed my window."

"I won't keep you, then," Boggs said. "But I just talked to a friend of mine from Channel Seven. She said they're doing a story on you and Anne on the five o'clock news. Just thought I'd give you a heads-up."

Toni glanced at her watch. It was almost five now. "Thanks, Boggs. And hey, do you know who cleaned up in here? When I got home everything was done."

"That was Patty and Frank. Can you believe it?"

"Jeez. It looks great. I need to thank them." She paused for a moment. "I'll talk to you when my folks leave, okay?"

"Perfect," Boggs said. "Try to get as much rest as you can, okay?"

After disconnecting, Toni switched on the TV. Her parents joined her on the couch with cookies and coffee. "The story is going to be on the news," she explained.

The story began with a statement from Captain Billings. The next clip was from a reporter describing both Anne's attack and the one at Toni's apartment, all in graphic detail. A photo of Paul was being shown in the top right corner of the screen. The story ended with the reporter standing outside the hospital where she gave an update on everyone's injuries. Toni's graduation photo, captioned "Assistant Prosecuting Attorney," flashed on the screen when the reporter gave the update. Toni turned off the television after the story ended.

"Did you all see that?" asked Toni. "They put my title under my name. And they spelled my name right."

Toni's mother was nearly in shock and looking pale.

"What's wrong?" Toni asked, perplexed. She thought they'd be happy.

"I think you left out a few details," suggested her dad. "Like the fact that one of your bodyguards was killed, another almost killed and the other seriously wounded . . . and it happened in this room!"

"Oh," Toni said softly. "I didn't want you to worry. And a couple people cleaned everything up while I was in the hospital last night."

"You had to spend the night in the hospital?" her mom asked in disbelief. "And you didn't call us?"

"Well," Toni explained sheepishly, "it was pretty late. I didn't want to wake you."

Both her parents were shaking their heads. Obviously they had raised a very independent child. They insisted that Toni should move back with them for at least a couple weeks, but she refused. They reached a compromise of spending the night with her and then letting her fend for herself. Toni's mom fixed dinner while she and her dad played cribbage. The phone rang every few minutes and Toni finally turned off the ringer and the volume on the answering machine. Most of the calls were either from the media, gun fanatics, religious nuts or "friends" wanting to get the real scoop. By the end of the evening she was exhausted. She convinced her parents to sleep upstairs and she and Mr. Rupert curled up on the couch together. As much as she hated to admit it, she was glad her parents were there.

# CHAPTER 25

The next couple of days were uneventful but busy for Toni. She returned some of the phone calls and retold the story at least a dozen times. Vicky had been discharged and was staying at her mother's house. Toni talked to her several times and visited once. Boggs's sister had come into town and although Toni went over there once, she wasn't able to spend any time alone with her. She spent two afternoons at her parents' house helping with the Christmas baking, but mostly she slept. She hadn't realized how exhausted she had become, both physically and emotionally.

This afternoon was the memorial for Judge Haley. Vicky was determined to go, so Boggs offered to pick her up so she could ride with them. Later that evening the plan was to go out to dinner with Boggs, Vicky and Patty. Toni was looking forward to that, but more importantly she was looking forward to the time after dinner when she and Boggs would have some time alone.

When they arrived at the funeral home there were at least one hundred cars already there. Boggs pulled up to the door to let Vicky out. Vicky was wearing her dress blues as was Captain Billings, who was standing outside. He saw them and he recruited a young officer to park the car for Boggs. Even though she had shed her crutches the day before, it was still difficult for her to walk long distances. She was dressed in a black pantsuit and wore low heels. Toni had on a dark gray suit with a skirt that fell just at her knees. Luckily Toni found them seats in the back, and she spotted Patty sitting on an aisle amid the sea of blue uniforms in the front. Toni nodded at her and smiled.

The service was fairly short, but several people took the podium to share their favorite stories of Judge Haley. There wasn't a dry eye in the entire room when the last speaker stepped down. Slowly the room began to empty. As Toni, Boggs and Vicky made their way to the front door they were pulled aside by Captain Billings. He took the car keys from Boggs and sent the officer to get her car.

"We found out a little more," he told them. "We still have a lot to figure out, but here's what we know now."

He told them that the name "Dexie" was mentioned several times in Paul's writings. Dexter Crown was his half-brother and it looked like he had killed him shortly after he was released from jail. The captain wasn't sure, but it appeared Paul buried him near someone's cabin at the lake.

Captain Billings had also talked to one of Crown's doctors. Apparently Crown talked about Paul all the time. He idolized him. He talked about taking the blame for some of the things Paul had done when they were kids, but he was proud of it. These things weren't just breaking windows or spilling something on the floor. These were major things like torturing the neighbor's cats and making threatening calls to female teachers. The doctor had said that Crown would have done anything that Paul asked him to do.

"We're still not sure what type of medication Paul was taking," Captain Billings continued. "Whatever it was, he stopped about ten months ago. That's all I know."

Toni was grateful for the information. At least things made more sense to her now.

The officer pulled up in Boggs's car and the women got in. Boggs dropped Vicky off first.

"We'll see you at Aunt Hattie's at about seven," Toni said as Vicky slowly climbed out of the car. "Are you sure you're up for it?"

"I'll just catch a quick nap and I'll be fine," she said. "I'm ready to go out and have some fun. Maybe we'll hit the clubs and dance all night."

Toni was still chuckling when Boggs dropped her off at her apartment. "You'll pick me up at six thirty, right?" she asked.

"Yep," Boggs said. "A couple hours off this leg and I should be as good as new."

Once inside her apartment Toni decided that she too could use a quick nap. She still had three hours and that would give her plenty of time to get ready. She set her alarm and stretched out on her bed with Mr. Rupert.

The alarm went off at five thirty. Her showers still took longer than normal because of her arm and her head. She'd yet to wash her hair, which made her crazy, but the stitches would come out on Monday. She stood in the shower and let the warm spray of water engulf her entire body. She closed her eyes and let her mind wander. As was happening more frequently, the image of the dream she had weeks ago came to her mind.

This was the kind of dream she wanted to relive over and over. She was standing in some room and the lights were low. Boggs would step a little closer and Toni would nervously take a step back. In the dream it seemed to go on forever, until finally Toni could back up no farther. There was a wall. Boggs came closer. Toni could feel herself breathing heavier. In the dream it had ended there, but Toni had fantasized about various endings for weeks. This time was no different. When she opened her eyes she found she was again breathing heavy. How long had she been in the shower? She felt that the water had definitely gotten cooler. Worried that she might now be running late, she hurried to finish.

She was still feeling the effects of her shower experience when she picked out her outfit for the night. She knew exactly what she wanted to wear—a long-sleeved, white cotton shirt that buttoned down the front, jeans and her boots. This was the same outfit she was wearing in the dream. She finished it off with gold hoop earrings and a delicate gold bracelet. A touch of perfume and she was ready. She went downstairs and considered pouring herself a glass of wine but decided against it. Instead, she got her dad's letter jacket from the closet, located her wallet and keys and sat on the couch to wait. The doorbell rang at exactly six thirty.

Toni leaped from the couch and peered through the peephole. She opened the door and let Boggs in. Mr. Rupert was perched on the end of the couch. This was the first time Boggs had seen him. He'd been inside the carrier when they returned from the vet and she'd only seen his face.

"Nice hairdo," Boggs said.

Toni stared at her. There was something familiar about her outfit, but Toni was sure she had never seen Boggs in it before. She was wearing a pair of faded blue jeans, a pale yellow oxford shirt and a thick ivory cardigan sweater. It took her a minute before she remembered that was the outfit that Boggs wore in her dream. Her heart was pounding and she was having a difficult time concentrating. She realized that Boggs was saying something.

"I'm sorry," she said, stammering a bit. "What did you just say?"

"I asked Mr. Rupert if he had a hot date tonight," Boggs repeated.

Toni was able to pull herself together. "Oh, no," she said. "He's staying home and watching *America's Most Wanted*. He's taking crime fighting very seriously now. Ready to go?"

"Sure," Boggs said.

Toni went in the kitchen and turned on the light above the stove. She hated coming home to a dark house. Then she picked up her jacket and flipped off the light in the dining room. The only light left on was the one in the kitchen and it gave a warm glow to the room. Toni froze. This was just like her dream. She looked at Boggs, who just smiled. She was standing only a few feet away. *Holy shit.* Boggs took a step toward her and Toni took a step back. *Oh, my God.* Boggs moved still closer, smiling. Toni backed up again. She was nervous. Boggs took off her sweater and put it on the couch. Another step. This time Toni was stopped by the wall. *Oh, jeez.* She swallowed hard. Her gaze moved down Boggs's body, stopping at the holster fastened to the waist of her jeans. Toni felt her knees get a little weak. The woman of her dreams, literally, was standing before her.

Boggs followed Toni's gaze, reached down and pulled the holster and gun from her waist. Without breaking eye contact she put the holster on the back of the couch. Then she took another step toward her. Toni looked at her and unconsciously her tongue slowly moistened her lips before smiling.

She couldn't move. Even if there hadn't been a wall behind her, she couldn't move. Boggs was now only two feet away from her. Toni heard a slight moan coming from somewhere. It took her a second to realize it came from her. The tension was almost intolerable. She could feel her chest rise and fall from her own breathing. She could smell Boggs's perfume. Toni stood there against the wall, her hands by her side. She was trembling with anticipation.

Boggs reached down for Toni's hand. Their fingers met. That was the first contact. Toni could feel the electricity pulsing through her body. Boggs was only inches from her face. She took Toni's hands and pressed them against the wall. Then she slowly moved them upward. Toni was breathing hard now, and her heart was beating so loud she was sure Boggs could hear.

Boggs continued to slowly pull Toni's arms up the wall. They were just above her head when she stopped. Their fingers were interlocked as Boggs gently pressed Toni against the wall with her body. Toni heard herself moan again, only this time louder. She felt the heat from Boggs's body envelop her.

Boggs's face was a fraction of an inch away. Toni's mouth opened slightly in anticipation, but Boggs's lips brushed against her cheek and lightly kissed her ear. The feel of her breath on her ear was maddening. Toni felt her knees go weak. Another kiss on the ear. A little more pressure against her body. Toni thought she might lose it right there. Her body was aching for more. She was at the very edge. Then she felt the tip of Boggs's tongue on her ear and her grip tightened on Toni's hands. One more kiss on the ear. Toni could barely stand. She pushed back against Boggs's body, then relaxed. Again. A rhythm developed. Boggs slowly moved her head toward Toni's mouth, kissing her cheek gently. Her body movements didn't change. Neither did Toni's. They were slow and deliberate.

Boggs's lips reached the corner of Toni's mouth and she lightly kissed her. Toni wanted more. Much more. She pulled away from Boggs's grip and put her hands on both sides of Boggs's face. She looked into Boggs's eyes for just a moment before pulling her close again. The kiss began tenderly, but soon Toni's hunger overpowered her and the kisses became deep and passionate.

They kissed again and again, still standing with Toni's back against the wall. Toni's hands were behind Boggs's head, pulling her close. Boggs caressed Toni's hair and cheek. Their bodies continued to move in rhythm.

Minutes passed. Toni was lost in the feel of Boggs yet she could barely stand. Just then Boggs pulled away. Toni looked into her eyes and smiled. Boggs let her fingers linger on Toni's cheek, then went to the opening of her blouse. Lightly she touched bare skin, then followed the line of the soft white fabric until she encountered lace. Boggs unbuttoned one, then two buttons. Toni felt her trace the outline of her bra with the tip of her finger and she moaned. One more kiss and then Toni grasped Boggs's hand and pulled it away. She looked at Boggs and smiled again.

"I'm feeling a little faint," she said as stepped away from the wall. Boggs frowned slightly. Was she worried that she may have gone too far? Toni wondered. Boggs started to speak but Toni shook her head and held out her hand. She led Boggs up the stairs to her bedroom.

She left Boggs at the doorway and crossed the darkened room. She lit a candle and placed it on the headboard. She pulled off her boots, then motioned for Boggs to join her. As Boggs got closer, Toni reached to pull her close. After one long kiss, Toni pulled away again. She smiled and then slowly began to unbutton the remaining buttons on her blouse. Boggs watched as she slipped off her blouse and let it fall to the floor. Toni reached for Boggs's shirt, but Boggs was already ahead of her. She was kicking off her shoes and fumbling with her boot-cut jeans. Toni followed suit.

Toni saw the bandage on her leg. "Are you sure you're up for this," she asked.

Boggs grinned and put her arms around Toni. She answered by slipping her fingers underneath Toni's lace bra and caressing the bare skin of her breast. Toni's knees wobbled again, but this time she let herself fall back on the bed, pulling Boggs on top of her. She unfastened Boggs's bra and moments later their bare skin touched. The feeling and excitement was escalating as Toni's hands and mouth searched every part of Boggs's body. Toni was teetering on the very edge of ecstasy when . . . the phone rang.

And rang and rang. It was hard to ignore completely. The answering machine came on, then the beep.

"Hello? Hello?" Vicky yelled. "I know you're there. Does this mean you're not coming to Aunt Hattie's?" Vicky was laughing. The phone disconnected.

Toni pulled away slightly from Boggs. "I guess we missed dinner."

"I guess so," she said.

Toni laughed before she pulled Boggs close again. "Now, where were we?"